Once an English an
Jackson is at present fortunate to write our
passions are social history, gardening, cooking her
own produce, travelling, walking coastal paths and of
course writing. Diana's love of the Channel Islands,
UK, is never far from her novels, this time with
connections to Jersey and Alderney.

'Murder, Now and Then' is Diana's third novel
and was inspired whilst researching for *'Ancasta
Guide me Swiftly Home,'* historical fiction set between
1910 and 1920, a very different story at the time of
The Great War. She stumbled upon an unsolved
murder close to her home in Bedfordshire, which
happened back in 1919. At first she began to write a
short story but, prompted by meeting many readers at
events who claimed that they only liked to read murder
mysteries or horror, she took up the challenge and
planned a full novel.

'Murder, Now and Then' is set in the future in
2019, with flash-backs to 1919, adding another
dimension where different styles of language were
needed. This novel reflects Diana's interest in family
and social history and she has also enjoyed writing a
book based mainly close to her home in Bedfordshire,
a county with places of interest and little known
treasures which she hopes to reflect in her book.

Diana Jackson's other works

The Riduna Series:
    Riduna
    Ancasta ~ Guide me Swiftly Home

Memoir:
    The Life and Demise of Norman Campbell

To find out more about Diana Jackson's writing check out
her website:
    www.dianamaryjackson.co.uk

Her two blogs:
www.dianamj.wordpress.com
www.selectionsofreflections.wordpress.com

Riduna on Twitter

'Diana Jackson's Author Page' on Facebook

Diana Jackson

MURDER,
NOW AND THEN

EVENTISPRESS

A CIP catalogue record for this title is available from the British Library.

ISBN 978-0-9572520-8-0

Published by Eventispress in 2014

Printed & Bound by Createspace

DEDICATION

To my husband, who is very much alive, working hard and supporting me on this venture and has been checking food and drink for anything suspicious for the last year or so!.

ACKNOWLEDGEMENTS

Heartfelt thanks go especially to my editor Marcus Webb and my proof reader Brenda Webb, who have both given me so much enthusiasm for the project as a whole, and also supported me in aspects of farming. Many thanks to my Beta readers Colin Calvert and Adam Croft who have helped to give the novel a final polish.

Thank you to the Bedford Archives, the library in St Helier-Jersey, The Channel Islands Great War Study Group who gave me the initial inspiration and a special mention to Mike Clear who took the trouble to show me around Pierrepont Farm in Surrey, where cows do virtually milk themselves!

Students from North Herts College have taken part in a competition to design the cover and I'm delighted that Emma Black has designed this paperback version. I am so grateful to all the students, including William Smith, whose design was used for Kindle.

Also, many many thanks for the support of all my friends, and followers on Facebook and Twitter too!

THE PROLOGUE

May 9th 2019

'I wouldn't kill my husband. How could you think such a thing?'

Joanna sat on the grey plastic bench, her hands in her lap, absentmindedly tearing tiny pieces from a ball of spent tissue and watching them drift down on to the brown tiles; droplets of tears joining the snow-flaked floor.

Even though Joanna was alone, she could feel the glare of DI Norton boring into her, willing her to confess. How easy it would have been to halt his incessant questioning and say 'Yes, I did it,' just to silence him? His voice still lingered in her head.

Numb with the enormity of her situation she closed her eyes and sat in a sleepless trance, her hands now motionless and her mind free–falling in a bottomless void.

May 9ᵗʰ 1919

"Sergeant Major Alfred Donald Keith Regmund appeared before the Bedford Division Bench on Wednesday morning. Crowds waited outside Shire Hall to see the prisoner arrive and depart, which he did in a closed cab. Three or four rows of public gallery were filled, as also was the grand jury gallery.

Mr P D Holmer presided, the other Magistrate being Mr A C Greenachre. Superintendant Patterson went into the witness box and gave evidence as follows.

'On Tuesday May 13ᵗʰ I arrested the prisoner at Haynes Park. He was conveyed to Bedford. On arrival I charged him on suspicion of murdering a girl, Lucille Vardon at Wilshamstead on 9ᵗʰ May. I cautioned him and he said,

'I understand my unfortunate position, and your justification for arresting me, but I am innocent, and I shall be able to prove my innocence. '

The prisoner was then remanded until 11.15 am on Tuesday next. " [1]

1. *Bedfordshire Times and Independent May 30ᵗʰ 1919 (names have been changed)*

7

PART 1

HAYNES, BEDFORDSHIRE

CHAPTER 1

July 2017 Joanna and Bob Thomas at Pear Tree Farm

Joanna, a farmer's wife of forty two years of age, whose youthful make-up-free complexion was more like that of a woman in her early thirties, looked out of the yellowing UPVC faux Georgian windows of their old farmhouse. She smiled at the sight of the small herd of prize Jersey cattle her husband had purchased when Britain had won back independence from the EU. The cows, she felt, were a symbol of that independence since the little island of Jersey had enjoyed self government for centuries.

Britain and the farmers especially, were enjoying the freedom which some couples experience after the break-up of an unhealthy marriage - that of mutually beneficial friendship, without binding ties. Of course all the countries involved had undergone the pain and bitterness of a difficult and lengthy divorce, with complicated legal proceedings stretching both lawyers and politicians to the limits, but now all of that was behind them. In fact, some said that many nations still in the EU, held a silent respect for the British spirit that was willing to believe that it would be best to go it alone.

Still maintaining brotherly and sisterly links within the former British Isles; England, Scotland, Wales and even Cornwall and the South West now enjoyed their own governing body. For England that had been a great victory and each country had celebrated the occasion in style with street parties, the likes of which had not been witnessed since the dear Queen Elizabeth's Diamond Jubilee back in 2012. Ireland too now held

9

three councils, one in the north, one in the south and a further umbrella council. This worked much like the Parliament in London had done in the past; a matriarch overseeing the British Isles as a whole.

The Jerseys provided local milk for local people, as did many small herds of cattle which had reappeared in the last few years all over the English countryside. There had even been a revival in friendly milkmen. Though in Joanna and Bob's case she was a milk lady called Fiona who called three times a week, a young lady pretty enough to pose for Hello magazine.

'Coals to Newcastle!' would be her cheery greeting to Bob, Joanna's husband, if she passed him in the yard returning from the milking barn to have a break before checking the Jerseys. It seemed ironic that they had their own milk delivered, but that was the law. Even for their own use, the unpasteurised milk needed to be checked, cooled and bottled in the normal way, for which the dairy charged Bob an astonishing 40p a litre for his own milk!

Joanna focused on the cattle. Was it their panda-like saucer eyes which amused her or their upturned haloed noses? Bob was experimenting with a new purely organic herd of Jerseys which provided delicious unpasteurised milk for his friends and neighbours. It was like a 'trendy' hobby for him, but he was astute enough to foresee this becoming a dairy product of the future. Their son Paul had even persuaded him to introduce the most innovative milking system of its day, where the cows choose when they want to be milked and are milked by a robot. It was the only time Paul had paid any attention to life at the farm and he looked with disdain on the old fashioned parlour they still used with the Friesians.

Joanna's eyes panned over the scene and focused on the wind turbine which stood boldly on the hillside away from the woods. What an outcry there had been when plans were afoot to install it on their land.

'Self interest!' 'Waste of money!' 'Useless and inefficient!' 'Vital for our future!' 'Beneficial for the whole community!' 'Low cost power!'

Whatever the arguments at the numerous meetings Joanna and Bob had attended, each side seemed to have reams of evidence to back their own case, but in the end it was government policy and that was that.

Bob thanked his good fortune that he only rented the land to the council and did not have to maintain the monstrosity. Rumour had it that, five years after its installation, it was costing more to repair the damn thing than the electricity it produced. Such was the advancement in technology.

It took a while for all factions in the village to speak to one another after that. In their local, The Greyhound, Joanna perceived a drop in temperature the moment she and Bob walked through the door. It was strange that there had been little or nothing like those levels of resentment when they had been approached to have a mobile phone mast installed just a few years earlier. In the end most understood that Bob and Joanna had little or no choice in either matter and certainly the phone mast helped to compensate for the lack of subsidies no longer provided by the EU.

Joanna's daydream was disturbed by a movement behind her and she turned around, her face a mixture of surprise and concern. Inadvertently she flicked her shoulder length wavy auburn hair behind her ears.

'Hello Helen. I wasn't expecting you in today. You don't need to worry about us for a while if you'd rather stay at home.'

'Oh, I don't think so, Joanna. Best for me to be busy. Time goes quicker that way.'

'Let me make a cuppa then, and we'll sit down and have a chat. How are you coping?' Joanna's eyes were full of genuine concern.

Seeing Helen's startled face obviously fighting to hold back the tears, Joanna realised, too late, that she had said the wrong thing.

'I understand Helen,' she said gently. 'Just do what you feel you can cope with. Come and go whenever you want to, but I'm always here if you'd like company.'

Joanna did not add - like you've always been here for me - but hoped that Helen understood.

Helen just nodded and went straight to the broom cupboard and Joanna did not see Helen's almost imperceptible wince at her last statement.

'I've just got some paperwork to do for Bob and so I'll shut myself in the office for a couple of hours. Help yourself to tea Helen, and there's cake in the tin.'

'Ta, Joanna, but you get on. Don't mind me if I just need to be alone.'

Joanna walked sadly into the office, a muddled den she and her husband shared, and closed the door, carefully putting her hot mug down on a mat of St Aubin's Bay. They had honeymooned in Jersey, as Bob's mum and dad had also done years before. Bob had no wish to go abroad and Jersey was about as overseas as he would venture. Joanna had, on the other hand, spent all her holidays whilst at university travelling to exotic places like India, to do some voluntary teaching, and backpacking across South America from Argentina to Ecuador. Those were her Bohemian days when she had worked at a cafe all term and during the Christmas holidays to save for the long summer of freedom.

Joanna frowned as she stared at the screen coming to life. They had never found the money or had the inclination to update to the latest technology, like wall computer screens linked to gadgets she had seen in the homes of some of their friends. Their's was just the old familiar laptop, still with its reassuring wires leading to plug sockets; even though their son found it hard to hide his contempt at his parents' ignorance.

'Even your old thing is wireless, mum. You only need to recharge it from time to time. You don't even need trailing wires,' he had said pointing to the printer / cum fax / cum copier / come phone cum...he had helped his father choose during his last holiday.

Joanna picked up her mug and sipped. How could they help Helen? She had been such a friend and so supportive since Joanna and Bob married over twenty years ago. Through Helen, Joanna had got to know all the gossip about the locals and been guided as to the best way to win their hearts, even her mother-in-law Madelyn.

'Ask Madelyn if she'll show you how to bake cakes and make pastry,' Helen had said wisely. And she was right. Soon Joanna and Madelyn were laughing and sharing a kitchen as if they had known each other all their lives, Joanna showing obvious admiration for Bob's mother's skills in the art of cookery. For Joanna it opened up a whole new world. She had lived with a nut allergy and had to be careful all her life, but now they could be sure of the ingredients in their baking rather than scrutinising every single packet.

When Joanna moaned once that she still felt a stranger in their local pub nearly three years into her marriage, Helen had suggested,

'Ask for the same drink each time for a while and don't be too shy to use Bill's name.'

It was odd at first. Joanna was a free spirit and liked choice, but since the pub usually had a guest cider she opted for that. It worked like a treat. Not only did Bill, the landlord, have 'their usual' ready almost as soon as they appeared at the door, but after she had said 'thanks Bill' a few times and smiled at him shyly, he began to ask her opinion on the new brew.

'So Joanna,' he said one day with a wink. 'What's your verdict on this one? It arrived only yesterday,' and then he waited expectantly for her reply.

Taking a slow sip Joanna savoured the cider like she would a glass of her favourite Rioja. 'Umm. Bill. I think it's the best I've ever tasted.'

'You're not just saying that to please an old man,' Bill replied, his face beaming with pride.

'No, Bill, it's the truth. What's it called?' she peered at the pump label. 'Ah, Cibernicks. It's sweet and appley enough, but with a twang to make you smile.'

He had chuckled at her response and from then on he had always made a point of stopping at their table to have a chat.

Her thoughts switched back to Helen Carter. The once exuberant wholesome lady, full of mirth at the slightest notion that caught her imagination, once pretty in a charming earthy countryside sort of way, had aged before their eyes. Two months ago her only daughter Kirsty had died of leukaemia at the age of 21. It was such a tragedy. Helen had brought Kirsty up on her own and had always been dismissive of the father and so no-one knew who he was. Many had wondered if he might reveal himself at the funeral, but no strangers had appeared. Of course it did not have to be a stranger, but the community did not like to look inwardly to seek the truth.

Anyway, Helen had always been adamant, on the few times she had been pressed, that the father was living abroad. Since Helen had once worked in Italy at a restaurant by Lake Como and had returned in the family way, they had no reason to doubt her. But, to the disappointment of some of the villagers, no olive skinned Italian appeared in Haynes churchyard two months ago at the funeral and so Kirsty's father remained a mystery.

Although Joanna's fingers hovered over the keys, her eyes had still not focused on the screen in front of her. She heard the sound of the Dyson overhead and wondered what Helen would do next. Since Kirsty had been born, Helen had been content to find numerous cleaning jobs in order to make ends meet, but a recent conversation over breakfast with Bob came to mind.

'It's a pity Helen can't find something a bit more rewarding now she's only got herself to think of,' Joanna commented as she served up the bacon and eggs.

'You'd be surprised, Joanna. Our Helen was always quite bright at school.'

'I don't doubt that, Bob, after all, you should know. You went to school with her but....'

'I'll have you know she even won several prizes for best pupil of the year and highest achiever in mathematics.' Bob interrupted without giving it a second thought.

'What happened then?' asked Joanna frowning as she stared down at her plate. It was one of those rare moments that Joanna had dared to ask, but was afraid Bob would clam up again, like he always did.

'Well, she'd planned to go to university but decided to have a gap year in Italy. I think there were some family connections, you know. There have been many Italians in Bedford over the last century, of course.'

Joanna waited. Maybe he would reveal something she did not know already, but unlikely.

'Then she came home...well you know... Is there anymore Daddies sauce, Joanna?' He looked up expectantly and Joanna realised that the matter was closed.

It made Joanna smile to think that Bob was unable to say that Helen was pregnant, even though he dealt with the facts of life every day on the farm.

Back to the present she heard the sound of the toilet flushing upstairs and the frantic scratching of a loo brush. Surely Helen could be free to do something special with her life now, if she could only recover from her overwhelming sense of loss. Joanna shivered. How would she have coped if she had lost either of her children? However annoying and worrying they were at times, they were adorable nevertheless and such a vital part of the life she shared with her husband, even though both of her offspring were now making lives of their own.

It was early days though, for Helen. She would talk when she was ready but she had to grieve first. It was not only natural but vital for her recovery. After about an hour there was a small tap at the door bringing Joanna abruptly to her senses. As Helen walked in without waiting, Joanna tried to look as if she had been busy rather than daydreaming, whilst Helen had strived so hard to make their home clean and tidy. Joanna turned a shade of pink.

'I'll finish for the day Joanna if you don't mind and do another hour downstairs tomorrow. There's a meeting of the

Leukaemia Society in Bedford after lunch and I'd like to get involved. I've got to do something worthwhile,' she exclaimed with a determined expression in her watery eyes.

'Come whenever you want to, Helen, but don't worry if you don't feel like it. I understand.'

'Do you really?' Helen said, unable to hide the sarcasm in her voice, her eyes giving Joanna a piercing stare.

'I admire you Helen, for going this afternoon. I hope you get some support too,' Joanna replied, determined to ignore Helen's tone and to be warm and friendly in return. 'See you tomorrow then.'

Helen closed the door behind her without saying another word and Joanna heard the rattle of Helen's bicycle as she rode over the bumpy farmyard. Joanna switched off her PC. Now alone in the house she climbed the stairs and went into their bedroom to make the bed. Gazing momentarily out of the window on the south side of the house, she looked over towards a field of wheat, which shimmered like rippling sand.

CHAPTER 2

Summer to winter 2017 Helen in Haynes

Grief comes in waves

Don't worry about keeping your usual schedule

After Kirsty's funeral Helen longed to be on her own, but once she had shut the front door of her two bedroomed ex-council house, a massive wave flooded over her and she sank on to her sagging velour sofa, hands falling defeated by her side. With eyes closed, she felt the rising tide of anger. Anger at God for taking away her most precious daughter. Anger for having to cope on her own all these years for what? Pain. Just more pain.

Helen could hear the sounds from next door; the stairs climbed with heavy thudding footsteps - fifteen year old Joel, no doubt, up to the barracks of his room, a door slamming then, moments later, the thumping of an over-emphasised base. Another generation and things had not changed, just the eerie wowing of the most up to date technology producing an innovative sound they called music.

'It was never like that when I was a girl,' Helen's mother had said to her one day, forgetting that her own era had been heavy metal - Deep Purple and Led Zeppelin and her mother had boasted of going to Knebworth in her youth to see the latter. Helen had even turned into the clone of her own mum later in life, wearing ill fitting baggy skirts and blouses, she realised with a shudder. Heavens, at least her own daughter would never turn into a clone of herself. Helen sobbed a tearless cry of agony. She did not even have her mother to turn to now.

Suddenly she raged round the house snatching photos and stuffing them into drawers, pulling down any ornaments her daughter had bought, the little windmill proclaiming 'Great Yarmouth' painted roughly on the base, bought on one of their numerous cheap caravan holidays. Come gales or heat wave they had made the best of them. She grabbed a bin bag from a kitchen drawer and threw in each item, not caring if any would break, systematically going through each room - the ornaments which littered the window sill in their pokey lounge diner and the print on the wall in the kitchen of a black Labrador, bought in memory of their only pet. He had been much too painful to replace when they had to put him down. Even the kitchen clock, a quirky thing that read backwards, Kirsty had bought to make them laugh. There was nothing to laugh about now, was there?

Next Helen raced up to the bathroom - toothbrush, flannel, creams and potions, medication in the cupboard. Helen doubled up as pain hit her abdomen and she leant against the bath. A few moments later she straightened before glancing around and tying a knot in the bin bag, her expression set in a stubborn glare.

Next she cleaned everything - the surfaces, the cupboards, every crevice, not even the walls avoided her frenzied activity until everything smelt of bleach, antiseptic and impersonal. The only room she left perfectly alone was Kirsty's bedroom and in her present state of mind she dare not even open the door.

The next week Helen spent holed up in the house. She was not hungry, but if she felt a twang of need for food she ate anything - stale bread, a chocolate biscuit, handfuls of dried fruit, a bowl of dry cereal - the milk had long gone off, a packet of crisps. She drank water from the tap, not even bothering to boil a kettle. A bag of food left on her doorstep by a kindly neighbour was left untouched. Although that was not strictly true - last night it had been ravaged, probably by a fox, and debris was scattered around her porch.

She had a few phone calls from concerned people - Joanna, her cousin Adam who she said lived in Newcastle, Penny the only person she had ever considered a friend, who was wheelchair bound and living north of Bedford. Each time the phone rang she had taken a deep breath and braced herself, putting on as normal a voice as she could muster but she just brushed each of them off,

'I'm OK thanks. I just need to be alone for a while with my grief. I'm sure you understand.'

Then they all left her alone. Only the vicar was persistent. He called at the door and waited patiently to be let in. When he realised that Helen had no intention of opening it he went away, but half an hour later he was back. This time he did not knock but slipped a letter through the door, glancing back over his shoulder with concern before opening the gate and was gone.

That letter sat on the door mat for another three days, as a couple of items of junk mail covered it. They no longer had bills. When Kirsty had turned eighteen, she had said,

'How you pay bills, Mum, is totally archaic. I don't know anyone who insists on having paper bills anymore. Think of the rain forest. I'm just stuck here half the time and you trust me. Why don't you let me deal with all that on-line; take away some of the strain of having to do everything for me?'

In fact, it had been an excellent move and such a relief too. There was always enough money in the bank and they discussed what they could afford and what needed to be bought or saved for.

Another sob. Another realisation. A bereaved wife must feel like this when her husband dies after he dealt with all the financial arrangements in the house. Slowly Helen climbed the stairs. It was exactly one week since the funeral. She braced herself and reached for the door knob.

Everything was all there, just the same as the moment they had taken her precious girl. The medics had carried her away that last time and covers still lay strewn on the floor. Everything else was spotlessly clean and tidy. With the windows tight shut there was hardly any dust on the ledge and the PC screen sat opened on the bedside table, one of those you could wheel away and adjust to the height of the bed. Helen looked at it with dread. She had never used one since her school days and she had not been any good at it then, so her teachers had told her anyway. There were too many geeks in the class who were streets ahead of her. The technical world absorbed 90% of their waking hours, whereas she would still prefer to go for a walk or to read a good book, admittedly these days on a Kindle Blaze her daughter had bought her for Christmas a couple of years ago.

'Mum,' Kirsty had exclaimed in disgust as Helen had picked up another dilapidated paperback from the church sale. 'Yuk, you just don't know where it's been. Someone might have been reading it on the toilet!'

In one of her daughter's short periods of remission she had bundled all of Helen's old books into a sack and put them out for the bin men, ignoring Helen's protests that she had kept them because she might read them again, or at least make a bit of money for street kids in Guatemala by selling them.

Helen could not even face turning on the computer. Memories flooded back. Waves. Massive waves.

'Look Mum, come and sit with me for a moment. You never stop. I've got something very important to say.' Kirsty had paused, waiting until Helen had perched on the corner of the bed.

'I know you're finding this harder than I am.... that the second transplant didn't work...... but we must face facts and prepare ourselves.'

Helen had made to get up, wanting to brush away her daughter's comment with some meaningless platitude like, 'It will be OK next time' or 'Let's not worry about it,' but Kirsty had placed her hand firmly on her mother's arm and looked into those all so familiar sad eyes, her own shining with the life she still had, but resolute that she would help her mum to cope.

'Mum!' She had exclaimed in frustration. 'Sit down and listen to me.'

Helen had sat back down, resting her head against the wall this time, trying to look more comfortable than she felt.

'Firstly I think we need to have a holiday together. It would have to be in the UK. I've had a word with the doctor and he said that it would be fine. It only takes a couple of hours to Great Yarmouth and we can afford a week in a caravan. I would enjoy seeing the sea again and we'd be near the shops if I'm up to it.'

'That's a great idea. Arrange it and I'll let everyone know, but are you sure you'll cope?'

'I'm positive. We've got a wheelchair that we've hardly ever used. It would be wonderful having some time together. Just the two of us.'

Happy with that Helen started to get up.

'I haven't finished yet Mum. Can't you stay still just for five minutes?'

Helen sat back down frowning.

'If and when I'm not here anymore, I've written a list of all the passwords and all the sites you'll need for our bank account and all of the bills. They're paid automatically so you don't have to worry about that. It's just that if you want to check them. I've put the list in an envelope at the bottom of my knickers drawer....' her voice trailed off.

Helen could not trust herself to reply. Bile had filled her throat, as it did again now, as she stared down at Kirsty's dreaded computer. Back then she had leant forward to give her daughter a hug before rushing from the room to vomit in the toilet. This time she glanced at the offending drawer and again retreated, slammed the door loudly behind her and sat on the top stair, head slumped in defeat.

Slowly over the weeks Helen tried to recover some kind of routine in her pointless life. Two months after her daughter's death and she felt ready to get involved in fund raising activities for leukaemia.

She sat in the St Mary's Church Hall, Goldington listening to a speaker say, 'Nine in ten sufferers are cured of the disease, usually surviving after their second transplant.' Helen felt a stab in the back. Unfortunately, her Kirsty chanced to be the child that didn't[2].

'We have sufferers who are so brave that they raise money for others,' the woman continued. Helen's daughter had been so brave. She bore the chemotherapy and periods in hospital with unstinting optimism, always thinking of others rather than herself.

'Thank you for travelling all the way to visit,' she would say to a friend. 'I hope the train fare wasn't too dear,' she would say to another visitor. 'Can you spare any of your loose change?' She would always ask just before they left, even when she had just come back from surgery. Everyone would drop their loose change in her charity box beside her bed and, even at her worst they had been rewarded by her dazzling smile.

'Then there are periods of remission and that's the time to live life to the full.' The speaker finished, showing snapshots of families on holiday, in the park and one girl even bungee jumping off a cliff!

'That's certainly true,' Helen conceded, remembering that Kirsty's periods of remission were the most precious moments of her life, but each time hope had been snatched away she had been devastated, as any parent would be. The successful treatments just delayed the inevitable, and now Helen could not believe that she was still involved in organising cycle rides and sponsored walks to find a perfect cure. Mankind had progressed very little in her eyes, but she signed up for a few events and made her escape before anyone came to speak with her. She could not face that. Not yet anyway.

A chance coincidence though had brought another purpose to her otherwise fruitless life, when she was placing flowers at her daughter's grave. She had noticed a gravestone, a cross as it happened, of a young girl who had died at the same age as her daughter, at 21 years, but what was surprising was that the date of her death was nearly 100 years ago. Feeling an affinity to the girl, whose name was Lucille Vardon, Helen decided to make it her quest to try to solve the mystery of her early death. Not having the mega speed access to the Futurenet, she frequently took herself off to the records office in Bedford. It was as she was getting to grips with the technology installed there, that she decided to update her own skills and attend an IT course, much to Joanna's relief, who thought that Helen was tentatively beginning to think of the future.

Helen felt guilty that she had denied Kirsty such technology at home, always claiming that they did not have the spare cash. She felt now that maybe she had handicapped her daughter, compared to her friends, although she knew that Kirsty had managed with her laptop and her latest '4 phone', enabling her not only to access Futurenet, but also to keep in touch with her friends, especially when she had been poorly and bed ridden.

Helen began her search with the help of the archivists, who guided her to the instant browser. This soon located relevant documents which she could study on the screen.

Occasionally she asked for the originals, filling in an on line request form, and within minutes the items were brought to her numbered booth. The first time a collection was brought to her it arrived in a comfortingly old fashioned cardboard box with a pair of white gloves and padded resting mat.

'Don't forget that some of these are over 100 years old,' the kindly archivist reminded her unnecessarily, although he could probably read 'novice' all over her forehead.

'I'll be careful, truly I will,' Helen reassured the man, whose receding hairline and large rimmed spectacles were unable to hide his friendly features. He retreated silently, but not before he had left a pencil on her notepad.

'I'll put my pen away, don't worry,' Helen whispered, pre-empting his final instruction before retreating behind his desk. His eyes smiled a silent thank you in return.

Helen settled, slipping on the gloves like a detective at a crime scene, but soon she was deeply absorbed in what she was reading. She discovered an amazing amount of information about Lucille Vardon, but to her dismay the story was more tragic than she had imagined. Lucille, by all accounts, was a pleasant good natured young girl, much like her own daughter, and she came from the island of Jersey. It was on the night of May 9th 1919 that Lucille was found murdered in Wilshamstead Woods at the back of Haynes Manor, where she was serving in the QMAAC, the Queen Mary's Army Auxiliary Corps.

Over the next few months, Helen gave herself no time to brood. She still cleaned for Joanna and other folks in the village during the mornings, but each afternoon was filled with activities related to her charity work, a 'Make Yourself Techy Savvy for the Nervous' course at Bedford College, and researching in the archives, and soon she was even in the library in the evenings using Futurenet with a confidence she still found hard to believe.

One day her kindly archivist brought her a set of old postcards and photos and, handling them reverently in her white gloved hands she studied each image. It was fascinating to see how Haynes had changed in the last hundred years and yet there were familiar buildings; the old school house, the blacksmith and the laundry, all of which had been homes for decades and the church and manor house on the hill remained as they were a century ago.

It was the postcards of life at the WW1 camp at Haynes Park which caught Helen's attention most. There were officers posing individually in one and parading en masse in another.

26

There was one picture showing the officers' mess and another of row upon row of tents, obviously for the men.

It was a couple of details in this picture which caught her eye. First of all there were two young girls, who could easily have been Lucille's age, or Kirsty's for that matter, but they were standing next to a car which looked strangely familiar. With a shiver she recognised it instantly as the pride and joy of Bob's great grandfather, an Austin 7hp which was still lovingly preserved and driven by both Bob and his father Peter. The highlight of their year was when they entered the 'Haynes 100,' when a vehicle from each year of the previous 100 years pulled up on the recreation ground and then paraded twice around the village. The show was very popular and people travelled long distances to participate.

The more Helen stared at the photo the more she was sure that it was one and the same car, but whether this was the fanciful imaginings caused by the delicate balance of Helen's mind it was hard to tell.

2. *These are predicted figures for 2019. Statistics in 2013 showed that fewer than 7 in 10 children are cured*

CHAPTER 3

2018   Pear Tree Farm

Joanna tried to work but was distracted by thoughts of Helen.

She was relieved that Helen still called twice a week to carry out vital cleaning work at Pear Tree Farm even though it was obvious that Helen was living a full life. She still arrived on her rickety old bicycle but what intrigued Joanna was that she now wore designer clothes to village events and services at the local church and she had certainly lost weight.

When she was at Pear Tree Farm she avoided any conversation, in fact she often called when Joanna was out. If they did happen to meet, to Joanna's annoyance, Helen would never discuss her personal circumstances and so Joanna and many of the village gossips were in the dark as to how Helen obtained these clothes or more importantly the money to purchase them.

Once when Joanna could bear it no longer she approached Helen at a village meeting,

'You're looking well Helen. How are you?'

'I'm fine thanks Joanna,' she had replied before turning to ask someone else a question, making her reluctance to talk quite clear.

It upset Joanna when she thought that they used to be quite close, even more so when she realised that Helen treated others quite differently. On one occasion when she came home from a trip to see their daughter Emily, who was finding pregnancy a daunting prospect and just needed her mum, she had found her kitchen full of people. Her husband Bob was discussing schedules with John his cowman, whilst Helen was deep in conversation with Peter, Joanna's father in law.

'I'm sure it's the same car, Peter,' Joanna heard Helen say quietly.

'There must be a few hundred of them still in the UK, Helen. Pure coincidence and anyway the picture's not very clear. I'm sure it's not an Austin 7hp. It looks more like a Model T Ford to me; far more popular at that time.'

Glancing up and noticing Joanna enter the room, Helen slipped the picture into her bag.

'Must be off, anyway. I have a meeting at 2 pm.' Without saying goodbye, Helen slipped past Joanna.

'Hang on, I'll walk with you,' replied Peter, disappearing out of the door too. Joanna watched though the kitchen window as the two of them walked across the yard for Helen to retrieve her bicycle, their discussion looking quite heated. Joanna's curiosity was heightened but she was even more concerned that she might have offended Helen in some way.

At Christmas she had confided in her daughter when they were alone in the kitchen washing the pots and pans,

'I can tell something's on your mind,' Em said. 'Can't you tell me about it?'

'I don't know Em but I'm a bit mixed up. I'm not getting along with Paul so well at the moment. He's decidedly frosty with me and that's not like him.'

'That's not strictly true, Mum. I thought the problem was with Dad about the farm and not you. That's the impression I get, anyway.'

'It's not just Paul, its Helen too. She hardly speaks to me now; in fact she seems to go out of her way to avoid me.'

Emily frowned at her mother.

'Give Helen a bit of slack Mum, and Paul too for that matter. After all Helen's been through, she just needs you to be there for her.'

'I know, Em, but it's strange that she seems to be turning to Paul of all people. All they ever talk about is computers.'

'You should be proud of Paul that he's shown an interest. It's Helen's new hobby and it keeps her mind occupied. Don't begrudge her that, Mum.' She paused. 'Why are you so against Paul going off to uni to study computer science anyway?'

'It's not just the farm, Em. Your dad and grandfather will be heart-broken if they can't pass the farm on to him but I suppose they'll get over that. It's the cost too. Why doesn't he study nearby if he has to go to uni?'

'It's the best course in the country for his discipline, that's why Mum, and he's going to work through college to help pay for it, isn't he?'

'I wish he'd talk to me more like he used to. He barely says more than one syllable at a time.'

'That's hardly surprising until you shift ground a bit Mum. "*Give and Take*" as they say.'

Their conversation came to an abrupt halt as Bob came into the kitchen. He saw the look pass between mother and daughter but he did not comment. He just went up behind Joanna and tickled her, which she hated him doing when she had rubber gloves on.

'Don't do that Bob,' she had exclaimed.

'Well, come back in to join us so that we can open our gifts.' He winked at Em.

'You're up to something, Dad,' she had laughed.

Joanna tried to focus on the farm accounts, but it barely filled the yawning gap in her life. Occasionally Joanna day dreamed that she might have the chance to finish off her degree, but knew in her heart that this was unlikely. She was needed far too much on the farm to concentrate on anything so frivolous.

Thank goodness she and Emily still maintained a positive relationship. Emily had always been such a good natured kid and Joanna was comforted that, with a grandchild on the way, demands for her support would surely increase. Joanna hated to admit it but she was suffering from *"empty nest syndrome"* and knew that if she did not find something personally fulfilling in the next few months she would go mad.

CHAPTER 4

February 2019

Bob slipped out of bed. A moment longer snuggled next to the warmth of Joanna and he would have slipped into oblivion once more. It was a game he played every morning. Dreaming of the time he would just say 'blow it' and turn over, overcome by Morpheus's temptations and wake up at a civilised hour. It was 4.30 am, pitch black on a damp February morning. He felt his way to the landing where he switched on the low voltage light.

After searching in vain for his lost sock in the glimmer of light from the passageway, Bob gave up and crept to his bedside cabinet to rummage for a fresh pair. Anyway, Joanna was always nagging him to change his socks everyday and a wry smile passed over his face as he imagined her predictable reaction to finding the elusive sock half under the bed later on that morning and she would huff and puff as she retrieved it to pop it in the laundry.

He glanced down at her sleeping features in the gloom. It had not always been easy but, all in all, it had worked out pretty well for them and now that the children were both safely off their hands, surely they could look forward to winding down soon; fairly soon anyway. At Christmas he had tentatively asked their son Paul whether he would be interested in taking over the farm one day.

'I know you're at uni for three or four years and I don't begrudge the good times you're having in Exeter, but do you think you'll come back?

'What are you driving at Dad?' replied Paul, knowing full well what was on his father's mind and skirting the issue. 'I'm studying computer science for three years, Dad, but I thought I might have a gap year. Go travelling like Mum. What do you think?' he added, neatly manoeuvring the subject.

'I can understand that Paul. I sometimes wish I'd been able to do the same.'

'Don't talk fibs, Dad. You know you're about as adventurous as a dormouse but I must take after Mum.'

'But your mother was quite happy to settle down here at the farm when she was ready.'

'I know what you're getting at Dad. Why don't you just say it?' returned Paul, a little frustrated that his dad never took the hint that the thought of farming for the rest of his life left Paul cold.

'But I followed in my father's footsteps, Son - and the farm has been in the family for generations.'

'What about Emily and equal opportunities and all that?'

'You know full well that Emily is pregnant and will have her own family to look after. Her husband has a good job in local radio and they're settled in Bromham. Emily's out of the question.'

Paul looked at his dad's pleading eyes and he felt trapped. Caged in a destiny he neither wished for nor could imagine. He had never liked the outdoorsy sort of life. Even when he was little and his granddad tried to get him interested in shooting rabbits or growing veg, he had found any excuse to get back inside and on to his computer.

'You don't even listen to my suggestions about the farm. I've told you that I think the milking should be fully automated for over a year now but you still get up at that ridiculous time every day.' *That's not for me,* he wanted to add.

'But I do listen, Paul. The Jersey unit is fully automated and it works a treat thanks to you. Yields are far higher than my expectations and I can't believe how happy the cows are.'

'But they're only your hobby Dad. What about your main herd of Friesians?'

'It would cost a fortune Paul. Where do you suggest we get capital like that from?'

'Oh Dad, it always comes back to money doesn't it.' He sighed in pure frustration. 'Anyway, the Jersey herd are going so well that maybe we should put our resources into expanding them and possibly running the Friesian side of things down. Anyway, I'm sure John would do a much better job than me. He was born for it. I must be a throw back. Maybe I was from the milkman,' he joked trying to make light of their argument, knowing full well that they had only had milk women as far as he could remember. 'Anyway, must get on. I've got an assignment to hand in after the hols,' and with that he walked back upstairs and shut himself in his room, leaving Bob staring up after him.

Bob sighed. What with his frustration over Paul's decision to leave home and his argument with Joanna about the shower, he too felt a little trapped. Mind you, thinking of Joanna made him smile. They had had quite a row in The Greyhound just before Christmas and he loved to wind her up.

He knew that their shower lost pressure in the winter; old pipes and all that, but he had had every intention of surprising her and the plumber had duly arrived early in the New Year. She had opened the 'Instruction Book' which he had carefully wrapped up and put it under the tree on Christmas morning and he would always remember her face. She had thumped him affectionately. Then he had seen the glint of pleasure in her eyes; not so much of thanks but certainly claiming 'I've won!'

His son Paul was another matter. Despite the fractious atmosphere between them, which he had attributed to normal ongoing teenage angst, Bob knew in his heart that he had to be philosophical about the future of the farm. He too had begun to hope that John, his cowman might be interested in taking on more responsibility soon. He knew that this would upset Peter, his father, who wanted to see the farm passed on to Paul but to Bob it made perfect sense.

After a cursory wash, his shave could wait 'til later, he dressed and passing the empty rooms along the landing he stumbled quietly down the stairs. He tapped the old barometer as his father always had. It was already above freezing for the first morning since before Christmas and rain was on the way. Good, he thought. The icy paths and roads were beginning to get him down. He was happy to do his bit for the local community and clear the lane of snow with his tractor when needed, but finally he would able to have his breakfast in peace, knowing that he did not have to go out again straight away to beat the local rush hour.

He stoked the embers in the range and threw in a couple of logs he had left in readiness the night before and moved the warm kettle on to the hottest plate so that, by the time he had retrieved his favourite mug from the cupboard and popped in a tea bag, a familiar hissing sound signalled that the water was boiling - much more satisfying than the electric kettle which they resorted to using through the hottest part of the summer, when to light the range would be an utter waste.

As he drained the dregs of his mug he glanced at the kitchen clock. 4.40 am. John would be at the gate by now, expertly guiding their main herd of Friesians from their winter shelter across the track towards the milking parlour. Without so much as a thought about his empty cup left on the kitchen table he grabbed his thick parka from the back of the door, pulled on his Wellingtons in the porch and strode across the now slushy snow towards the barn. By the time he had switched on the pumping equipment and checked it over he heard the latch as John guided the first of their herd into position, in rows of two either side of the pit. The two men worked in smooth conjunction for the next hour until most of the cows had been milked and the tank was full of gallons of white liquid.

Leaving John to finish the milking, clean up and switch off the equipment, as he always did, Bob walked back to the farmhouse. It was twenty to six. He could hear John's soothing voice as he coaxed the cows and he enjoyed a few moments peace before checking the Jerseys. He enjoyed another cup of tea, instantly brewed from the Aga hob.

It was still dark outside when Bob went out again at 6 am. It was not strictly necessary but he could not resist just checking on his Jerseys in their own purpose built barn. He loved to say hello to his animals every morning.

Primrose brushed up to him for some fuss. She had just come from the automatic milking unit and looked relaxed and content. As he checked the computers, the next cow, Jenny, peered under the barrier at him, quite unconcerned as the robotic arm located her teats. Behind her Poppy was awaiting her turn for milking. The other 27 Jerseys were in their cow kennels resting. Reassured that all was well he headed back to the house.

Once he had removed his boots he picked up yesterday's newspaper and sank down on his kitchen chair beside their large traditional farmhouse table, worn with years of healthy use, and enjoyed his second cup of the day. He sighed with pleasure as he turned to the sports pages and read that England was heading towards an unexpected victory with Pakistan in Karachi; first Australia, then the West Indies and now Pakistan. His cup of happiness was overflowing.

They would be able to continue trimming the hedges on the Haynes Park boundary today if the rain stopped, he thought, but for now he relaxed for a well earned break.

Joanna switched on the shower, the pleasure of the surging heat of water like a pounding orgasm on her skin. She smiled. It had taken many months of arguments of a 'waste of money' and 'there's nothing wrong with the one we've got.' Some women would only be satisfied with clusters of diamonds, an amber necklace or even a new outfit. Some of her friends' husbands had even bought frilly underwear thinking that their other halves would be pleased, but Joanna was totally satisfied with her Christmas gift which gave her pleasure each and every morning. She relished in her joy.

She remembered the day an early boyfriend she had shacked up with at college had bought her a pressure cooker as a peace offering after an argument. Her feisty retort had made it quite clear just where he could stick his pressure cooker and on the rebound, as the steam of her anger had dispelled into the autumn fog, she had bumped into this handsome farmer whilst standing on Silver Street Bridge in the heart of Cambridge.

Bob had been in jovial spirits that day, following a Young Farmers' meeting to discuss possible jointly organised events for the coming year. This was one of his rare visits to the city, since he was a country boy through and through. He was being groomed to take over his father's dairy herd next year, following three years at Shuttleworth College. There was not a lot the college could teach him that his old man did not know about animal husbandry, but it had been an eye opener to learn about up to date practices and rules and regulations. His father had argued with him when he had said he wanted to enrol.

'No need for that Bob. Hard graft here on the farm is all you need.'

But even his father had to admit that Bob's ideas of modernisation had been an improvement. Bob had dreamed of the time when the farm would be his to manage and then he would bring in many of his efficiency and time saving ideas into practice. This was not to please his ego, but as a means of survival. Bob had already seen the smaller dairy herds going under or been swallowed up, but for now, as a medium sized enterprise, they were making ends meet - just. It did not occur to Bob that his reluctance to rush into updating the farm was pushing their son Paul even further away.

That day in Cambridge Bob had strolled down to the river for some air before finding his way back to the car park when he had caught sight of this pretty young girl about to throw what looked like a new pressure cooker into the river. Knowing how his mother had pleaded with his father to buy one, his natural instinct was to be appalled by the waste and so, without thinking as to the state of the young lady's mind, or how odd the scene looked, he had called out.

'Wait, don't do that!'

The young girl had been so surprised to be interrupted. Tears were streaming down her face and her outstretched arm paused momentarily. This gave Bob just enough time to reach her, stretch out and gently retrieve the offending article. His only reward was a piercing yell by the young girl,

'How dare you!'

Their eyes met; his with an amused concern which seemed to defuse her anger, as if her madness had been plunged into the cold water of the river below and only the gentle steam of her breath was hitting the cold evening air between them. After a moment's silence she spoke in exasperated frustration,

'What the hell did you go and do that for?'

Bob had smiled. 'Well, if you dislike the pressure cooker that much then my mother would be delighted to have it. To dump it in the river would be such a shame: bad for the environment too.'

They both looked down into the dark swirling waters and Joanna looked back at him about to say, well it's none of your goddamn business, is it, but something stopped her. His smile had calmed her and she began to see the futility of her defiant gesture.

'Would you like to buy me a drink then?' She had asked, for the first time noticing the tweed jacket, cap and polished shoes; much too fuddy duddy for the twenty something, handsome young man in front of her. Mind you, there were all sorts at Cambridge.

'It's the least I can do,' replied an equally surprised Bob as they headed for The Anchor. He smiled at her, his glance taking in her Bohemian apparel, floor length ethnic skirt, flowing scarf and long wavy hair. Whatever would his mother say if she could see him now?

Years later it was no surprise that Bob had turned out to be just the same as his father. He had a routine of a lifetime which followed the seasons, or just followed the habits themselves, and the closer they became, Joanna began to understand that it was like father like son, like grandfather like father like son, as the farm had been passed down to Bob. The Thomas family did not like change, but with each generation they brought new ideas and to a certain extent managed to keep no further than half a century behind the outside world. None of Bob's family liked to spend money though.

Joanna learnt quickly that waste was an anathema. In the early years of the century she soon realised with surprise that the 'modern concepts' which were all the rage then, of conservation, recycling and reuse, were in fact like second nature to a farmer. Eat naturally healthy food; compost green waste for the vegetable plot; save other food waste for the pigs (not that there was much food waste in the Thomas's household) and any stale bread was soaked in water before supplementing the diet of the farmyard ducks and hens.

It had taken Joanna a long time to adapt to their way of life, but since they had moved into the large old Georgian farmhouse, she had finally settled into the full role of a farmer's wife and she really enjoyed it. Bob's mum and dad had finally splashed out on a world cruise before moving into the little farm bungalow, which Bob and Joanna had been cooped up in for the first fifteen years of their married lives.

The farmhouse was a bit empty now, since their youngest, Paul, ever stubborn to the last, had gone to university, as far away from home as he possibly could have chosen. Where had that idea come from? wondered Joanna. School, no doubt. Ever a disappointment to his father and grandfather, he had ignored the current trend of studying near to home to keep costs down and save the planet.

'I'll work my way through college. You'll see,' he had replied defiantly, wanting to keep the upper hand in their conversations.

'You'll end up with a mountain of debt,' his father continued in dismay.

'It's only ever about money Dad, isn't it? That's all you think about!' With that Paul had stormed upstairs and slammed his bedroom door, a habit he had got into of late.

Mind you even Paul was speechless when, just before he left for Exeter, his grandfather had bought him a second hand Mini.

'You spoil him,' was all Bob would say, but Joanna was the only one who could see that her husband was quite touched by this rare gesture of his father's generosity. In fact Bob went off to tend to his precious Jerseys, not even waiting around to wave his son goodbye and wish him luck.

Now that both of their children were away Joanna filled her time with jobs around the farm and had become an excellent cook, impressing any friends honoured by a rare invite, with good wholesome mouth watering meals. Her Aga cooked beef casserole was a legend. Did she have any regrets? Her only regret was that she never did finish her Classics degree or make use of its knowledge.

'I'm afraid I'm leaving,' Joanna had told her professor one day and in answer to his raised eyebrows she had replied, 'I'm going to be a farmer's wife!'

'No knowledge is a waste Joanna, and now you're going to learn about true life, closer to reality than many of your peers.

I envy you in fact. You'll be surrounded by the excitement of new birth, the art of nurturing to maturity, life coming to ripeful fruition, the joys and tribulations of harvest and finally death as everything turns in its natural cycle back to the soil.' He had paused a moment before continuing. 'Most of us just play at life but you'll be living it every day of your life.'

Her tutor had hugged her then and it was the first time that she had seen him as a man and not a teacher and could see the longing in his eyes.

Joanna turned off the shower and put on her clothes in an unhurried fashion, thinking about her friend Diane who still commuted to London each day, and she smiled. For a moment she stopped to stare out of their bedroom window. The snow had almost cleared now, the rain washing it away. In one direction the field looked the same sandy brown, with a marbled effect of white patches of snow still clinging to the earth, but if she turned her head just slightly and gazed across the furrows there was just a hint of spring green in places, a promise of the crop to come. She threw her favourite burgundy cardigan, which Madelyn her mother-in-law had knitted for her, around her as she walked downstairs.

CHAPTER 5

Thursday 9th May 2019

It was 4.30 am and Bob was up as soon as the alarm went off. The dawn chorus was reaching its crescendo as he headed for the bathroom. He frowned. He could also hear music from Paul's bedroom and so he knew his son had either been up all night, probably on the computer with a can of lager in his other hand, or he had fallen asleep in the early hours leaving the music blaring. Paul had driven home to see his family during reading week this May, knowing that he would be working down in Newquay for the summer surfing season. He had also reasoned that there were fewer distractions at the farm to revise for his exams than there would be at uni.

Bob had been glad to see Paul make the effort, especially for Joanna's sake and, not wanting to create any more aggro with his son at this time of the morning, he forced himself to walk past the door and down the stairs, saying nothing.

In fact Paul was asleep when his father went downstairs. He had been up until late on Futurenet but had fallen into a fitful sleep where the mind barely gave him pause to rest, and registered his father's footsteps on the stairs. Half an hour later he stirred once more, aware of light creeping upon him. He groped for the curtains he had failed to draw the previous night in his drunken state, but as he peered out into the dim light of dawn, his attention was distracted by a figure walking on the other side of the field. Absentmindedly he had picked up his binoculars which his grandfather had given him for his eighth birthday, always hoping to inspire Paul's interest in the nature around him.

Well, he was certainly interested now, and the binoculars had come in handy on more than one occasion. This was not the first time he had seen this attractive young girl, who looked as if she might be bird watching. He had seen her before a few times, either cycling or walking in the area. Once he had even spoken to her and he was annoyed that she had spurned him.

It had been during February reading week and he had driven by her on his way to The Stone Jug, his favourite local.

'Want a lift anywhere? I'm just off into Clophill myself,' he had asked as casually as he could, his heart beginning to flutter faster at the sight of her close up.

He had not expected such a startled look on her face.

'No thanks,' she had replied more sharply than she had intended. She looked as if she had come out of a trance, momentarily wrong-footed by a hint of recognition.

Paul had found her stare unnerving and yet appealing in a weird sort of way. She was almost a challenge. He was certain he did not know her and was sure she was not local, but what was she doing today, three months later, out on his father's field? She had certainly roused his curiosity. He had smiled.

A moment later it was as if her binoculars were locked in his direction, staring back at him. He glanced down at his naked body and involuntarily took a step back into the protective shadows of his room. When he had looked up a second later she had disappeared into the woods. Disappointed, Paul shrugged and decided he might just as well try to have a kip, before his mother started nagging him to get up. He glanced once more towards the now empty field before closing the

44

curtains. The moment his head had hit the pillow, Paul fell into a deep and dreamless, lager induced sleep.

For Bob the morning's milking went well, as it usually did, and he felt comforted by the familiar rhythm of his life on the farm. No ugly words had actually passed between him and his son since Christmas and he wondered whether the continuing bad feeling was his fault or Paul's. Personally Bob hoped he would let it go but maybe it was Paul who felt a trifle guilty.

Once back in the kitchen Bob stoked the range, still handy in the chill of the early mornings and settled down to enjoy his favourite cup of tea of the day. As usual he could hear the sound of Joanna taking a shower over-head, signalling that she was up and that she would soon be down to cook him a hearty breakfast, while he was checking on his Jerseys. Although he was health conscious, starting the day with a 'Full English' had never done him any harm yet, and he was sure he worked it off through the day.

He had just turned to the sports pages at the back of yesterday's paper; never did get the hang of e newspapers and never would, when he heard a sound at the back door. Thump. An excruciating pain shot through his spine and he slumped forward on to the table. Suddenly, it was as if the whole of his insides were torn in two and his shoulders went limp and lifeless.

Upstairs Joanna sang to herself as she got dressed. Throwing her cardigan around her shoulders, more for familiarity than warmth, she crept past Paul's room, though the music would have drowned even the heaviest of footsteps, and walked on down the stairs. She knew full well that her son wouldn't surface until lunch time and, however much she knew it irritated Bob, she well remembered her Cambridge days, sneaking back into her room at four or five and sleeping it off until surfacing at lunchtime on a Saturday morning. She glanced out as she always did, never tiring of the daily changes to the landscape. The field of wheat had taken on a blue-green hue, the grain swelling with the spring rains in their unripe state, swaying like the ocean on a restless day.

Joanna was totally unprepared for the sight before her as she opened the kitchen door. At first she thought Bob had fallen asleep reading the newspaper, which he did occasionally, if he had not slept well. Then she saw the blood behind him and dripping down the leg of his chair, making silent pools of red on the grey flagstone floor.

She screamed, but there was no answer to her cries of anguish. Without thinking she grabbed Bob's shoulder and shook it, shouting for him to wake up until she slumped down, almost insensible, her face contorted with disbelief and shock. Blood stained her hands and cardigan as she sobbed into his head, his hair dampened by her tears.

After a few minutes which felt like an eternity she stood up, her whole body shaking with shock but it was at that moment that Sally, the post woman, hearing Joanna's shouts of distress from the end of the yard, gingerly peered round the open door. She took in the scene; Mrs Thomas with her blood stained hands and pain stricken face, her husband slumped before her and the floor splattered with blood. She summed up the situation in an instant. Without thinking of the consequences she rushed back outside and retrieved her mobile phone. Keeping a watchful eye on the farmhouse as she spoke; she dialled 999 and asked for the police.

Nervous now that the deranged woman would come after her, she rushed towards the gate and was relieved to regain the relative safety of her red van. She locked the door as a precaution and turned the van around in the gateway. Then she waited for the inevitable sirens, checking her watch. With hunched shoulders she wrapped her arms tightly around herself. Only five long minutes had passed. It would take the police at least fifteen to reach her, if the roads were clear. Never once did she imagine that Joanna, this usually calm cheerful lady whom she had known all her life, could be innocent. After all, the facts spoke for themselves, didn't they?

There was a tap at the window and she jumped, startled like a frightened rabbit in her headlamps on a dark morning. It was John, who had been paged by the Jerseys' computer. Puzzled that Bob was not there to sort the problem, which was almost certainly a blocked pipe, he had walked back to the farm, his Border Collie Bengie at his heels.

Sally wound down her window, her eyes darting over his shoulder towards the farmhouse.

'What's the matter Sally? You look ghastly. Are you not feeling well?'

'I'm waiting for the police to arrive, John. It's awful in there.'

'What on earth are you talking about, Sally? Slow down, you're talking in riddles.'

'It's Mrs Thomas. She's murdered her husband,' she said, her trembling hand wiping the tears from her eyes.

John stood there a moment, trying to keep control of his dog, barking at him and tugging at his lead. He did not know what to think. He realised that he could not get anything sensible out of Sally and so he began to walk towards the farmhouse,

Bengie dragging him along. Frantically Sally pressed the button to wind down the passenger side window.

'Don't go in there John. It's far too dangerous.'

John ignored her cries as he walked through the open kitchen door and took in the horror before him. Bengie strained at his leash to run forward, but John pulled him back tied him securely to the boot scraper, where the dog barked in frustration. John stood at the door for a moment, stunned with the shock of it, but as he stood in silence his common sense clicked in, telling him not to jump to the most obvious conclusions. He could see Bob slumped over his newspaper and the floor covered with blood. Joanna was sitting opposite Bob talking quietly to him, encouraging him to wake up, with her blood stained hands resting on his.

At that moment he heard the siren of the approaching police car. He knew that it had stopped at Sally's van and could imagine what she was telling them. He had to know the truth.

'Did you do it Joanna?' he asked gently.

It was as if Joanna was being called out of a trance but had no wish to be woken up. She closed her eyes. She could hear by the quiet firm tone of John's voice that it was imperative for her to answer, but she was paralysed with fear.

John repeated his words, more urgently this time, since he could hear a police car pulling up outside the house and then two uniformed police officers came up behind him and glanced into the farmhouse kitchen before stepping back into the yard.

Joanna's eyes snapped open.

'Of course I didn't, John. What on earth made you think I could do such a thing? I just don't understand.'

John heard more vehicles arrive and turned to see a man wearing an old, ill fitting dark suit, who he assumed was the inspector, walking towards him, the two police officers standing back to let him pass. The inspector, whose lined face looked more than his 59 years, surveyed the farmhouse kitchen for several moments, the video camera on his jacket automatically making a record of the crime scene. Then he nodded to a uniformed policewoman to come forward. Joanna began to sob uncontrollably as the policewoman came and encouraged her to stand before leading her out to the waiting police car. Another uniformed officer was cordoning off the crime scene for forensics. The inspector turned to the man standing in the farmhouse doorway, whose concerned face was watching Joanna's slow progress.

'I'm Inspector Norton and who might you be?'

'I'm the cowman John Cookham. I work with Bob and bring the cows in for milking first thing every morning. He was all right when he left me to finish the milking.' He paused. 'She didn't do it you know,' he added firmly.

'That's for **us**, not you to decide and if Mrs Thomas didn't do it, then **who** else do you think had the opportunity? Is there anyone else in the house?' The inspector stared at him with his piercing eyes and it was not until that moment that it dawned on John that he would be a prime suspect too.

'There's only their son Paul who is probably fast asleep upstairs, but I really have no idea who might have done this Inspector,' John replied quietly.

'We'll ask you to accompany us to the station for questioning nevertheless,' DI Norton barked. 'My officer will show you into a waiting car.' He turned to DC Peterson and DS Brown, plain clothed detectives who'd arrived in a separate car and gestured upstairs.

'You'd best check to see if the lad's upstairs and glance around his room before bringing him down. We'll do a complete search of the house next.'

'Yes sir,' replied DC Peterson as they headed up the stairs, followed down a few minutes later by a bleary eyed, angry young man of about twenty years. The Inspector gestured that the lad be taken out of the front door and away from the scene in the kitchen. Whatever he might know of the incident, and DI Norton imagined very little, the lad should be protected as much as possible from witnessing his father in such a condition.

PART 2
ANNA BERET

CHAPTER 6

Easter 2018   Jersey, Channel Islands ~
Bedfordshire and Cambridge

Anna stared through her binoculars out over towards Noirmont Point from Portelet Common, a favourite spot if she wanted to be alone but to feel out in the wilds too, within easy cycling distance from her home on the outskirts of St Helier. With the cycle path along the Promenade on St Aubin's Bay she was at the harbour within minutes, a popular spot for tourists in all seasons, and then she pedalled the steep and winding back lane towards Noirmont.

She knew every sea bird likely to inhabit these islands, having followed her father on endless forays as a child, but it did not stop the adrenalin rush of maybe, just maybe, sighting something unusual. This time last year she had spotted a pair of gadwalls just off shore here, the unmistakable black rear end of the male grey duck disappearing below the water. It was a rare enough sighting for Anna to report it to the Société. Today she was reassured by the return of the more common fulmars. These white sea-birds with grey wings and yellow beaks, often mistakenly called gulls when in fact they were petrels, were always a comfort to Anna. At least these beautiful birds were still at liberty to choose Jersey as their home, unlike human beings for whom the restrictions of residency were purely financial, 'successfully keeping the riff raff at bay,' her father would say.

Anna was an attractive 20 year old, with shoulder length fair hair and blue-green eyes, reflecting the mood of the sea.

Like most students of her age she wore predominantly casual clothes, although she had a couple of jump suits, one in pale green and one in electric blue which she could dress up or down, depending on the occasion or how the mood took her.

Tomorrow Anna would fly back to the mainland. She had enjoyed a month's break which was to give her time to return to college with the draft of her major second year study. Not quite a dissertation at this stage in her course, but a substantial project nonetheless.

She was heading back for her last term in her second year at Cambridge where she was studying Ornithology, her passion, but she was taking some time out to do her own bit of sleuthing. It had all begun when her aunt died a year ago and in her will she had left Anna a box of books. Not just any books mind, they were her great-great-grandfather's collection and also his travel log - a painstakingly accurate record of birds he had witnessed first-hand in his travels, all beautifully hand drawn and labelled with care; the time and place of the sighting, whether they were alone or in a pair or group. Thus, she had followed not only in her father's footsteps, but in her uncle's, grandfather's, great-grandfather's and great-great-grandfather's too.

Occasionally Anna and her cousins had been allowed to look at the travel logs when they were young and with near reverence Anna had handled the corner of each page with her finger tips, not wanting to damage the drawings in anyway. It was as if she had an inborn respect that they were not only beautiful but priceless. She knew that the family had taken them to be valued in London when her grandfather had passed away, but she also knew that they would never part with them. They were part of her rich heritage and as valued as her family history; good Jersey stock far back to the early nineteenth century when her descendents had come over from France.

She was excited to tell her new boyfriend Nick about it when he called from Cambridge.

'It's not just the journals. Of course I'll treasure those, but there was a scroll of letters too.'

'I suppose you've dug up some family secret Anna. A bit of a cliché isn't it. When are you coming back to Cambridge?'

'My flight's next Tuesday, but Nick, these are so special. They're sepia with age and the handwriting is hard to decipher, but they were written between 1914 and 1918.'

'From a long lost relative,' I suppose.

Anna ignored the mocking in his voice and continued speaking quickly, 'They were from a young girl called Lucille Vardon and she signed her name Lucy. They were written to my great-great grandmother from a place called Haynes in Bedfordshire where she was stationed at an army camp I think. I gather Lucy was my great-great grandmother's cousin. Anyway they stopped abruptly in May 1919 and I'd love to know why.'

'That's obvious isn't it? The war was long over by then. I expect she came home.'

'Oh I'm not sure Nick but..'

'So I'll come and see you as soon as you get back then Anna. Are you looking forward to seeing me too, or will you be so engrossed in reading those letters?'

'That's not fair Nick. Of course I'm looking forward to seeing you. It was lovely of you to drive me to the airport and see me off.'

'Would you like me to pick you up again? We could stop somewhere for a picnic, or a bite to eat at a pub if the weather's not great.'

'That's OK Nick. I've booked my flight to Gatwick this time and my train ticket too. I'll see you in Cambridge.'

'Promise?'

'I promise.' With that she switched her phone off and went back to her task.

That night Nick was far from Anna's mind. She dreamt she was in uniform, serving cheeky officers in a make shift tent and followed by laughter and song as she danced the night away. Not the glaring music of today, but soft and romantic as she was whisked around the sandy dance floor by her handsome uniformed partner.

The letters were so compelling that she decided to take them back with her to Cambridge rather than the books, although she knew that her professor would have been fascinated by the log, and she might have gone up one notch in his expectations of her. After all she was a woman and he was of the old school, soon to retire; long past retirement age, over 80 in fact. He would never say it, because he knew what PC meant, but everyone was aware that he tolerated women at Cambridge like a doting father of past times. He would much prefer to see daughters occupying themselves with child rearing and home making.

On her last evening she visited her grandmother, a formidable woman who still walked her dog for miles every day along coastal paths and inland tracks. Her grandmother parked her old Peugeot at the Corbière end of St Owen's Bay. They headed for the sand dunes of Les Blanches Blanques, more popular with locals than holiday makers, and wove their way towards the Standing Stones, setting Saucer, her oddly named mongrel, free from her lead to run among the tall tufts of grass-topped dunes. As they climbed higher, the views of the bay were spectacular, but it was as they approached the Ossuary, a ring of stones denoting the site of a Neolithic tomb, that grand-daughter and grandmother paused. In a different life Anna might well have chosen archaeology. She loved this place almost as much as the nearby St Owen's Pond, with its ever changing abundance of wildfowl throughout the seasons.

She sighed.

'Grandma, did you hear your parents talking about Lucille Vardon when you were little? She called herself Lucy?'

Anna could not fail to notice her grandmother's initial surprise and discomfort over the question.

'Oh, that was a very long time ago Anna. Why do you ask?'

'Because I've found several letters written from Lucy to your grandmother in the box of books Auntie June gave me.'

'Then I expect that you know far more about her than I do Anna. Anyway, how are you enjoying college?'

Ignoring her grandmother's expression, which had changed into dismissive contempt, Anna replied,

'I love it Grandma, but...

'Do you think you'll ever return to Jersey to live, now that you've tasted the outside world?'

'I've only been as far as Cambridge, Grandma. That's hardly the world.'

'What's Cambridge like? You know your family are so proud of you.'

Realising that her grandmother had gained the upper hand in steering the conversation Anna replied, 'It's a wonderful city,

Grandma, but what I really want to know is why the letters stopped so abruptly.'

Her grandmother stooped down to ruffle the shaggy fur of Saucer before the dog scampered into the scrub-land in search of rabbits and she turned to face Anna.

'I believe strongly that some things are best left well in the past Anna.' Then turning away she called out 'Saucer', signalling that the matter was closed and that it was time to return home, which left Anna frustrated but nevertheless determined to find out the truth.

The following day, on May 8th, Anna took a flight from St Helier to Gatwick. From there she took a train directly to Flitwick Station, not far from the village of Haynes in Bedfordshire.

Anna had booked a night's stay at a little B & B in the village of Clophill. The taxi driver had quite a job turning in the narrow rough road where the quaint Broom Cottage stood. She introduced herself to the landlady Mrs Broom, a cheerful widow who smiled indulgently. Anna was shown up the steep crooked staircase to a cosy little wild rose patterned room with a smoky pink bedspread and old fashioned blankets and sheets.

'I'll make you a cup of tea if you'd like; but I'll put it down in the front room in a few minutes, leaving you time to settle in.

'Oh thank you Mrs Broom. This place is just what I need. It's so lovely and quiet.'

'Call me Mrs B dear. Everyone else does.' And with that Mrs B turned and Anna heard her footsteps retreating on the creaking stairs.

Ten minutes later, when she headed back down, she found a tray with a small willow patterned pot of tea for one, matching jug of milk, cup and saucer and a piece of homemade Victoria sponge which melted in her mouth.

'Umm, this is delicious Mrs B. What a welcome!'

'Oh, I do like to make my guests feel at home. Is there anything else you need, Miss?'

'Call me Anna, please do. Well, as it happened there is something. It seems a bit of a cheek but I saw your bicycle leaning against the wall outside and I was wondering, since I have no transport, if you'd mind me using it this afternoon. That's if you hadn't planned to use it yourself of course.'

'No problem Anna. I cycled over to the store in Maulden to get a few things just before you arrived and I won't be going out again. My daughter's helmet should fit you too. It's in the cupboard in the hall. Just one thing though, you do remember that I don't serve an evening meal don't you?'

'Oh yes, thanks Mrs B. I saw that there were places to eat in the village on the Net.'

'There are three as a matter of fact. There's The Flying Horse. It's a bistro. I've never been there myself but I hear it's popular. It's a good sign that you always see plenty of cars outside and you don't have to book. Then there's The Green Man, opposite on the green; serves Italian food and its run by Italians, so they know their stuff. I can certainly recommend it. Then there's The Stone Jug just up the road from here. It's the locals' pub; lots of atmosphere but it only serves food at lunchtime.'

'After this lovely cake I don't think I'll need another thing till this evening, so maybe I'll treat myself to an Italian meal. Sounds fun but do I have to book?'

'I think it's probably best but I'll do it for you if you like. Will 7.30 be all right?'

'That would be great Mrs B. I think I'll get changed and borrow your bike if I may.'

'No problem my dear. Help yourself.'

A few moments later Anna was on the rickety bicycle. She checked the map that she had printed from the Futurenet and within minutes she was passing an orchard on her right hand side and heading up Great Lane. She enjoyed the exhilaration of pedalling as fast as she could up the slopes and freewheeling down the next. It was a beautiful day. Within minutes she paused to take in the sight of a large country manor in front of her and she tried to imagine what had happened to Lucille Vardon nearly a century ago.

Turning right at this junction she cycled more slowly into Church End and with the iron stone church nestled to her left, she slipped up the side track towards the churchyard. She left Mrs B's bike locked securely to a fence before creeping inside. Churchyards always made her feel like she did not want to make a sound, not so much out of reverence but because the atmosphere was so peaceful. Today there was just a gentle breeze which caught a wisp of her fair hair escaping from her helmet. She removed it and shook her head, her hair falling around her shoulders as she looked around her.

Anna walked slowly amongst the gravestones, but after a few moments was drawn towards a large age worn stone cross which was leaning at a disturbing angle, as if the occupant might be pushing her way out. Anna shivered. She stooped and peered, first at the embellishment denoting that it was a military WW1 grave and then to the inscription.

IN MEMORY OF

LUCILLE VARDON

QUEEN MARY'S ARMY AUXILIARY CORPS

who died age 21

9 May 1919

REMEMBERED WITH HONOUR

Here you are Lucy,' Anna whispered. 'What secrets do you hold, deep below the earth? If only you could tell me your story,' Anna sighed. After taking a few photos and writing down the inscription, which was weather worn and hard to decipher, she sat down on a wooden bench nearby.

Anna daydreamed taking in the scene, Haynes Park standing majestically on the hill with the drive sweeping down and passing what must have been estate cottages. As her eyes continued to follow the drive towards the rustic church, Anna became aware of another lady in the graveyard, who was tending a more recent grave, not far from where she sat. Anna did not like to stare because the lady looked soul stricken as she knelt at the foot of a recently dug grave with a small wooden cross. Anna would have liked to comfort her but instead she turned away, aware that the lady needed some privacy to arrange her flowers in peace. Anna wished that she had also brought some flowers to pay tribute to Lucille Vardon, this member of her family who had died here nearly 100 years ago, so young and so far from her island home.

Her cycle back was faster. It was warm now in the late spring sunshine, but the hills seemed gentler on her return. Finally, as she neared the edge of Clophill she paused to gain her breath and looked over the hillside towards an old church set amongst the trees. Then within a few minutes she was back at Broom Cottage.

'Is there anywhere local I can buy flowers,' she called through the kitchen door.

'Yes, my dear,' said Mrs B, coming out of the kitchen and wiping her hands on her apron. 'There's a place at the far end of the village towards Shefford. You can't miss it but it's a cycle ride rather than a walk.'

'Thanks Mrs B. I'll have a bit of a rest in your garden and then try to find it if I may.'

'You're welcome,' Mrs B replied retreating behind the closed kitchen door.

After sitting for five minutes Anna set off again and with ease she found the small nursery and bought some vivid yellow chrysanthemums, aware that her choice of flower was in line with her family's French custom. She would take them the following morning before heading back to Cambridge.

That afternoon Anna retraced some of her route on foot and, taking her binoculars up to woodland near the old church on the hill, she spent a pleasant hour bird watching. The fact that she noticed nothing unusual did little to lessen her enjoyment. During the evening she ate deliciously prepared sea bass at The Green Man. 'As good as at home,' she complimented the good looking waiter.

Feeling truly replete, Anna ambled past the Stone Jug where there was a group of young men sitting on the benches outside. She felt their admiring looks which made her smile, but one young man, the one with jet black hair and piercing blue eyes, captured her sideways glance in a meaningful millisecond.

Back at the B & B she spent an hour skimming though the local magazines before she headed for bed. Just before she turned in, a small article caught her eye about migrating waxwings visiting the area each February. They were cheerful migrating birds and so she made a note of it in her diary. After that she retired for the night and slept soundly.

Early the following day Anna borrowed Mrs B's bike before breakfast and pedalled back the couple of miles or so to the churchyard in Haynes. It was a misty morning, but it promised to be another fine day. This time the churchyard was deserted, her only companions being the finches and blue tits, hopping in and out of the hedgerows. She went directly to Lucy's grave but, to her surprise, there were already white carnations at its foot. The surrounding area had also been tended to; the grass clipped and weeds removed.

Reverently Anna placed the yellow chrysanths dotted between the white carnations and, standing back to admire her handiwork she smiled; pleased that Lucy had not been completely forgotten, but rather puzzled as to who might have been looking after the grave so well.

With a hearty breakfast awaiting her she hastened back to Clophill, after which she walked down to catch the bus into Bedford. There she did a detour to the Bedford archives, which she had contacted a week before.

'Strangely enough we know exactly where to find pictures and information about Lucille Vardon because a lady has been carrying out some research on several occasions in the last few months. Look, here are the references for pictures and postcards of Haynes Park and these are the references to the local newspaper accounts of Lucille Vardon's murder. Would you like to fill in the screen requests and I'll have them sent up?

'What do you mean by newspaper reports of Lucille's murder?'

'I thought you must know. Lucille Vardon was murdered in Wilshamstead Woods near Haynes Park back in 1919.'

In a daze Anna filled in the details while the man continued enthusiastically. 'There's an article on a web site too, from a young lady who called in nearly ten years ago. Have you seen it yet?'

The man, who must have been in his mid fifties, was bearded with glasses, hiding his bright brown eyes which shone with enthusiasm for his job of unearthing details of the past. He bent down to click on his search engine and, as he typed in the name 'Lucille Vardon,' almost instantly an account of her life flashed up on the screen before them.

Anna scanned through the article and was even more surprised to see her cousin's name at the end. She had not thought to get in touch with Kate or her sister Dawn. They were several years older than Anna and had both settled on Jersey. Kate had trained as a dental nurse and Dawn was a hairdresser; both were married now. She was surprised because she did not think they had been the least bit interested in family history since last time she had met them at Dawn's wedding they had been keen to get married and start a family. She could have kicked herself for missed opportunities.

I could send Kate a message, Anna thought. What a shame I'll not be back on Jersey to talk to her until the summer. She must have carried out the research when she was studying dentistry in England a good few years back. Where did she study now? Wasn't it Barnfield College in Luton? That's only a few miles from here isn't it?

While Anna was lost in thought she barely registered that the bearded man was talking to her again.

'The writer was from Jersey too I believe, though it was several years ago and it's hard to remember the details. It just came to mind as being rather odd when we had another request for information less than a year ago. Although the recent request was a local lady I believe.'

'Do you have any contact details?' Anna asked.

'I'm afraid we are not at liberty to give details but she did say she was setting up another website. I have it here I think. There you are.' The man wrote down both of the websites on a piece of scrap paper and passed it to Anna, who folded it up and put it in her pocket.

A few moments later the helpful man brought several boxes and some white gloves to Anna's table.

'Do you know the author of the article then?' he asked as he placed the items reverently in front of her.

'Yes, she's my cousin.'

'Oh, how odd,' the man replied and it was obvious to Anna that a light had dimmed in his eyes. Any serious researcher would have exhausted the avenues of close family well before arriving in an archive. 'I'll leave you to it then, but we'd appreciate that you wear these gloves to protect the items, please. After all they're nearly 100 years old,' he added, stating the obvious and making Anna squirm.

Anna lost track of time, fascinated as she browsed though photos and postcards, gleaning a picture of what Lucille's life might have been like. It was when she began reading through the detailed newspaper reports of Lucille Vardon's murder on the old 'Reader-Copier' machine, that she was gripped by an overwhelming sense of injustice. It appeared that no one had been convicted for the murder and the more she read the more she was hooked by this tragic story and felt empathy for this young girl, whose life was snatched away from her so young.

Suddenly aware that time was passing all too quickly Anna printed out a couple of the pages to read later. Picking up all her acquired notes, she thanked the man, paid the lady at the front desk for the copies, retrieved her belongings from the locker and strolled along the river, the short distance to the town centre and bus station and caught the Cambridge bus.

That evening back in her digs, she was glancing through the letters, when the door bell rang. It was Nick. Though reluctant to leave her task, she was pleased to see him.

'So what's new?' he asked. 'Glad to see me?' he grinned.

'Of course I am but I've made this exciting discovery.'

'Some unusual birds have arrived on Jersey's shores no doubt. Why don't we talk about you and me instead? That's far more exciting. Like when are you going to allow us to...?' He leaned over the table putting his hand underneath and stroking her leg as high as he could reach.

Anna unconsciously shifted out of his way. 'Soon,' she replied, seeing a shadow of anger cross his brow.

'No listen,' Anna exclaimed, adept like her Gran at changing the subject. 'You know those old letters I found in my great great grandfather's belongings about a lady called Lucille Vardon. Today I found out that she was murdered.'

'What, murdered today!'

'No, Nick, I told you on the phone. This girl lived in 1919, and just like me she travelled from her home in St Aubin's Bay, but she joined the QMAAC. That's the Queen Mary's Army Auxiliary Corps. She was stationed at a training camp at Haynes Manor, not far from Bedford one hundred years ago. Then, today, I discovered that she was brutally murdered just outside Bedford.'

'Up to no good was she? A bit of a tease' Nick added with a knowing look in Anna's direction.

'Don't be like that Nick. No, I've read she was a popular, pretty young lady, who served as a waitress in the officer's mess.'

'Why was she still there in 1919? Didn't she go home to Jersey at the end of the war?'

'I know she went back home for a short break before returning to Haynes, but the troops still had to be in readiness for war even in 1919.'

'A bit of a serious lass doing her duty then?'

'By her letters she sounded a lovely girl with quite a sense of humour.'

'A bit of a good time girl was she?'

'No Nick. You're not listening to me. She was a good girl, though it appears she had admirers. One letter hinted that any relationships she enjoyed were innocent. She seemed to be a girl who rarely took life seriously. Maybe that was the effect of living through The Great War or perhaps it was the girl's true nature.' Anna paused. Nick was looking thoughtfully at her.

'As I say, a good few parallels to you then Anna and, like you, she was probably a big tease. You should loosen up a bit; after all I can't wait...'

Anna did not want Nick to finish the old cliché so she leant over and kissed him suggestively.

'I rest my case,' replied Nick with a satisfied grin.

'Anyway, I'm shattered. It's been a long day and so if you don't mind...'

'You'd like us to go to bed,' smiled Nick, getting up and moving towards her.

'I'd like to go to bed on my own,' replied Anna firmly, opening the door for him to leave.

'Whatever you say,' replied Nick, 'but...'

'No buts, Nick, but perhaps we could meet up later on in the week.'

Nick took her into his arms roughly and kissed her passionately; Anna relaxed and returned his kiss.

'Like I said, a big tease,' he grinned back over his shoulder as he marched out.

Despite trying to have an early night Anna could not sleep. The letters had inspired her to discover more about this distant relation and so she vowed that she would find out all she could, not knowing that this investigation would ultimately change her life.

On her second evening back in Cambridge she refused invitations to join her many friends for a night in the city, claiming tiredness after her journey, and ignored Nick's calls too. Instead she stayed in and began to read the letters from Jersey again, using some thin gloves to handle the letters with delicate reverence.

'Umm, that distinctive smell of aged paper,' she said out loud as she opened the frail folds.

Before settling down for the night she sent her cousin Kate a message through Facebook, the only way they ever kept in touch these days and by morning she had received a brief reply.

'Hi Anna. Lovely to hear from you. The story was spoken about quite a lot as I grew up, so I did some research in my teens both here at home and in Bedford when I was studying. Put together the website and forgot about it to be honest with you.

Work and family took over. I've never seen the letters though. Hey, get in touch Cuz next time you're home. Love Kate'

Anna resolved to be more methodical and to transcribe all the letters, a job made relatively easy by voice activated software, although irritating when she made frequent errors as she misread the now almost illegible writing.

Over the next few weeks Anna spent a great deal of her free time on the Futurenet. On the most recent website there was a link to a blog which published posts related to Haynes, Haynes Park and Lucille Vardon twice a week and so she decided to become a subscriber. Some of the information she had gleaned already, but there was also much which surprised her. It was like the tide turning to reveal fragments of ancient wood. As the tide recedes an outline of a wreck becomes more obvious. Then with research, careful observation and an element of intuition it may be possible to draw a picture of what it might have been like, but you may never know for sure. Snippets of the features may be revealed but not enough to understand the complete picture. On this website it was like that. The writer always left with a question and in the end Anna could not resist having a guess at some of the answers.

'Do you think Lucille was innocent?' The Webmaster asked.

After much thought Anna had answered,

'Maybe Lucille was not so innocent after all. Maybe she was pregnant or stringing along a couple of admirers.'

The answer came back sharply.

'I disagree. Many witnesses claimed that Lucille was a good girl, well liked but one who protected her virtue.'

And so it continued; compelling and time wasting, as Anna juggled her studies with an ever growing desire to know the truth.

After about a month Anna read a question which made up her mind to divulge a snippet she had found in Lucy's letters which puzzled her:

'*Could someone else have been involved?*' The screen asked.

Anna was excited to answer,

'*One of Lucy's letters to my great great grandmother mentions a farmer with an Austin 7hp motor car. What do you think?*'

There was no response at first then Anna opened her email box the following day and saw that she had a message from the site.

"GOOD NEWS! YOUR LAST PIECE OF INFORMATION YOU SUBMITTED TO THE SITE WAS DEEMED TO BE SO USEFUL TO OUR RESEARCH THAT YOU HAVE WON A PRIZE JUST TO SAY THANK YOU.
REPORT TO WAYBACK CLASSICS, CLOPHILL FOR YOUR PERSONAL GUIDED TOUR OF BEDFORDSHIRE ON SATURDAY JUNE 26TH AT 10 AM.
The tour will take approximately six hours and will include a picnic lunch!"

Anna printed off the page with a sense of shock. She tried to find a way of contacting the website manager for more information but there were no contact details and so, finding the number for Wayback Classics on their website, she phoned them. The helpful man confirmed that the booking had been made and that it was all genuine and so, excitedly she called Mrs B at Broom Cottage to book a room for another stay.

CHAPTER 7

June 2018   Anna in Bedfordshire

Anna woke up in the now familiar wild rose patterned room and sighed. She had stretched over to where Nick was still asleep, glad that he had come along with her. She would have been too nervous to have come on her own.

'What's it worth,' he had exclaimed with a cheeky grin, when she had asked him.

Last night they had dined at the bistro at The Flying Horse and giggled back in the dark, stopping off at The Stone Jug for another night cap for courage before reaching the B & B. In fact, it was such a beautiful night that Nick had pressed his finger to his lips as he retrieved an old car rug from his beat up Mini Countryman, very popular in their revival ten years ago and now that it had been converted to electric by its previous owner, quite economical too.

He took her hand and they crept up the lane, Nick shining a torch back to her to guide her safely over a nearby stile and into a little spinney. They found a spot away from the track and Nick pulled Anna towards him. Their lips met with passion and soon his hands were running smoothly over her jump suit. With a dexterity which surprised Anna he quickly undid the buttons and the suit slipped to the ground revealing her body which glistened in the moonlight glimmering through the branches over head. Within seconds he had slipped off his clothes too and gently laid her on the rug. With no need to hurry he kissed her, starting with her neck and slowly down to her breasts, releasing her bra strap to gently suck her nipples. She arched

70

up to him as his hands explored her secret parts and as they made love there in the woods, Anna had never felt so satisfied and at one with her world.

It was as they sat up afterwards that she felt a sudden cool breeze on her shoulders. Lucille had been murdered in woods similar to these only a few miles away. There was a crackle deeper in the woodland. Anna shuddered. Thinking she was cold, Nick draped the rug around her and pulled her to him once more.

'No Nick, I think we'd best get back now. It must be gone eleven and I said we'd be in by then.'

'Mrs B said she would leave the latch up for us. You worry too much Anna.'

'I know, but we've got an exciting day ahead of us and I for one want to enjoy it. We should go back now.'

With that, she had stood up and slipped on her jump suit and put out a hand to pull Nick up by her side.

'That was a lovely way to begin our weekend,' she had said as she gave him a reassuring hug.

The following morning they were enjoying Mrs B's hearty breakfast when they heard a knock at the door.

'I'll be a couple of minutes,' called Anna as she headed up the rickety stairs to fetch their jackets and her handbag. Nick followed the driver, who introduced himself as David, out to the waiting car. It was a beautiful white Mark Two Jaguar, which Nick stood admiring until Anna joined them.

David, who was dressed for the part of a chauffeur with a cap over his greying hairline and a black brass-buttoned jacket, held the car door open for them.

'Just a few important points to mention,' he said once they were settled. 'Before you ask, there are no seatbelts in the back of this car because it was built in 1966 before seatbelts were compulsory. I won't be going very fast but I'd rather you didn't lean forward to ask questions. Just sit back and listen and I'll explain the tour as we go along.'

Anna and Nick smiled at each other in a conspiratorial way as they relaxed in the luxury of the red leather upholstery. She was surprised that they were heading up the now familiar Great Lane and even more puzzled when they pulled up outside Haynes Church.

The driver opened the door for them to step out and began to give them a short history of Haynes Park, mentioning the period of history, during The Great War, which was of interest to Anna before leading them through the churchyard to where Anna noticed there were fresh flowers on Lucille's grave. Anna felt a sudden chill in the air.

From there they drove along country lanes and wound their way through the quaint little village of Old Warden, with its thatched cottages and gardens overflowing with an array of pastel shades. They pulled into a place called The Shuttleworth Collection but to Nick's disappointment the driver explained that they were not here to look at the museum of old aircraft. Instead they pulled up outside the entrance to the Birds of Prey area where they spent a delightful hour watching displays of falcons, owls, a golden eagle and even a vulture.

'I've never thought of vultures as beautiful before,' Anna remarked.

Nick shuddered.

'Not sure I'd like to come across one in the desert.'

'I know about their reputation but look at it circling. It's so graceful.'

'Umm,' said Nick as it landed and was treated to a bit of meat from the handler. 'Ugly bastard close up though.'

After the show though, Nick had to admit that he was impressed.

After a quick cup of coffee their route took them back to Haynes where the whole village was preparing for the Haynes 100, the village event of the year. David parked the Jag carefully between a 1965 Rover P4 Saloon and a 1967 Sunbeam Alpine sports car.

'The Haynes 100 marks a centenary of motoring and the organisers try to represent a vehicle for each year for the last one hundred, and more some years,' David explained.

Nick nodded, smiling in anticipation.

'You have just over an hour to wander around the cars while I set up a picnic for you on a rug in front of the car. Then, after lunch, we'll join the parade; an exciting event where we'll drive in convoy around the village.' He looked up as if waiting for any questions.

'So I'll see you at about 12.30 then. Enjoy yourselves.'

'Thank you,' Anna replied, realising that Nick had already wandered off, his face like a boy on a Christmas morning grinning with anticipation with too many toys to enjoy.

'Incredible,' he exclaimed at a 1909 steam car, which had obviously been brought in on a trailer.

Just a few cars down Anna hesitated and caught her breath. If she was not mistaken it was the very same car she had seen in a photo of Haynes Park Camp back in 1919 with those two young ladies standing on the drive. It could be an unnerving coincidence though, she reasoned. 'I wonder who this belongs to?' she must have whispered out loud.

'This beauty is my father's but it's been in the family since almost new,' a greying but not unattractive man in a tweed jacket and matching flat cap exclaimed proudly. We're only from up the road; Pear Tree Farm near Church End Haynes. Are you local too?' he asked.

'Oh no! I'm from Jersey, but we're studying at Cambridge,' Anna answered. She was increasingly aware of the parallels between her and Lucy's life and even on this warm afternoon she felt her temperature drop as if a cloud had passed overhead. She could not help but wonder yet again why she had won this amazing prize from someone who obviously knew a great deal about her life and Lucille Vardon's. She was certain beyond all doubt that this encounter was not a chance happening but part of the tour.

'My wife studied at Cambridge. In fact we met there,' the man added. He certainly did not look like a murderer. Anna shook herself. This was becoming an obsession. She gave herself a mental telling off. After all, Lucy's murder happened a very long time ago didn't it?

Anna and Nick nodded at the man politely before moving on down the rows of spectacular cars.

'Awesome,' Nick commented an hour later as they finally reached a 2017 Lotus, which had actually been driven at Le Mans the previous year, and it's incongruous neighbour and the last of the exhibits was a 2018 electric Smart Car in mint condition. It was so narrow that it was designed to use the network of cycle lanes which now criss-crossed the country, with handy charging points at intervals along the way. It reminded Anna of the play vehicles her brother had drooled

74

over in Hamley's as a kid on one of their rare Christmas trips to London as a family.

'For someone studying English at Cambridge, your vocabulary this afternoon has been severely limited,' she remarked with irritation. 'I think it's time for our lunch,' she added trying to take her mind off the car and more especially the farmer.

'This is good,' Nick said, tucking into some game pie. 'What a treat. How's yours?' he asked, unable to hide his disdain at the sight of Anna's plate full of smoked mackerel and salad.

'Delicious thanks and this wine's excellent too. You'd hardly believe it wasn't French. Old Warden Sparkling.' Anna read out the label on the bottle. 'I bet you haven't any room for cheese.'

'You wanna bet,' said Nick taking a slice of an English Brie, not so local but from Somerset. Nick stretched out on the picnic rug. 'This is the life!'

Anna giggled, the wine softening her demeanour.

'You should have seen your face looking at all those cars.'

'Well, you have to admit it's quite a spectacular sight. A unique collection of vehicles and I expect it's different each year too. I wonder how much it costs to keep one of these going.' Nick waved at the Jag behind them.

'In your dreams,' replied Anna. 'Have you used up all the adjectives you can think of ....? Awesome, unique, spectacular. Any more?' Anna raised her eyebrows, her head tilted questioningly; just catching a napkin Nick playfully flew in her direction.

Before she could retaliate David, the chauffeur walked up to them. 'Excuse me. Sorry to butt in but have you finished your lunch. It's just that the parade begins in ten minutes and we should be getting in the car.'

'Oh!' said Anna jumping to her feet, starting to collect the debris from their picnic. Nick was still lying back observing the cars around them.

'I'll do that,' replied David, 'If you could both hop in the back.'

'Come on lazy!' Anna reached out for Nick's hand and brought him to his feet so that David could fold up the rug and put it in the boot with the basket.

Once back in the car he turned. 'We'll be taking nearly two circuits but then we'll veer off half way through the second and head back to Haynes for the end of our tour. I assume that you'll want to be dropped off back at Mrs Broom's.'

'That's fine thanks,' replied Anna.

David followed the '65 Rover around the arena and out on to the lane. Onlookers waved and cheered as each vehicle passed them by and Nick and Anna joined in the spirit of the parade and waved back, David tooting the horn to join the cacophony of sounds. They followed the convoy of distinguished vehicles, not just cars but trucks, motor bikes and even a hearse, winding slowly through the village, taking a loop along the country lanes and back to the village hall. There was a distinctive smell of engine oil as they passed by, intermingled with aromas from various garden barbeques.

In the middle of the second circuit David broke away and turned towards Church End and Anna was not surprised to be following the Austin 7hp out of the village too. This time a young man, probably the farmer's son, was driving. She tried to take no notice as it turned into what was obviously the track up to the farm, but the son pulled to a standstill and both farmer and son waved, the son's and Anna's eyes locking momentarily in a way which left Anna feeling decidedly uneasy and yet full of instant desire. She recognised him instantly but feeling compelled to return the compliment she smiled as she and Nick waved.

Very soon they were back at Mrs B's which was becoming a bit like a home from home for Anna. The driver passed over their Personal e-Scrapbook of their tour and Anna sat up in bed clicking through each page. Nick still irritated her, so that when he made advances to her that night she pushed him away claiming 'the wrong time of the month.'

'I thought you were a bit out of sorts today,' Nick remarked as he gave her a good natured hug and turned over, soon deep in the land of sleep.

For Anna, sleep was elusive. She could not get the farmer or his car out of her mind and when finally she did nod off, her dreams were a weird mixture of present day happenings and times when she was Lucy, working at Haynes Park. An army officer standing in the field in front of her held a large vulture on his gloved hand and in her dream she watched mesmerised as the bird flew high up above them, circled once, ever searching, before swooping down. When the bird flew back to its waiting handler it barely missed Lucy's head before depositing, not a mouse or a rabbit but a scroll of paper into his outstretched hand. Anna heard the sound of a car behind her and although she could sense that Lucille was in danger, it was as if she was also outside her own body and wanted desperately to warn Lucille but could not. She looked down and a bloodied old looking blade was at her feet.

She woke up soon after in a cold sweat and got up to fetch a glass of water from the bathroom before drifting off into a dream free sleep.

Once back in Cambridge she focused on her studies to complete the year successfully, passing all her exams and assignments with no marks less than an A. July on Jersey was uneventful although it was made more bearable by the frequent messages from Nick, who was working in a bar in Malaga.

Anna did not like Jersey in August, too many grockles and she had arisen at 5 am one morning just to enjoy the peace and solitude of Portelet Bay. It was a bit of a clamber over the rocks to reach the beach but it was blissfully empty. That was not to say she was entirely alone. Since the tide was low she noted a couple of fishermen who had already climbed to the farthest rocks below the tower, neither acknowledging the other in their bid for isolation. Like her, they would be long gone before the holiday-makers had even arisen for breakfast.

Her thoughts turned to Nick as she sat on the rocks looking out to sea. Yes, he was good looking and made her laugh. He fulfilled her needs and they shared a common interest in birds, the feathered variety, but she had a feeling that there was something missing in their relationship. As Lucille had hinted in her letters, she felt sure she had not met Mr Right yet. Anna thought of their last conversation while they sat at Gatwick Airport before Nick had left for Spain.

'Don't get so obsessed with this murder thing while you're at home. It's making you a bit dull to be honest.'

'Why do you say that, Nick?'

'Because it's changing your whole personality. You used to be so bubbly but now, well, you seem to be broody all the time; too serious by half.'

'What's wrong with finding out what happened, Nick? I just want to know who murdered Lucy,' answered Anna, eyes averted and her left hand toying with the tassel on her handbag.

'It was so long ago Anna,' replied Nick, his voice softening in the hopes of melting her into common sense. 'You need to let it go because you'll never find the truth now. Oh, I don't know Anna, I worry about you. How can I explain?' Nick scratched his head in frustration. 'You don't seem to be living in the here and now.' Nick turned to look directly at her, his eyes inviting her to lighten up and give him a passionate goodbye kiss before he left.

'It's important to me,' Anna replied, a determination in her voice, but relenting for a moment she had reached across and returned his embrace.

Nick had pulled away first.

'I must go now,' he had said, glancing down at his watch, and without another word he turned towards Departures, not looking back.

Anna tried to dismiss thoughts of Nick from her mind as she walked home to prepare for her journey back to England the following day for her final year at Cambridge. She had a dissertation to research for and so she tried to keep Lucille Vardon from her mind, too. Ideally she would have liked to have spent July on the Island of Burhou just off the coast of Alderney observing puffins. Her idea of heaven would have been to set up camp in the little tumbledown cottage on the island and spend two weeks there, cut off from the main island except for a delivery of supplies including fresh water every couple of days, if weather permitted. To watch the puffins leave, allegedly at 9 am, to be precise, on 26th July, would be amazing.

She had run out of time now, but maybe she could leave that for her Master's Degree. It would be fantastic if she gained an A+ in her finals and was sponsored to do the research by her college. She mused on this possibility during her short flight back to the mainland.

With this goal in mind Anna tried to focus wholeheartedly on her studies, although she could not resist taking another trip to Clophill in February in order to try and catch a glimpse of those elusive waxwings. She stayed at the B & B for a couple of nights and, borrowing Mrs B's bike, she managed to get about.

Up at dawn on both mornings and accompanying a couple of local enthusiasts in their vigil, she was delighted that her visit was not in vain. Several other twitchers had also joined them and set up no end of elaborate camera equipment in order to capture the moment. She could not compete with these professionals and yet she was proud of her photos nevertheless.

That afternoon Anna could not resist visiting Haynes churchyard once more. This time she had brought an ornament of a couple of metal birds on fine poles which she thought looked a bit like seagulls.

'There you are Lucy,' she whispered. 'They'll remind you of home.'

Having no reply she continued,

'I'll find him Lucy. I promise you I will. You and me, we sound so alike. I've got to go now but I promise I'll be back.'

Cycling to the B & B she happened to pass a battered old Land Rover and sitting at the wheel she recognised the farmer's son. Anna fixed her eyes on the road and pedalled furiously along Great Lane, relieved to arrive at Broom Cottage where Mrs B made her a lovely cup of tea.

'That'll warm you up,' she said.

'Do you happen to know the farmer over near Church End Haynes, who has an Austin 7hp,' she found herself asking.

'No I'm afraid I don't. I think I've seen one driving about but we villagers keep ourselves to ourselves really. I don't know many people in Haynes at all. Why do you ask?'

'Not to worry,' Anna replied, unable to hide her reddening cheeks.

It was a Friday night and Anna had decided to save money and buy some fish and chips at the van she had heard visited the village green once a week. Taking Mrs B's bike she was soon jostling with the pleasant natured crowd near to the post office.

'No love. There's no point standing here. We've already ordered,' explained a kindly looking middle aged lady.

'Go straight to the hatch,' chimed in a lad of about seventeen years, polite and unusually helpful for a boy of his age. Like home, thought Anna.

'55.' A man, with two young kids on small push bikes who had been meandering in and out of the queue, went to collect his large order at the hatch and the lady nodded with encouragement as Anna stepped behind him.

Curious to see Yellow Fin on the menu Anna placed her order before joining the patiently waiting group behind her who were stomping their feet and clapping their hands to keep moving in the chill of the early evening.

'So you're not local then,' the lady said.

'No, I'm staying at Broom Cottage. Come to see the waxwings,'

'Oh, I saw a bit about them in our village magazine, The Spotlight,' the lady answered.

'56'

'That's me,' she beamed. 'Enjoy your fish and chips,' she remarked as she headed off towards her car.

'Good that it's cooked fresh,' the young lad said, as if apologising for the delay.

'Oh, I agree,' replied Anna.

'57' was the cue for the lad to disappear too and his shy smile amused Anna that he was already smitten, but at that moment she was distracted by the Land Rover which was pulling up beside the green. Just as the farmer's son was walking towards Anna the number '60' was called and Anna rushed up to collect her meal from the cheery lady at the hatch, before she got back on the bike. The farmer's son raised his hand as she brushed past him. Lucky escape she thought.

Despite protests from Mrs B, Anna relaxed, eating her fish and chips at the garden table on the patio, wrapped up in her mock sheepskin coat. After supper she did not want to sleep on a full stomach and so she strolled up the track, torch in hand. It was spooky pitch-black, but soon she reached a clearing where horses were still grazing and the horizon was a beautiful shade of pinkish orange. Above her the stars shone in a deep purple sky.

Glancing towards the horizon, which she guessed was mainly light pollution, she headed in the opposite direction taking determined strides, both to keep warm and to walk off her substantial meal. She did not see a soul until she turned down Mill Lane when she heard the rumble of a car and lights come around the bend in front of her. She moved to the edge of the lane and shone her torch out to make sure the driver had noticed her, but was startled when the familiar Land Rover pulled up beside her.

'Can I give you a lift anywhere?' he asked.

Anna's complexion paled as she recognised the farmer's son.

'No thanks,' she stuttered. 'I'm just enjoying a walk.'

'No problem, but it's so dark now. You're staying at Broom Cottage aren't you?' he asked. 'I'm going to the pub so I drive almost past there,' he added hoping the girl would change her mind to satisfy his curiosity if nothing else.

'Um, yes, but honestly, I'd rather walk if you don't mind, thanks.'

'OK then,' replied the farmer's son. After a pause he added, 'My name's Paul by the way.'

Although he seemed friendly enough, Anna could not fail to notice his disappointed frown before he drove away.

Anna took a deep breath to slow her beating heart. Her fear was irrational but who should you really trust? Quickening her pace she was soon passing some scattered houses and bungalows, but it was not until she had closed the old oak front door of Mrs B's and snapped the bolt that she sighed with relief. It did not occur to her to wonder where he had been since she had bumped into him at the chip van or why he should offer to go back towards Clophill when he was heading in the opposite direction.

As Anna headed back to Cambridge she vowed she would leave this sleuthing behind her and focus on her studies. She certainly needed to concentrate on her final dissertation and so she pushed Lucille Vardon and the farmer's son firmly from her mind.

Her relationship with Nick was a bit frosty too. The last time they had spoken on the phone she had nearly finished it but hesitated because it was a bit cowardly not being face to face. She had her principles and would hate to be treated so appallingly herself.

'Come out for a drink tonight. You're working too hard,' he had said.

'Oh no Nick if it's all the same to you. I'm so close to finishing this that I'd be terrible company.'

'Even more reason to take a break. You know what they say about "*All work and no play*"?'

'Thanks Nick for that vote of confidence,' Anna snapped, hurt by the implication that she was dull. There was an awkward pause.

'I've missed you,' began Nick in a more conciliatory tone. 'That's the truth,' he added softly, as if warming to his theme.

'I've got to wash my hair Nick,' Anna replied, wishing she could end the conversation abruptly, but was too polite to do so.

'That old cliché!' stormed Nick slamming down the phone.

Anna sighed and went to have a shower and as the water ran through her silky hair she imagined all her pent up emotions running down the plug hole. She only saw Nick a couple of brief occasions after that until he announced that he had arranged to take her away for her birthday in May and no excuses this time. So it was with nervous surprise that he drove her up to Broom Cottage once more.

'Hello dear. Happy Birthday,' Mrs B beamed, leading them into the front room where a special birthday cake greeted them.

'Oh you shouldn't have gone to so much trouble Mrs B but thank you. It's very kind of you.'

'A little bird told me,' she winked as Anna noticed the amazingly detailed iced robins on the log cake.

'I know it looks a bit Christmassy but I knew you'd like them,' Mrs B apologized.

'It's beautiful Mrs B. A lovely surprise.'

When she had gone to collect the tea Anna frowned, reminded of the old wives tale about robins and death.

'I thought you'd be pleased,' sighed Nick, crestfallen that Anna looked so dejected.

Anna forced a smile as Mrs B came in with their tea but it soon disappeared the moment Mrs B's back had turned.

'You save your smiles for everyone else but me,' Nick said running his hands through his hair, his bottom lip twitching - a sign of his subdued anger.

'I thought you wanted me to forget all of this. Put it behind me!'

There was a long silence as Anna poured their tea.

'You've changed so much, Anna,' was all Nick could think to say.

At this remark Anna lost patience.

'I'm going out,' she said as she stormed out of the house, taking Mrs B's bike without asking and pedalled furiously out of the village towards Church End Haynes.

As Anna knelt beside Lucy's well tended grave floods of tears started to flow.

'What happened to you, Lucy?' she whispered as all her pent up emotions were finally spent. A little robin sang his song of mourning from the nearby hedge.

Anna walked slowly back to the bicycle, her hands absentmindedly thrust deep in her pockets. She felt a slip of paper and as she focused on the print an eerie realisation dawned. By chance, or was anything purely by chance, the following day was the centenary of Lucille Vardon's murder,

9th May. She had even had a DM$_3$ inviting her to a memorial gathering in the churchyard at dawn. A chill filled her being and she shook her head as if trying to forget. That's the last place she wanted to be in the morning. She had deleted the message but as an afterthought, had scribbled it down on the piece of paper in her hand.

As Anna cycled back to the village she decided to apologize to Nick for being such a fool. He had probably booked supper for them somewhere nice but after waiting until after 10 pm, eating only a bag of crisps and an apple she headed up the creaky staircase to bed. It was midnight before he stumbled in beside her, drunk out of his mind from an evening at The Stone Jug so it was not difficult to fend off his advances and soon she heard the reassuring sound of his heavy breathing. Anna turned over but sleep eluded her and she tossed until almost dawn.

At 4 am she slipped silently from the bed and hurriedly dressed in their small bathroom. She crept downstairs and was relieved to step out into the fresh early morning air. By 4.30 am she found herself near the woods at Pear Tree Farm and, hiding her bicycle behind a bush, she strolled up the path, the natural beauty of her surroundings calming her. She retrieved her trusty binoculars and little notepad from her rucksack and out of habit started to note which birds she saw or heard in the woods and she was truly lost in the moment. By this time the dawn chorus was in full flow and she revelled in its riches.

The farmhouse was like a magnet to her and, as she stepped out in the clearing, she could not resist pointing her binoculars towards the farm.

Her eyes locked with his.

For what seemed like a lifetime they stared at each other, as if destiny had planned that very moment, but it was by no means a pleasant one. All of a sudden Anna broke the spell when she realised with horror that the farmer's son was standing in full view of the window stark naked.

It was at that instant that he must have been filled with sudden embarrassment too, because he stepped back into the shadow of the darkened room, whilst Anna disappeared into the cover of the trees like a startled deer.

Running blindly she tripped over a tree stump and lost her footing flying head first into a slender sapling, big enough, though, to knock her out. When she came to, several minutes had passed. Disoriented, she tried to sit up and untangle brambles gripping her padded jacket. She struggled to her feet but had to sit back on the tree stump for a few moments to regain her breath and still her shaking hands; questions buzzing though her mind.

Was Lucille talking to her from beyond the grave?

Was this just coincidence or just her vivid imagination?

Why did Nick have to bring her back here?

Anna shivered as she carefully retraced her steps, her mind flitting between her vivid imagination of the tragedy of Lucille Vardon's death, listening out for noises in the wood, and the frustrations of her own life. She cycled frantically but as she passed the church track she was reminded of the strange message.

She saw a taxi pull out and she slowed down, stopping just outside the churchyard, the grave compelling her to follow the man from the taxi. By 6 there was a small gathering and a few had wreaths to place at the now familiar grave. She had nothing, although the little metal birds were still poised where she had pushed the wires into the ground on her last visit.

The group remained respectfully silent and Anna felt herself relax. This was where she was meant to be and it was if all the weird happenings of the past few years were focused on this point in time. Surely this was her moment to let go of her quest and be at peace about Lucille Vardon. As everyone dispersed, Anna cycled at a more leisurely pace back to Clophill, letting the early morning sunshine soothe her soul.

Later at breakfast Nick was subdued. Both knew that it was the end. Nick was angry but he could see that Anna was distracted and upset, which soothed his wounded pride.

They hardly said a word as they travelled back to Cambridge but as Nick dropped Anna off at her lodging house he remarked, 'That's it then?'

'That's it,' was all Anna replied and without a smile or thank you she walked away, hearing the sound of Nick's car speed dangerously into the crowded streets and disappear.

She had one more phone call from Nick just a week later but it was not begging her to resume their relationship.

'Anna, sorry to disturb you but a friend's just found something on Futurenet and it made me a bit scared for you, to tell you the truth.'

'What are you talking about Nick?'

He cleared his throat. 'It's sick really but we think you're being watched.'

'What do you mean 'watched'?' Anna snapped.

'I don't know how to say this but my mate has found a video on Futurenet.' Nick stopped, running his fingers through his hair, sweat appearing on his forehead.

'Spit it out Nick!' Anna moved the phone to the other ear and slumped down on her sofa. 'Go on,' she said in a calmer voice.

'I'm only frightened for you and wanted to warn you to take care. There's a video of you cycling around Haynes but there's also …' he paused again, sucking in his breath. Anna waited. 'What's worse is there's a video of me and you making love in the woods near Mrs Broom's cottage. It must have been taken with a night vision camera.'

There was an unnerving silence as Anna tried to make sense of it. She sat bolt upright, 'Do you know what, you're sick! If there's a video of us making love then I bet you put it there. How dare you! I trusted you. Now get lost out of my life and I never want to hear from you again. Ever.'

'But...' then the line went dead.

---

3. DM: a direct message. A private message sent via social media

PART 3

JAMES BOUCHARD

CHAPTER 8

Spring 2018   James in Canada

Over 'the pond$_4$' in Halifax, Canada, James Bouchard stared at the large screen above his desk. By the movement of his eyes the screen would instantly change appearance as it searched for information. It could not quite read his mind but he believed that soon technology would advance so much that it would. Within seconds he had discovered so much.

A few months ago his mother had nagged him to carry out some research into their family history. She did not like recent technology and found Futurenet, the replacement of the internet quite frightening, however hard James had tried to explain that the internet just could not cope with the overload of information. They were chatting about this when James had called in for his obligatory Saturday morning cup of espresso.

'I'm happy with what I do James. Emails to my friends are good enough for me.'

'But Mother, your machine goes so slowly. If you updated your system to a ZX then you could have everything on one screen on your fridge if you like. It would alert you if I'd sent you a message and even open the fridge for you when you reached for the milk. As simple as that.'

'But, Son, I don't want anything in my kitchen. I'm happy to come up to the spare room like I've always done; keeps things tidy up there. Come up and have a look at something I've been working on.'

Elizabeth Bouchard could be irritatingly demanding. James was proud of his mother though, an elegant lady with immaculate coiffure and wearing a stylish deep blue shift dress. She led him upstairs, switched on her old laptop and loaded her online album.

'My word, Mom! You must've been working hours on this. I didn't realise.' He was clicking through the pages of her on-line family album with newspaper cuttings, photos, house details, travel documents, announcements, a multitude of artefacts, tracing their family history almost back to the Pilgrim Fathers. James was speechless.

Misreading the silence as disapproval she said, 'Don't you like it Honey?'

'It's fascinating Mom. I never knew even half of this. Where did these photos come from?'

'I found lots of things in my grandfather's trunk. He served in England in WW1 or at least I think he might have been injured in France. I'm not sure of the whole story but...'

James had brushed his finger to turn the page and a newspaper cutting caught his eye. He drew in a sharp breath.

'Every family has a dark secret or two and I'm afraid that's one of ours,' his mother said looking a little smug that she had caught his attention so easily.

James scanned the print but it was illegible in parts.

'So my great-grandfather might have been a m..'

'Yes and no,' cut in Elizabeth. 'It's a bit of a mystery though don't you think,' but seeing her son's frown she added, 'nothing was proved. The murder was unsolved and still is, I should think.'

Silence.

'It was a long time ago James. 100 years in fact.' Pause. 'I was wondering..'

Suddenly James was alert to the tone in his mother's voice like police giving a warning shot.

'No, Mother. Whatever it is you are going to ask, I'm far too busy with work,' and he glanced at the time on his ephone.

'Just a minute more, Son. Just come and look at this.'

'What is it, Mother?' James had replied guardedly. He only said 'Mother' and not 'Mom' when he could see Elizabeth wanted him to do something time consuming, and time was a precious commodity when you were middle management, had a growing family and a mother, recently widowed, living only two miles away.

'That album's OK on the computer but, like I say, I prefer doing things the old way. Here is your true family history.' James heard the emphasis on the word 'your', a hook to catch him and make him feel guilty that it was really his responsibility and not hers. 'Come and have a look at this.'

Elizabeth unrolled a beautifully set out family tree with exquisite line drawn branches, photos stuck strategically, and his mother's beautiful, almost calligraphic writing scribing births, marriages and deaths in pencil beside each name. James could not help but be impressed.

'Oh Mom! This is beautiful.' He was drawn to follow the lines from his children Beth and Jonathan all the way through to his great-great-great grandfather born in the early 18th Century. There was a photo of his great grandfather standing proudly beside an enormous hangar and under the photo was scribbled, 'Louis Bouchard April 1919.' In fact, the man in the picture was just a speck, emphasising the vastness of the construction. This must be connected to the newspaper article he had just seen entitled 'Murder Mystery.'

It had been a year, almost to the day, since his father had passed away and he was impressed that his mom had been able to concentrate on something as complicated as this.

'You **have** been busy but it looks like you've finished,' James said with relief, since the last thing he needed right now was poring over websites for any missing links. It did not matter that neighbours far older than his mom had embraced the new technology. The silver surfers did not impress Elizabeth, who still preferred a good old conversation on the telephone. For her, there was nothing like the joy of seeing a letter from a dear friend drop on to the mat in the morning to read with a morning Americano.

'Would you do me a favour, James?' Elizabeth asked as her son studied it further.

James tried to ignore her. 'This is incredibly detailed. So you found most of this stuff in the attic. I knew we were a family of hoarders, but this is amazing.'

'I was so excited when I discovered every family document imaginable, and all was carefully sorted in order. I've tried to trace each one, cross referencing where I can, and match the more recent ones to photos where possible, for the last century at least.'

'Here's that article you were looking at on the computer.'

James read the short newspaper article. It was carefully cut out with the date January 1924. He could feel his palm begin to sweat. Whether this was due to shock about the content, or fear that he was already being sucked into his mother's time consuming project he could not tell.

'That was a very long time ago Mother. Maybe it's best to celebrate what you've achieved rather than try to dig up the dirt.' He was pretty sure he would rather leave the past a mystery. He stood up to give his mother the expected peck on the cheek before heading back to the more mundane job of washing his car.

'But it wouldn't take you long. Not on that computer of yours. You're always nagging me how useful it would be if I updated mine. All you have to do is what do you call it? Google it, isn't it.' She smiled her never to be refused smile, knowing full well that she had won the argument.

'We'll see if I have time Mother,' James prevaricated as he headed for the door. 'See you next Saturday,' he called from the drive, sure that he had already forgotten her request.

Finally, on Friday lunchtime James sat at his desk frowning.

It's funny, he thought, how something I just want to ignore, especially a task given to me by my mother, just sits on the verge of my consciousness twenty four hours a day.

He sighed.

Usually James tried to leave the office for at least a half hour break, but today he had asked his assistant Jane to fetch him a cappuccino and a sandwich. He clicked on Google and typed in Louis Bouchard, Illinois. His finger paused momentarily before clicking 'Search.'

It was an hour later that Jane, his efficient assistant hovered behind him.

First she cleared her throat. 'Here are your notes for the meeting in ten minutes, Mr Bouchard,' she said firmly. Usually her boss was alert and nagging her to be prepared and so she was inquisitive, verging on the suspicious, as to what claimed Mr Bouchard's undivided attention, and as far as she could see from her surreptitious glance over his shoulder, he was just surfing the net. How odd, she thought.

'Oh yes, thank you Jane,' he said, waving her away with a flick of his hand and so, still in frustrated ignorance, she headed for the door.

James switched off the screen and tried to concentrate on the papers before him. He longed for the afternoon to be over so that he could get home and back on the Futurenet, in fact during the next month he spent all of his spare time searching for clues, so much so that his wife was concerned that he had started a cyber affair.

What had he discovered so far? That his great-grandfather served in the 1st Army Headquarters unit as a 1st Lieutenant until he contracted influenza and was sent to St Nazaire American Military Hospital. James was unable to surmise how his great-grandfather found himself in England, but after looking for American servicemen in Bedfordshire he got sidetracked, as one often did when carrying out research. He read about the 306th Bombardiers who were based at Thurleigh, a small village north of Bedford next to what must have been an enormous airfield in its day. Of course this was even the wrong war. As James was led down what appeared to be a blind alley, he read about the famous member of the 306th, Glenn Miller, who had also disappeared without trace only a few miles from Bedford at Twinwoods during WW2. This was a slim unrelated coincidence because records showed James that his great-grandfather had vanished too but during WW1. Louis Bouchard must have come home after the war, he reasoned, otherwise none of his family would be alive today, would they? James smiled.

The newspaper cutting his mother had shown him said that his great-grandfather was alleged to have worked in the Short

Brothers' factory just outside Bedford at a place called Cardington, where they built those huge airships. What a history he had discovered there! Of course this only confirmed the location of the photograph in his mother's possession.

James searched for 'Short Brothers Cardington.' He found pictures of the vast hangars, first built in 1915 during WW1, the place where his great-grandfather must have worked as a deserter, and photos of the R31, R32 and R37 - airships he might have worked on. James wasn't sure which, and the photo wasn't clear. Neither was it dated. Most likely it was the R32 which made her maiden voyage after the war in the autumn of 1919, he thought. Whichever it was, James was pleased that his great grandfather had continued to do his bit for the cause.

The next Saturday they were talking about it again. 'There's a lot about Cardington where they built airships and you might have heard of the R101, Mom.'

'What's the R101,' she asked, 'and what has it to do with us?'

'Nothing to do with us really. The R101 was the airship they hoped to use to fly passengers all over the world but a tragedy struck and so many people lost their lives - but that was much later, in the late 1920's.'

His mother looked a tad impatient so James continued. 'Great Grandfather must have worked at Cardington, near Bedford and Haynes as a matter-of-fact, on a much earlier airship which was built for the war effort. I'm not sure which.'

'But your great-grandfather came back here, so it couldn't have been him.'

'I know Mother,' replied James, trying hard to hide the exasperation from his own voice. 'But it's interesting all the same.' He could see she was disappointed so he changed the subject to his children's exploits.

Later that evening he was on the Futurenet again. Just like any research into history, he got sidetracked down interesting cul-de-sacs, but by fine tuning his quest he found web pages on the R37, the airship which was in the process of being developed in the final months of The Great War and for a moment James allowed himself to daydream of his great-grandfather, working on such an unusual vehicle of war.

He had said little to his mother, since he had really discovered no more about the life of his actual great-grandfather than they already knew. Nevertheless the quest had sown a seed deep within him and it grew like bindweed; as each flower opened to reveal more information within its grasp, the roots below took greater and greater hold of him.

4. Over the 'pond' ~ colloquial expression for the Atlantic Ocean

CHAPTER 9

Summer 2018   James in Bedfordshire

By now James had found a website on the village called Haynes mentioned in the cutting and there'd been a quiz about family history. He had answered the quiz greedily hoping that more information might come to light, but instead he had received this strange message which caught the flow of his enthusiasm short.

'YOU HAVE WON A WAYBACK CLASSIC TOUR OF BEDFORDSHIRE;

A delightful day in a classic car visiting sites key to your ancestral past. You just need to contact Wayback Classics by email and all we ask is that after your experience you give us an honest account of your day. We can assure you that no personal details will be asked of you and no registration fee. This is not a scam. We look forward to hearing from you soon.'

James closed his eyes, signalling a shutdown of Futurenet and his screen went obligingly blank, then he tried to forget about the prize but try as he might he knew that he was going to investigate it further. His curiosity was like a fish lured by bait, although his head was still struggling with its implications and searching for a hidden ugly hook. Usually a cautious guy, his instinct was to accept the prize regardless.

Going over to England was no problem. One of the line managers was scheduled to visit their sister company in London at least twice a year and he usually made some excuses to refuse.

He could offer to do the summer visit to coincide with claiming this prize. Not only that, but he longed to see some of the places he had discovered on Futurenet and walk in his great-grandfather's footsteps.

The following evening, against his better judgment regarding IT security, he had responded to the email, drawn in by the allure of winning the prize, and such a personal one at that. How could he really refuse?

James went to see his mother on the evening before his flight.

'I'm not sure how much spare time I'll have Mom, but I've booked a couple of nights at The Swan Hotel in Bedford and I'll see if I can find out anything for you.'

'Oh thank you Son. I wish I could come too but I'm glad that you'll have Trudy for company.'

'She's not too enthusiastic about us spending two weeks of her precious summer holidays over in England Mom.'

'Oh, I know James. Your wife's a creature of habit. She likes nothing better than to spend each summer at your cabin on the lake, and who can blame her?'

'It's not only that Mom, but she has such a stressful time teaching that she needs the summer to unwind and travelling can be a bit harrowing.'

'I'm sure you'll enjoy yourselves Son. I'll be thinking of you.'

James gave his mom a hug, a rare sign of affection between them, so much so that it brought tears to her eyes. Misreading it as a sign that she did not want to let him go, James quietly replied,

'Cheer up Mom. Two weeks'll go by in no time.'

And so here he was on the plane to England. He had retrieved some notes out of his briefcase from the overhead luggage compartment and was staring at their sister company's figures. Another down turn in the economy had made its mark but, since leaving the EU, the UK branch was still holding its own, only just. James frowned and he thought about the days ahead. Trudy sat next to him with a face mask over her eyes and she was snoring quietly. He nudged her gently so that she rested her head sideways on the head-rest and breathed more quietly. He smiled. She had made such a fuss about coming. She even suggested that he came over on his own, but selfishly he did not want to do that.

Trudy was still an attractive lady. Their children were now at university, and she had supported the family through every sort of trauma in her unflappable fashion, as well as working full time at a local school, but the only lines on her face were laughter lines. He wanted to stroke her hair, to thank her for being by his side all these years when so many of their friends' marriages had disintegrated. He knew the kids were grateful. They had ridden any storm in their marriage and remained locked together. Not that it was a 'ball and chain' relationship. It was more a silken thread of memories and shared dreams and experiences.

He made his way to the toilet, more to stretch his legs than with necessity, and squeezed himself inside a vacant cubicle. For a moment he stared at himself in the mirror. Not bad for a man of his age, he thought. A bit of a belly was the most marked sign of middle age creeping in, and maybe a few grey hairs. Nothing that a bit of colour and getting back into a routine of an early morning jog before breakfast could not handle. He did the necessary and then returned to his seat, just in time for lunch.

He smiled at the air hostess. Yes, his face could still hold its appeal as the pretty young lady smiled back.

Trudy, awake now, dug him in the ribs with her sharp index finger.

'Ouch, there's no call for that,' he grinned at her, noticing not for the first time that a little anger seemed to enhance Trudy's beauty.

'Just you remember what I've sacrificed to come with you Honey, before you eye up all the ladies.' She grinned back at him. It was a joke they frequently shared.

'I only have eyes for you my love, you know that,' replied James with an expression of mock hurt. It was the banter that kept their marriage fresh. He stretched over to kiss his wife on the nose, not a mean feat, even with the extra leg room paid for before the flight.

'And don't you forget it,' Trudy replied softly, returning his smile. She knew they were lucky. They defied the statistics but someone had to be the one in three still with a happy marriage after the kids had flown the nest.

James and Trudy spent the first week in London.

'What are you going to do today while I'm at work?' James asked over breakfast.

'Oh Honey, there's lots to see. I'll take a cab to The National Gallery first and see how it goes from there. What time will you be back?'

'About 4.30 I should think. Why don't we meet in Fortnum and Mason's for afternoon tea?'

'Oh how delightfully English, James. Do you think it'll spoil our supper?'

'Not if I book a table in the Diamond Jubilee Salon' for 5pm. We never eat 'til 8, anyway. What do you think?'

'How appropriate! We can always have a lighter supper in our room later.'

Trudy spent a whole day enjoying the luxury of second guessing the minds of The Great Masters. If she had lived near London she would spend days of her holidays here. Some of the paintings took her by surprise, like Dante's Inferno which she had expected to be floor to ceiling in its detail of hell but instead it was no bigger than the prints she and James hung on their living room walls.

The taxi pulled up outside the famous store at 4.30 and James met her and ushered her into the lift to the top floor.

'How quaint,' she whispered to James as they were seated by a waiter wearing white gloves, her chair pushed gently beneath her.

'I think we should go for an 'English Cream Tea,' but which tea? I'm sure I've no idea,' James remarked.

'It's like going back 100 years. I really can't believe it. I could be a character in a Regency novel and you my suitor,' Trudy winked. 'Shhh. The waiter's coming. We'll ask him for his advice.'

'Has madam chosen?' the waiter asked.

'We'd like an English Cream Tea for two, but,' said James lowering his voice and leaning towards the waiter, 'could you advise us on the best tea, please? We have no idea.'

'I would suggest Russian Caravan sir. That would be my choice; a good flavour, but not so different from normal English breakfast tea that you won't enjoy its aroma.'

'Thank you, we'll have that then.'

The waiter took their elaborate and lengthy menus and while they waited Trudy's eyes gleamed as she saw the towers of cakes and scones being brought to nearby tables. When theirs arrived she was not disappointed. A silver cake stand, piled with delights to feast on, was placed ceremonially in the centre of the table alongside the silver service.

'My, Honey, I must take a photo to send home,' and she reached for her bag and surreptitiously snapped a shot with her e phone and clicked send.

Later that night, full of home baking, cream and conserve Trudy lay on their bed.

'Do you know James, but I couldn't eat a thing tonight.'

'We could always have some exercise instead!' James replied, laying down beside her and dimming the lights above their bed.

Over the next couple of days Trudy visited the National Portrait Gallery and Tate Modern, but the latter did not inspire her nearly as much. She spent half an hour admiring the statue at St Pancras Station, which she passed on her way to the British Library. Oh what a joy her last morning had been as she drooled over original copies of Jane Austen, Alice in Wonderland and versions of The Bible dating back hundreds of years.

On their last night they sat at a candlelit table in their Hilton Hotel.

'I expect you're rather cultured out Trudy. Have you enjoyed yourself?'

'Oh James. If I lived here in England I'd be down in London at least once a year. It's been such a pleasure.'

'So what have you planned for your last morning? We catch the train to Bedford at 2 pm.'

'Oh, I can't leave London without a bit of retail therapy, but you must be quite proud of me. I've hardly bought anything so far, apart from a few mementos.'

'I must admit I had expected our room to be overflowing with shopping bags by now. Your restraint has been admirable.'

'Talking of which I'm going to get off to Bond Street early.'

'We'll meet back here at 1.15 then. Don't be late. I've booked first class seats on the train.'

'Bye Honey.' Trudy pecked James on the lips before slipping out of the hotel to find a taxi.

Later on, once they were seated in the comfortable rail compartment Trudy looked a bit miffed.

'What's the matter Trudy?' James glanced over the many extra bags they had accumulated since morning. 'You seem to have had a successful shop.'

'But there's so much more I wanted to see in London. I can't see the attraction of going to Bedfordshire. I'd never heard the place mentioned before your mother started talking about it. Why can't we go to Scotland or Wales or even York or Oxford?'

'Give me this little indulgence Trudy please, without all the fuss. After all, it's only a couple of nights.'

Trudy pursed her lips, unable to hide her frustration. It was her precious holiday after all. 'I know you've won this prize James but surely it's no big deal.'

'You've had a great time in London but I'm sure you'll enjoy this too.'

'You're as obsessed with this family business as your mother,' Trudy replied in frustration. Since his mother had set him on finding out about his family tree James had been so secretive. It was beginning to irritate her. She took a deep breath and looked out at the monotonous countryside and small town developments.

'What's happening tomorrow, Hon,' she asked later over supper. She realised that her frustration was also due to the fact that she had lost that independence she had revelled in during their stay in London. She had begun to warm to their new environment though.

They settled into quite a luxuriously traditional room in The Swan, which spoke of an English Country Hotel with timeless elegance.

'It's a bit of a surprise,' James explained guarding the real truth, not knowing quite what to expect from this prize he had accepted. In fact he was a little nervous as to what tomorrow would bring too.

'We'll be picked up at 9.30 am at the hotel for a tour with a difference and that's all I'm going to say. It'll be a surprise' and James would say no more, however much Trudy needled him.

When the flat capped chauffeur arrived in the lobby the following morning James was flooded by an irrational relief. To Trudy's delight he led them to their awaiting Mark 2 Jaguar, aptly in Old English White, and opened the door for them to slip inside. James finally relaxed when he saw the joy on Trudy's face as they settled into the soft red leather seats, anticipating the day ahead.

'Oh, what a treat,' she exclaimed, as they wound their way south out of Bedford. After a while the driver, David was his name, spoke over his shoulder,

'This is a bit of a mystery tour which will include an evening's entertainment, but I have been instructed to say no more about it.'

'So there's no itinerary you can give us?' James asked but the driver did not reply.

As they reached what was obviously a bypass James felt prickles on the back of his neck as he spotted the enormous hangars at Cardington, towering above the landscape. It was quite an extraordinary sight. Sure enough the driver headed in their direction. He paused at the memorial to the R101, which to James looked so familiar from Futurenet, and it was there that David showed them pictures of the airships including the R37, making it easy to imagine the scene over a century ago. His great-grandfather would have been just one of those ant-like bands of men in the photo, preparing the great vessel to depart.

'As you may know Short Brothers, or Shorts as they were known, set up business in England building planes down in Rochester and airships here in Cardington during WW1. This was the site of the Shorts factory and they built the small Shortstown nearby to house their workforce. Here is a copy of a newsletter of the day.' David held the album open in front of him but did not offer it to James. His secrecy was unsettling.

'This will be a souvenir for you once the trip is over,' David explained as he closed the book and put it under his arm. 'We'll continue when you're ready.'

James stared at the closed book wondering what else it might reveal about his family's past.

'Are you OK Hon?' Trudy asked. 'Are you having one of your turns? Maybe you had too much greasy food for breakfast.'

'I'm OK, don't fuss, Trud,' James snapped as they climbed back into the car.

'We have a little detour next,' David said as they ambled down small country lanes, through a place called Haynes. The name rang a bell in his mind. He wished he had brought some notes with him but that would have made Trudy more suspicious. They drove out of the main village and passing the church on their right hand side they pulled up in view of a large manor house set up on a hill behind the church. David showed them the next picture in the scrap book of their personal tour. It was of the same drive up to Haynes Park with tents lining one side and a couple of young ladies with floor length dresses standing next to an old fashioned motor car. It was labelled 'Haynes Park Training Camp during The Great War 1915.' James shivered even though the temperature was in the mid 70's. Trudy looked at him with concern.

'Have you seen a ghost Honey?' she asked jokingly.

'You could say that,' James replied thinking about the ghosts in the churchyard just over the hedge. He forced a smile.

'Where next on this strange mystery tour, driver?' he asked, his brow turning more into a frown than he had intended.

'We just have to pay our respects before we continue,' answered the driver cryptically, pulling up beside the churchyard and opening the passenger door for Trudy and James to step out.

The driver opened the boot and taking a small bunch of flowers he walked under the lych-gate, glancing over his shoulder to encourage them to follow him. Without saying a word he led them to a cross, bent over at a now familiar angle, and James had no need to read the inscription as the driver placed the flowers neatly at the foot of the grave, topping the pewter vase with water before standing and bowing his head.

Trudy bent down close to the grave and read the name out loud.

'Lucille Vardon,' she said. 'I wonder who she was.' She looked questioningly between their driver, whose blank expression revealed no secrets, and James, who by now was a touch grey. Trudy linked her arm in her husband's.

'Only 21 years old,' she said, thinking of their daughter and leading him away.

They followed the driver in silence back to the car.

'I can now say that the next stop is to The Shuttleworth Collection, sir and madam. Just relax and we'll be driving through one of the finest villages in Bedfordshire.'

James sat back and stared out of the window trying desperately to collect his thoughts. It was as if the person who sent him the prize had been watching over him and his mother in recent weeks.

They drove through the picturesque village of Old Warden with its thatched cottages and twee gardens. The Horse and Jockey looked a welcoming place to stop and James could really do with a drink.

'Do you think we could stop here for a quick one driver? I do love these English pubs.'

'It's a good choice, sir, but I can only stop for a twenty minute unscheduled break. I can recommend the local wine though. Old Warden sparkling white is quite famous and has Royal approval, you know.'

James had a far stiffer drink in mind and ordered a double Glenfiddich for himself and a sparkling white wine for his wife but as he drank it down in one gulp Trudy raised her eyebrows.

'Are you gonna to tell me what all this is really about or are you gonna to keep me in the dark until the shock gives you a heart attack?'

James took in a deep breath. 'There's nothing much to tell Trud, but in some ways it's unbelievable. A bit spooky if you must know.' He shook his head struggling for words. 'It was a prize I won on Futurenet and yet nothing is quite what it seems.'

'You're making no sense at all Honey, but we'd best get back to the car otherwise our driver will be fretting. If you promise you're not going to peg out on me, I'll enjoy the day, but only if you tell me the whole story over supper.'

'It's a deal,' said James, 'I promise,' and he kissed Trudy on her forehead. 'What do you think of the car?' he asked attempting to change the subject and get the vision of the stone cross out of his mind.

'It's quaint enough, a bit like these cute old villages. A day to remember,' She paused. 'As long as it's for the right reasons.' Her glance pierced through him.

'I'm OK, Trud. Don't worry!'

He smiled and turned to stare out at the passing scenery, cricketers playing on the village green. He tried to shift the unnerving awareness that someone knew far more about his family history than he did and the irrefutable truth that someone had tracked him down.

A few moments later they pulled up outside The Shuttleworth Collection, parking the car right next to the airfield and hangars, making it quite atmospheric, even before they had entered the museum.

'You only have an hour here I'm afraid. There's a garden included in the entrance fee,' he smiled knowingly at Trudy, who happily headed for the tranquillity of the beautifully secluded Swiss Gardens, whilst James headed towards the museum. He was surprised that David the driver followed him.

'You should be here on a flying day,' David said enthusiastically. 'It's one thing to see these beauties here in their hangars but it's another experience entirely to watch them fly.'

'Awesome,' James exclaimed. Not knowing quite what else to say.

'I must just show you one of the exhibits and take a photo before leaving you to browse in peace.'

James was led though to Hangar 2 and sure enough there was a Shorts Biplane amongst others, all of different eras.

David saw his puzzled look. 'They mix up the different types of aircraft as a safety measure. They used to keep all the WW1 'planes together and so on, but it occurred to someone that, if they had a fire, a whole collection of a particular era might be wiped out. Some call it The Shuttleworth Shuffle!' he chuckled.

'I can see why it's caused a bit of controversy.'

'Well sir, if you could stand next to the Shorts plane, I'll take a couple of shots and one will be delivered to your hotel as a souvenir before you leave tomorrow.'

James did not know what to say, so he posed for the camera.

After that he wandered around in a daze.

'1909 Bleriot,' James read. My, that's over one hundred years old, he thought.

'Bristol Boxkite. Replica of The Magnificent Men in their Flying Machine's Box plane,' he read.

'Does that thing still fly?' He asked the driver.

'Certainly sir,' David replied. 'I'll leave you to browse on your own now sir.'

James wandered from hangar to hangar but before his hour was up he returned to the Shorts Bi-plane. He looked closely at the wings whose wood and fabric structure amazed him.

How brave those early pilots were, he thought. How daring! He knew that, in the war, they had often returned to base with the plane riddled with bullets. Unbelievable!

Reluctantly he tore himself away from the museum and met Trudy in the cafe. They had a quick coffee before joining David once more.

'We have about half an hour's drive to the north of Bedford now to the little village of Bromham where we'll stop for lunch.' And no matter how many questions they asked him, David had been instructed to give no more details.

They pulled up at The Swan, a very English establishment, with its oak beams and original fireplaces. James and Trudy enjoyed a lunch of roast beef and Yorkshire pudding, setting them up for the remainder of the day.

It was gone 2 pm when they set off once more, weaving though little villages, over ancient bridges and streams until they reached what was obviously an industrial site on the edge of an old airfield. James had already guessed the connection before they set foot in this little museum at Thurleigh, where he felt more comfortable wandering though the WW2 exhibits with Trudy.

'Just think what it would have been like to have been a GI bride, Hon; all those dashing American pilots. The girls didn't stand a chance.'

'It wasn't all glamour, Honey,' James observed as they stood respectfully next to a memorial to the many men who had lost their lives. David next led them on a pathway to the edge of the airfield. James took a deep breath and closed his eyes. It was not difficult to imagine the guttural sounds of the planes as they readied for take-off and think of the pilots giving a final wave before opening the throttle to speed along the runway. It was a calm day today but even so a breeze whipped past them, blowing so many memories in its path. James sighed. 'We have so much to be grateful for, don't we Honey?'

'We certainly do.' Trudy linked her arm through his as they strolled back to the waiting car.

David glanced in the mirror at his passengers. 'We're on the last leg of our heritage tour now.'

They headed across country and down a small track. The sign read 'Twinwoods.' Now where have I heard that name before James wondered.

'There's time for you both to take a stroll around the event while I set up your champagne picnic,' said David. 'It's fascinating, although I find the old airfield watchtower a bit creepy with all those old photos and haunting music?'

Although Trudy and James enjoyed the various exhibits James was not going to admit to feeling a cool chill as he wandered around the watchtower. It must be autosuggestion he thought, gazing out over the now empty field, his imagination on overdrive with visions of heavy bombers preparing for take-off. Suddenly he shook himself and realised that he was even dreaming in the wrong war, unlike at the graveyard earlier in the day. This was nothing at all to do with his family. He turned around, but finding the room strangely empty, he was full of an irrational foreboding and rushed to find Trudy.

'What's the matter with you now Hon? I'm beginning to wish we'd never come if this is going to make you ill. Look at all these posters of Glenn Miller. He sure was busy before he disappeared. What a mystery.' She peered sideways at her husband and frowned. 'I think it's time we had some fresh air and that picnic supper don't you?'

They stopped at the officers mess and fought their way through the crowded bar of people in period costume before finding David, who had arranged a table with napkins, glasses and even candles. The place was buzzing. Music wafted across from tents and barns. People were milling about, the majority in dress appropriate to the era, colourful and dashing. Each dance venue was vibrant, full of the excitement for life in days gone by.

James and Trudy enjoyed a meal of smoked salmon, followed by game pâté and salad, washed down by a bottle of Old Warden 2007 sparkling wine, as they sat and listened to a live swing band, playing hits from the 1940's. Trudy was mesmerised.

'Aint it wonderful,' she beamed. James relaxed and began to enjoy the moment. It was a memorable evening to end a truly remarkable day which James certainly would never forget. But how was he going to explain it to his wife? Just before they set off to return to Bedford, David passed James the Personal E Scrapbook, revealing the last two pages on its screen.

The left side held the caption,

'The Mystery of Glenn Miller in 1944 ~ Did he Die or just Disappear?'

This was followed by pictures of Glenn Miller and his band, Glenn Miller beside his aeroplane and the newspaper article account of his disappearance.

On the facing page was the caption,

'The Mystery of Louis Bouchard in 1924 ~ Confessions of A Deserter or A Murderer?'

James clicked the book off and glanced at his wife, who he was relieved to see had nodded off to sleep. He would return to that last page later.

On returning to their hotel Trudy had to pack, so James took a stroll along the Embankment to clear his head. He watched the swans and Canada geese. The latter so far away from home, like himself, and yet he felt akin to this place, drawn by a sense of shared history or was it shared mystery, he chuckled at his own humour.

Why was his great grandfather a deserter? How did he disappear? Was he injured and being cared for at one of the many make-shift hospitals in the area and heard about the Shorts factory? How did he meet Lucille Vardon and did he really murder her? He could neither answer these questions for his mother nor, more importantly, satisfy his own nagging doubts.

On returning to their room he sat in an armchair beside the great sash window and opened his Personal E Scrapbook, turning the pages of this now familiar story. He thought he now understood the inclusion of Glenn Miller, even though it referred to WW2, because he was beginning to read the mind of the compiler. (Or was the compiler beginning to read his?) His great grandfather was American and his disappearance was also surrounded in mystery. He had also fought for the freedom of Europe even though it was thirty years before. His great grandfather obviously chose Canada for a new start. What about Glenn Miller? Now there's a thought!

As James clicked to the last page his hands froze as he read a copy of the newspaper article from The News of the World dated February 1924. There in front of him were the allegations that his great grandfather, Louis Bouchard, had confessed to the murder of Lucille Vardon.

Back in Canada James relived the experience in his quiet moments. He wanted desperately to forget it all. He certainly regretted the day he showed the E Scrapbook of their tour to his mother.

'Oh James. How fantastic! I so wish I'd been there too.'

'Well, there you are, Mom. The story's told,' said James, glad to be putting the whole episode behind him.

'Oh no, James, it's only just begun. I'm sure of that. You need to carry on your research for me. It's important for the family reputation.'

She was so enthusiastic that he gave in to her, hoping that her nagging would cease but increasingly Saturday coffee mornings with her were less about the fortunes and misfortunes of his family life today, or even the state of the world, but more about her research.

'Look at this,' she said one Saturday, holding up a copy of an old photo of a camel grazing in front of what appeared to be an English stately home.

'What's that Mother?'

'It's a camel, dear,' she replied grinning wickedly at him. 'No, it's a place called Wrest Park near Bedford. They still do World War One re-enactment days when everyone dresses up for the occasion.'

James peered closer at the print out and saw nurses and army types in old fashioned uniform.

'So why a camel?' he asked to please her.

'It was brought in to cheer up the troops and aid a hasty recovery and I have reason to believe my grandfather must have gone there to recover from his war wounds.'

'He might possibly have done, but how did he end up at Shortstown?'

'I expect he didn't believe in war and thought he could do his bit by working in the factory. Anyway, that solves the mystery doesn't it?' Her eyes beamed at him.

'Maybe it does Mother.' Not very scientific but it's a solution, he thought.

Not to be disheartened by her son's lack of enthusiasm she had also enlisted the help of a neighbour's son who had registered on the forum on the Haynes web site in her name and he had been happy to ask the questions she had dictated.

'Look at this,' she said to James one Saturday morning, and he reluctantly took the proffered print out.

'INVITATION OPEN EXCLUSIVELY TO MEMBERS OF THIS FORUM

GATHERING ON THE 100TH ANNIVERSARY OF LUCILLE VARDON'S UNFORTUNATE DEATH. MEET AFTER SUNRISE AT 6 AM ON 9TH MAY 2019 AT HAYNES CHURCHYARD, BEDFORDSHIRE, UK'

James re-read the invitation several times, not trusting himself to respond, and then looked up into his mother's pleading eyes.

'I can't go to England again this summer Mother. The firm would assign me the role permanently and Trudy'd flip her lid!'

'I don't ask you to do much for your own mother James, do I?' said Elizabeth with her endearing refuse-me-and-you'll-suffer smile.

'I'll think about it.' James knew that he was defeated.

A few minutes before the taxi arrived to fly James back to England he had a weird phone call. It was from his mother's IT friend.

'Can I speak to James Bouchard please?' the young voice asked in a soft Canadian accent.

'Speaking,' replied James.

'Sir, I know your ma and I know you're going to England today but I just wanted to warn you.'

'What do you mean warn me?'

'Well, when I was doing some research for your ma I found a forum, quite straight forward at first glance.'

'Yes, I've seen it. What are you getting at?'

'Well, I found a small link to this other site.' He paused and James gripped the handset more tightly. 'There are some videos on it. Most of them seem innocent enough but some I'm not sure about. There's a restricted link that I haven't been able to access yet, but I'm working on it.'

'Videos, what videos?' James's voice rose a pitch and his eyebrows furrowed.

'One is unmistakably of you and your wife: one of you looking towards a large hangar, and another with you both dancing.'

The sound of James's breath sucking through his teeth was the only reply he had time for before he heard Trudy call out,

'Who's on the phone Honey? Your taxi's arrived!'

'I don't know who you are,' James seethed, but you leave my mother alone do you hear,' and he slammed his fist on the 'call cancelled' button on the wall, not hearing the man's reply.

'I was just trying to warn you,' the caller spoke quietly to the dialling tone. 'Well, I tried,' and he returned his phone to its cradle.

James travelled alone this time. Not only was Trudy's term still in full flow but he thought it best that way. He had never

118

really got around to explaining the last visit and he knew she would be cross that he had been manipulated again.

'Would you travel across the world on a whim for me?' he could imagine Trudy asking, with unhidden sarcasm in her voice.

Throughout his journey the young caller's voice echoed in his mind and once in England James kept glancing over his shoulder.

He slept fitfully and was up for a taxi early the following morning. The driver, who dropped him off at 5.30 am at Haynes churchyard when a glimmer of light was just warming the horizon, looked quizzically at him as he paid his fare, but James was too preoccupied to notice. He was still thinking of his wife. What would she have said if she knew what he was doing?

Half an hour early, James was drawn towards Haynes Park he strolled up a farm track adjacent to its long sweeping driveway. He stopped to stare over the grassy slopes towards the imposing house and could imagine the little tents of the WW1 training camp, mock battles, bayonet charges and men hiding in the woods behind. He closed his eyes and could even imagine holding a bayonet in his hand, covered in blood.

His vision of horror was shattered when a young girl on a push bike sped past him towards the church, her distraught expression adding to his sense of foreboding. He shook himself free of the memory, turned and retraced his steps and stood in solitude next to Lucille Vardon's grave. There was a posy of fresh wild flowers in a vase, bluebells and white-bells, with a pungent smell of garlic wafting up to him. He chuckled to himself, relieving his tension. Keep the vampires at bay, he thought. The soil around the grave was freshly dug.

Near to the hedge he noticed some small shrubs in pots with tiny blue flowers. Their smell reminded him of Easter and Trudy's roast lamb.

When he turned back he was not surprised that the girl he had seen on a bicycle had arrived, her cycle helmet under her arm. She still looked frazzled. He tried not to stare as she walked up and knelt down at Lucille's grave.

A man in his early twenties appeared next, whose tough expression was in complete contrast to the lady who followed him, eyes soft and full of concern. Probably his mother, James reasoned. The man fiddled with a device James had never seen before. Maybe some type of camera, he thought.

Next a tall distinguished gentleman with a moustache, who looked vaguely familiar, strode towards the grave and nodded. Army type, James thought, though his smart grey suit gave no real clues.

A few minutes before six he heard the sound of a motorbike, its exhaust noisily in conflict with the early morning air, heralding the arrival of two lads, maybe eighteen or nineteen; college types. James was amused that they neither looked up, nor acknowledged the expectant group as they sauntered towards them; their dexterous fingers busy on the keys of their E phones, taking photos and sending messages, barely noticing the world around them.

Just after the clock struck six the last arrival, a plump middle aged lady in a UPVC Burgundy cycle cape, joined the group. She was out of breath. She nodded to the lads and they returned a smile full of condolences. Strange, thought James.

He glanced around at the gathering, all by now standing expectantly beside this WW1 gravestone. James looked towards the army chap and wondered whether he was a spy, and all the assembled company characters in an elaborate film plot.

With reluctance James moved closer, aware of an air of nervous anticipation. There was hardly a murmur now, each with their own thoughts of Lucille Vardon and why in God's name they were standing together in this churchyard. Moments ticked by. The army chap cleared his throat and everyone waited, expecting him to speak, but after a few more minutes the lads shuffled their feet and glanced at their mobiles.

Gradually the gathering of eight people dwindled. The two lads left, shrugging their shoulders and muttering expletives under their breaths, until it was just the middle aged lady standing a little aloof, James and the army chap staring at the grave. Many had left posies of flowers and the 'spy' had placed a wreath of poppies, a befitting tribute to a QMAAC who died in service, however brutally. The man cleared his throat.

'Strange business.'

'Yes it is,' replied James as they began to walk away.

James glanced over his shoulder and the remaining lady was now tending the grave, her gloved hands were planting the row of small shrubs he had seen earlier.

'Ah, I remember,' he said out loud, 'rosemary for remembrance.'

'What was that?' asked the army chap who was waiting for him at the lych-gate.

'Nothing important,' James replied, reddening.

'You from America?' the man asked.

'Easy mistake! No, I'm from Canada. Are you in the army?'

'Is it that obvious? Was, as a matter of fact,' his car immediately responding to his signal from his key. With embarrassment he turned to James,

'Want a lift anywhere?'

'That's very kind of you, but I can call a cab thanks.'

James retrieved his E phone from his inside pocket.

'It would be just as easy for me to give you a lift. Which direction are you heading in?'

'Flitwick Train Station. I'm on my way back to Heathrow,'

'Hop in then,' barked the man, obviously not used to his orders being disobeyed and while James climbed in the man fiddled with his navigation system.

'Keith Regmund,' he said, offering James his outstretched hand.

'James Bouchard.'

There was silence for a few moments, as Keith Regmund and James Bouchard digested the unnerving truth that each recognised the other's name from extracts of 1919 newspapers they had seen. Both chose to ignore the fact, as they steered their stilted conversation to safer subjects; work, wives, children. Within minutes they had reached the station and shook hands politely.

'Only came for a picture for my son's school project.' Keith Regmund's moustache twitched nervously.

'I only came to stop my mother's nagging.'

They smiled empathetically.

'Thanks for the lift anyway.'

James strode to the anonymity of the station platform.

5. Predicted statistics for 2019

PART 4
KEITH REGMUND

CHAPTER 10

Easter 2018 ~ The Regmund family in
Godalming, Surrey

Toby Regmund, a gangly thirteen year old was poring over
his holiday homework. He had finished his maths and
geography but he was faced with an English essay about his
family history. His mother's side was pretty boring. They had
been bakers in the village of Godalming for years and he was
sure something more exciting was expected of him at
Charterhouse School. So many of his peers had links to
nobility or nouveau riches who had made their fortune in
some innovative way that he was raking his brain for stories
that would impress his well-to-do class-mates.

His father rarely mentioned the Regmund side, except that
they were an army family and that both his father and
grandfather had risen though the ranks, but that was as much
as he knew. He must quiz his dad later on that evening.

Feeling that he had done all he could and that the spring
sunshine beckoned, he ran downstairs to the kitchen to find a
cold drink. Not that Toby noticed, but their family home was
full of character, an old three storey Georgian terrace with high
decorated ceilings and marble fire-places even in the bedrooms.
His room was up in the eaves of the house, which he knew
would have been for the servants. It was not an ancestral home.
His parents had bought it when his father had retired from active
service and began to work in intelligence; the administrative
side, which was based purely in the UK. Even his mum did not

know the actual location, but it was not far from where they lived.

Toby had always been a boarder at school. As his parents had moved to places like Germany and Gibraltar, Toby had enjoyed the continuity of school life, although he never knew quite where he would be staying in the holidays. Toby's parents had bought this house in Godalming when his dad had been posted to Iraq. It was near to his grandparents' bakery and it made sense to settle there as much as anywhere.

He rushed out to fetch his bike and raced off along the quieter back streets towards Rodborough Common. It was good to have some exercise. He had no real friends in the area and his upbringing was quite unlike that of his cousins, who had grown up in Godalming and gone to the local schools. Maybe he would ask one of his mates from Charterhouse to come and stay for a while. Still, it was only the second day of his holidays so he relished his independence. He certainly never had time to call his own at boarding school, sharing the dorm with nine other lads.

Later that night after supper he approached his father's study. The sweet smell of pipe tobacco seeped under the closed door. He tapped quietly.

'Come in,' called Keith Regmund, who, instead of working, was day dreaming out of the window. His eyes lit up at the sight of his son. 'Toby, my lad, what are you up to for your holidays?'

'I'm trying to get my homework out of the way first Dad. Then I can relax, but I'm rather stuck on my English essay.'

His dad raised his eyebrows in surprise.

'That's noble of you. I used to leave it 'til the last possible moment. My parents used to despair sometimes. So what's the subject? Is it anything I can help you with?'

'You can as a matter of fact. I need to write about my ancestors; where they lived, what they did, any skeletons or surprises in the cupboard and that sort of thing.'

'Oh,' frowned his father. 'I can see why that's a bit tricky.' He did not have to add that he understood why Toby was reticent to write the essay, since his peers all seemed to come from such illustrious backgrounds. That was one disadvantage to sending Toby to such a highbrow school he supposed, but it was a decision he and his wife had not made lightly. The fact that the school was not too far away, if there was an emergency, was one of the deciding factors.

'Can you tell me about your family, Dad? I'm not sure that writing about Mum's would be suitable.'

'I can see your predicament, young Toby. It's a difficult one. My family's been in the army for several generations, but it would take a bit of research to discover the details of battles they fought in and the like. Why don't you do some searches of your own and I'll see what I can come up with too, and we'll reconvene say in a week's time for a debriefing.'

'That's great,' beamed Toby, smiling more because his father always turned a project into a military operation, rather than agreeing wholeheartedly to help.

Toby enjoyed the research and although Regmund was quite a common name he found several references to a Corporal Regmund in the Royal Tank Corps in World War Two.

'Is this my grandfather?' he asked holding out a print.

'That's right; your grandfather Donald Regmund was in France but was one of the lucky ones to be evacuated from

Dunkirk in 1940. Then he went on to North Africa and served at El Alamein.'

'This article said that he was in the victory parade at Alexandria, father. He travelled about a bit, didn't he, because he was also part of the Normandy landings in 1944? Can you imagine how he felt driving his tank off the ship and on to French soil?'

'I'm not sure he was driving son, but I get your drift. He was certainly a hero. I've got his medals somewhere in the loft. I'll dig them out for you to take photos for your project.'

'Look at this account. The lady says that the Tank Corps parked outside a house up their street and had a mascot, a huge St Bernard called Butch. Three of them came to live at her house and at Christmas the dog ate all her mince pies. Why do you think they parked near the houses?'

'I should think that it was a strategy to confuse the Germans while they prepared for the Normandy Landings. You see, they couldn't behave in the most obvious way and it was less likely that a residential area would be bombed, but an army barracks, well, that was an obvious target.'

'I hadn't thought of it like that. Oh, what fun it would have been to have tanks parked outside the house.'

'I'm not sure that fun is quite the word, son. Those were tense times. The future of the freedom in Europe, let alone England, was at stake. Don't go away with any romantic notions that the war was exciting. I'm sure it was at times, but it was also deadly serious.'

'I know Dad, but this gives me enough to write about, don't you think; especially if you get the medals down for me?'

As Toby rushed off to begin to write and to research about the conflict in North Africa and the Normandy Day landings he was pleased he could be proud of his heritage. Meanwhile his father, Keith Regmund, was relieved that his son had not delved further into the past and found the family's near brush with scandal in World War One when his great grandfather had been accused of murder. He shuddered to think how Toby's mates at school would have teased him if he had come up with **that** story to tell.

Keith sat back, leaning against the head-rest of his deep burgundy leather swivel chair. He absentmindedly stroked the highly polished mahogany desk with leather inlay in front of him and tapped in the name 'Alfred Donald Keith Regmund.' He had over-heard his father telling the story to his mother when he was just a young lad. He had been eavesdropping at the door of their front room, sitting silently on the stairs,

'I've got something important to tell you. I suppose I should have said before we were married but...'

'If it's your past love life before we were married, I'd rather leave it in the past.' She had replied pausing. 'That is if there's not someone clamouring for money, in which case I'll support you. The child will have to be paid for of course.'

If Keith Regmund had been able to see his father's face, it showed amusement rather than surprise at his wife's calculating acceptance of this mythical situation.

'No, it's nothing like that,' Keith's father had reassured her. 'My father told me a story once about my grandfather and just in case it comes out sometime, I wanted to warn you.'

His wife had looked uncharacteristically nervous. Usually nothing fazed her. Stationed at times during their marriage in outposts such as Germany and Cyprus, each time she had adapted like a young vixen in its new lair.

'My grandfather was once accused of murder. He was tried and acquitted, but the murderer was never found,' Keith's father had continued.

'Did your father think your grandfather was innocent?' his mother had asked.

'Undoubtedly. After all, he continued to serve his country in India.'

'So the man was sent out of the way, in other words, to reduce the scandal?'

'You might think of it like that but he continued to serve until the Second World War.'

'So how did you fit into the picture then?'

'My grandfather married in India and they had a child there. Women did that in those days; went off to look for a suitable husband.'

There was a pause but Keith's mother did not interrupt.

'Unfortunately, my grandfather died and so his wife came home to bring up my father on her own. It must have been tough. She lived with her parents not far away from where they live now. I think it's best that we don't tell Keith though.' Keith remembered slipping soundlessly upstairs to his room and until that moment the incident had been forgotten. It's best that I shield Toby from this chequered history for now too, he thought. Maybe one day he would sit down with his son and tell Toby all about his great grandfather, but not now.

He typed 'Alfred Regmund' on to his screen search and then clicked on a couple of references, surprised to read the whole story and find snippets of newspaper cuttings too. Delving further he clicked on a site which was a kind of forum about WW1 research. He clicked in the name 'Lucille Vardon' not expecting to find any references but was surprised to find that several people seemed interested in the story in the past year. How odd, he thought.

He followed a thread which seemed to be from a Jersey girl who implied that another person might have been involved; possibly a farmer's son. Then, a month or so ago, there was a chap from Canada whose name sounded familiar. He rummaged in the bottom of his cabinet and found an old file of papers. He checked the story he had printed out and sure enough it was the same surname 'Bouchard' that was mentioned in the original story. Something about a confession by a man nick-named 'Frenchy' but nothing was substantiated.

He held his fingers over the keyboard willing himself to write, but hesitant to do so, uncertain as to what his actions might unleash.

'Hi, I'm a descendant of Alfred Regmund. Since I'm convinced that my great grandfather was entirely innocent, how do you see your ancestor? Do you think Louis Bouchard was innocent of Lucille Vardon's murder too?'

He pressed submit and then was frustrated that a dialogue box popped up asking him to enter some information in order to join the forum. Unwilling at this stage to share any details, especially when considering the delicate situation regarding the nature of his work, Keith's eyes shut down the web site and he tried to forget all about it.

Unfortunately, this was bit like forgetting to clean his army boots. It niggled at the back of his mind. In the end he waited for an evening when his wife was out at one of her keep fit classes and logged on to her computer. It made him smile. She always used the same password. So predictable. He found the website with ease and decided to be a little vaguer in his comment. He also set up a new inbox for any responses, registering the minimum of details.

'*I was interested in your thread. I believe I am related in some way to Alfred Regmund, the man originally arrested for Lucille Vardon's murder but I believe he was innocent as he claimed at the time.*'

His eyes moved the cursor to send and within moments he was surprised to have a response.

'*What makes you so sure he was innocent?*' the webmaster replied.

'*His service record was exemplary.*'

'*Being in the army could hide a multitude of sins, don't you think? After all, if you can kill for your country then you might also kill for love,*' was the return from the webmaster.

Another member of the group, CanadaJM joined in.

'*On that basis I'm sure that Louis Bouchard was innocent too.*'

'*Why is that?*' asked the webmaster.

'*Because he was supposed to have deserted the army, so maybe he just didn't like killing people.*'

'*I believe Alfred Regmund was innocent too?*' Keith typed.

'*Why do you think that, TD?*' asked the webmaster.

Keith thought carefully; Pleased that his initials TD, standing for Toby's Dad, should be untraceable. He paused over the keys momentarily before his fingers tapped,

'*He was such a kind and gentle man we're told; firm but straight down the line. Everyone said so. It would be so out of character. Anyway, I'm sure he would have told his wife and that someone in the family would know.*'

'*True. Very few people can keep a secret like that,*' the webmaster acknowledged.

131

As Keith signed off he was surprised to see that he had mail in his new inbox. He was wary of clicking on it because the subject was:

'YOU HAVE WON A MILITARY TOUR IN THE HOME COUNTIES.'

Unable to resist, and reasoning that his new inbox should be secure, he clicked on the message which explained that he had won a trip in an old Jaguar being the 50th person to register on the site. It seemed genuine enough, so he fired an email to the company and in no time he had arranged to go to Bedfordshire one day in August.

Keith Regmund decided to take his son Toby, rather than his wife. After all, she would only be bored, whereas Toby would be as interested as he was.

They stayed over-night at 'The Woburn Hotel,' a delightful, respectable small country hotel, close to 'Animal World', which Keith had promised his son they would visit on the afternoon they arrived. It was hard to contain Toby's enthusiasm as they took the Jeep Safari through the animal enclosures. He could not bear to drive his own precious car. Perish the thought.

As Keith watched his son's face he experienced a pang of remorse that he had seen so few of Toby's growing up years, although he felt his son had come to no harm at boarding school. In fact he seemed older and wiser than his thirteen years. A little man before his time.

'Look at that Dad. I'd love to see lions in the wild in Africa. That'd be a dream holiday seeing them in their natural habitat, chasing their prey.'

'One day, son. Maybe,' was Keith's non committal reply.

The tour guide continued her interesting talk about environmental and safety issues. She explained their policy 'on close to nature' habitats for all their animals.

'Don't forget,' she said, smiling mainly at Toby. 'Even in Africa the animals are in enclosures. These may be many miles wide but there are fences and patrols nevertheless.'

'Is that true Dad?' Toby asked over supper that night.

Keith smiled, since Toby had dutifully dressed in a suit and tie for the occasion.

'What's that Toby?'

'That animals are caged in Africa.'

'You've got to remember, Toby, that though some of the National Parks in Kenya and South Africa are huge, the townspeople need protection. It's not just for the safety of the people but for the animals too.'

'How do you mean?'

'Well say, as sometimes happens, an animal kills a child.'

'In Canada a bear occasionally does that. Not often though. They usually leave people alone.'

'Yes, that's right Toby. It's unfortunate but it's nature I'm afraid. They are wild animals after all, but what do you think happens next?'

Toby frowned. Not sure what his father wanted him to say.

His father continued, 'If an animal hurts or even kills someone at a zoo or wildlife park in this country. What happens to the animal do you think?'

'Oh yes, Dad. They have to shoot it because it may have the taste for killing people. Isn't that right?'

'Yes, Toby. Unfortunately it is, so can't you see that it's best to keep the animals separate if we can?'

Toby was silent for a few moments while he digested the conversation and his supper.

'In that case, Dad, why don't they kill murderers?'

Keith nearly choked on his last mouthful. Regaining his composure and hiding his embarrassment with a cough he replied,

'Ah Toby. That's a conversation for when you're older. It's time for bed now because we've another exciting day ahead of us.'

The following morning an Old English White Mark 2 Jaguar pulled up in the drive of their hotel, where they both stood admiring the car and its upholstery.

'Where to first?' asked Keith expectantly, unaccustomed to relinquishing control.

'My instructions are not to say, sir, but I ask you to be patient. I will talk you through each part of the day as we come to it. I must explain though, that we have no seatbelts in the back because of the age of the car.'

They set off in the direction of Milton Keynes. It was when they diverted from the A5 towards Bletchley that Keith guessed their first destination, but he decided to play the game and look surprised as they drew up outside Bletchley Park. He had visited the site on several occasions over the years, each time reassured that, though improvements had been made, the 'attraction' had remained as faithful to the original park as was possible, which certainly added to its appeal.

His son was thrilled by the visit. When it was time to leave Keith bought Toby an illustrated guide book, with the promise that they would return.

'Did this bloke Turing really build the first computer, Dad?'

'Well I'm not sure that he built it himself, but he certainly had a handle on the first design. What does it say in your book?'

'There's not much detail here,' Toby replied. 'How did it crack the codes and what were all those tubes for? I wanted to ask the guide some questions but it was time to leave.'

Pleased that Toby showed signs of a healthy enquiring mind, and wishing to encourage it as much as he could, Keith replied, 'Look for a more comprehensive history on your iReader$_6$ when we get home and you'll be much more informed when we next visit.'

'We'll come back soon then?' Toby asked unable to hide his enthusiasm.

'How about next summer vacation?'

'Great Dad, thanks,' replied Toby, returning his attention to his guide book.

While his son was deeply absorbed Keith tried to second guess their next place of visit and was not altogether surprised to see a sign to Haynes. He had seen an image of Haynes Park on the net and it was instantly recognisable, as was the little church nestling amongst the trees. They pulled up by the churchyard as Keith thought they would, although how he would explain this to Toby, he did not know.

David, the chauffeur, retrieved a bunch of flowers from the boot of the car and they followed him towards Lucille Vardon's grave. Keith felt nothing as he looked down on the tilting cross; if anything he felt a rising anger that a member of his family should have been so wrongly accused.

'Why are you looking so cross Dad?' Toby whispered as they watched David kneel and arrange the flowers. 'Why've we been brought here?'

'Well son,' Keith began. 'This is a military tour and I believe that Haynes Park was used as a training camp in the First World War. Isn't that right driver?'

'Yes, that's correct sir,' and he led them back to the car where he pulled a book out of the boot of the car. 'Here's your Personal e-Scrapbook of your tour. Bletchley Park is on the first page but here is a copy of a photo of the Haynes Park when it was being used for military purposes in WW1. There'll be a record of each place we visit but it will be up to you to fill in the detail.'

'So who was that Lucille woman in the grave?' Toby pestered.

'It was a World War 1 military grave. You could see by the carving on the cross, although it was quite worn down, but the inscription said that she was in the QMAAC, or to be more precise the Queen Mary's Army Auxiliary Corps. I expect she was stationed at Haynes Park. What do you think?'

'That sounds plausible,' Toby replied slowly, surprising Keith with his vocabulary, 'After all; those men certainly needed looking after.'

Keith just caught a glimpse of the chauffeur raising his eyebrows in the mirror at his son's unfortunate sexist comment and he smiled.

'Maybe they did Son,' he replied, glancing toward the stately home and thinking about his great grandfather over 100 years ago.

A few minutes later they pulled up at a military checkpoint. Keith had heard about Chicksands but had never been there. There was no public access to visit The Priory, which now housed a small museum, except by a previous arrangement, and he had never got around to organising it. The site was relevant to him in his line of work because, not only was it closely linked to Bletchley Park throughout World War Two, but it was also infamously remembered for 'The Elephant Cage'; the Cold War intelligence gathering construction which had dominated this skyline for years.

As they enjoyed their private viewing of the museum, pangs of doubt began to invade Keith's mind. Maybe he should have discussed this excursion with his senior officer. It seemed innocuous enough on the surface but he deliberated, not for the first time, on the identity of the person who had arranged this trip and their motives. How did they know so much about him? Had he been vigilant enough at covering his tracks; avoiding compromising his position? Keith's feelings of disquiet tormented him. He tried to relax. Their next stop was The Greyhound pub in Haynes where he and his son ate a light lunch.

'It's a bit of a drive to our next destination,' their driver explained as he held the car door open for them. In fact it was half an hour until they pulled up outside an old, but obviously restored barn just outside Tempsford, with an inscription on the barn door. An elderly ex RAF gentleman met them, resplendent in his medals.

'I was stationed here in the war and we were a proud unit. We carried out secret missions and raids during WW2.'

'Were you based here because it was so out of the way?' asked Toby, seeing the edge of the nearest village in the distance.'

'That's right young man. Our feats of daring were planned in this very barn and played a vital role in bringing the war to a successful conclusion. Now, you look around and ask questions if you want to.'

'Thanks,' said Toby.

It had not failed to reach Keith's attention that the word 'secret' had been repeated at almost each venue so far, but the organiser had no way of knowing his current occupation. Surely this was just another surprising coincidence? Nevertheless his sense of disquiet grew.

Toby was quite tired by now, his sponge like brain was saturated with so much exciting information. Keith was relieved when he nodded off to sleep in the car, and the unaccustomed sensation of Toby's head resting on his arm, was surprisingly soothing. Keith frowned. Maybe he was just suffering from an over active imagination.

At 3 pm they drove through the gates of The Shuttleworth Collection, the world famous museum of aircraft. Toby was awake and alert once more as they scrambled out of the car to enjoy talking to the pilots and taking photos of these amazing vintage aeroplanes before standing back to watch the old birds fly. Both Keith and Toby were too excited to enjoy the picnic set before them as they rushed forward to view another spectacular take-off or landing. The climax of the evening was seeing the old Edwardians fly.

'You are most fortunate, sirs, that the weather is calm and dry. Of course the pilots only risk flying these priceless machines in perfect conditions,' explained their chauffeur, who was also enjoying the spectacle.

Dixie, The Sopwith Triplane, caused a stir as it dipped and dived. This was followed by the Bristol F.2B Fighter. The man in the rear seat of the cockpit was taking photos of the crowd below.

'He's called the observer,' Keith explained to his son.

'I know Dad. He'd take photos of what was going on in the fields of France to help in planning the next battle - a bit like a secret mission.'

'Not so secret really,' replied Keith, impressed by Toby's knowledge but there was **that** word again.

And then there was a sense of awe as the replica Bristol Boxkite, which featured in "The Magnificent Men in their Flying Machines," soared gracefully above their heads, the complicated contraption of cloth and wire flying, as if in slow motion.

The grand finale occurred just as the sun was setting. There was a magical hush in the crowd as the 1909 Bleriot, the oldest aeroplane in the world still able to fly, gently lifted off the ground. It was aided by a competent ground crew who expertly held its wings in balance before it was ready to roll along the grassy runway. The machine hovered at what seemed to be only tree height, before returning gracefully to the safety of the earth. To the delight of the crowd the pilot repeated this flight on three occasions, each time as the sun sank deeper, leaving a lasting imprint on the minds of all who watched her.

'Wow, what an amazing day,' remarked Toby, as they sat together over supper at their hotel that evening.

'I agree, son, and what did you enjoy most of all?'

'It's so hard to say, Dad. It was like a week of special days all rolled into one, but I must say I enjoyed the show best of all. I'd been to aircraft museums before, but there's nothing like watching them fly.'

'Yes, we've been to air displays, but the more modern ones. You've seen The Red Arrows, and jets from the 1950's and even people wing-walking and doing aerobatics, but I agree with you, this was very special.'

Seeing Toby's eyes fighting with tiredness in his enthusiasm to enjoy every moment of the day Keith remarked, 'Why don't you turn in now. I'll just have a cup of coffee before I come up.'

'Yes OK Dad but,' and Toby hesitated a moment. 'Thanks, a million,' he exclaimed and he gave his dad a hug, an unusual sign of affection between father and son, bringing a tear to Keith's eyes as he watched Toby make for the stairs.

Keith sat for a few moments slowly sipping his liqueur coffee. It had been quite a trip, one he and his son would treasure. His mind drifted over the events of the day and his nagging doubts, so that by the time he too headed for the comfort of his room, he was resigned to two uncomfortable thoughts. Firstly he would have to report the day in full to his superiors, but worse still he would have to explain about Lucille Vardon and his family's involvement. He had no doubt that more information than even he was aware of would be contained in an e file about him, and that the details would have been meticulously checked before he was appointed. Even so, he found the whole business quite disturbing to his usually ordered life.

He glanced at the last photo in his E-Scrapbook, one obviously taken from the bi-plane earlier that day. There in the centre of the shot were him and his son, faces gazing upwards in wonder. Keith Regmund shuddered. He must do all he could to protect his precious only son.

6. iReader : device more advanced than an eReader in 2019

PART 5

LUCILLE VARDON'S STORY

1919

CHAPTER 11

May 1919

Lucille Vardon was full of mischief as she completed her shift in the Officers Mess tent. It was not that she taunted or teased the officers. There was no guile in Lucille. No, it was just that her smile and her sense of humour lightened up even the dullest meal and she had the knack of making the men feel like princes. One officer in particular, a Sergeant Major Regmund, had been so taken in by her personality that he had a bit of a crush on her and somehow or other he was determined to take the relationship further. Their eyes had met over the table and her smile had softened his heart, so much so that on one occasion his favourite meal of devilled kidneys remained barely touched.

The Sergeant Major was a dichotomy of two diverse personalities. On the one hand, with his men, he was firm and authoritarian, as you would expect from an army Sergeant Major. On the other hand, with women, he was reserved and lacking in confidence. They say it was mainly due to being ignored in preference to his sisters, by both his nanny and his mother in his early years.

This tall handsome, moustached officer had been wondering how he could approach Lucille for some time, and to his delight she had danced with him on two occasions the night before, but he had been too tongue tied to arrange a date. His stomach was in knots trying to conceive the right moment to approach her.

His quick-witted neighbour had exclaimed, *'If you're not gonna eat that, then I certainly will!'*

'Be my guest,' replied SM Regmund getting to his feet and striding to the tent opening, timed at just the moment Lucille was returning.

'You off your food today sir?' Lucille smiled.

'Umm, not really, I'm just going into Bedford and I'll get something to eat there.'

'I'm going in later too, when I've finished here,' Lucille smiled encouragingly. She liked the shy young officer but could not work out if he was interested in her. There had been a few time wasters in the past who had only wanted one thing. She had kindly, but firmly, put them in their place and was well respected for it amongst all the girls. That's why she was so popular. But this officer was different. When they had danced the other night he had barely said a word to her, but there was just that feeling between them. Had she imagined it? The way he had held her as if he did not want to let her go.

Taking her cue as a sign Sergeant Major Regmund smiled nervously,

'There's a truck going to Bedford at about 3 o'clock. If you'd like to accompany me Miss Vardon, we could spend the afternoon on the river and then catch a bite to eat before returning later. What do you say? It would be my pleasure.' He hoped that he did not sound too eager as he waited for what seemed like ages for her response.

'I'm not sure when we'll finish clearing away here, sir, but I'll try to make it. Must get on now, but thanks for asking,' she added, bobbing her head as she brushed past him back into the tent, blushing slightly. Behind her Sergeant Major Regmund strode off; a lightness in his step.

Lucille had many jobs to do before she was free for the afternoon. After she had cleared away the tables, she and her best friend Margaret had the job of trundling the sack full of dirty linen down to the laundry in the lane near the church. It was a job they quite enjoyed, especially in the spring sunshine. They chattered as they walked.

Margaret, a tall girl with curly red hair, swept back under her cap, had taken to Lucille the moment they met, even though they came from diverse backgrounds. She was a northern lass from Leeds. She liked a laugh with the girls but with her young man away in France she had no patience with girls who were out for too much of a good time. Lucille seemed a bit of a mystery to her; her island home sounded almost tropical when compared to the back to backs where she was brought up. Even her name sounded exotic, which Margaret had shortened to Lucy, so she would fit in better.

'Will you go with the officer to Bedford, Lucy?'

'Oh, I don't know Maggie, what do you think I should do?'

'He seems genuine enough. You usually have a scent for the rogues. You've always been a fair judge of character but what do you really think of him?'

They continued to pull the heavy cart between them.

'I think he's nice. A bit quiet, but I'm sure it's just that he's a touch shy. He doesn't talk about his family a lot like the others. In fact he doesn't talk a great deal at all.'

'Yes, that could be a worry, but maybe he's a private sort of chap and he might open up if you get to know him better.'

'Maybe,' Lucy replied unconvinced.

Their conversation was brought to an abrupt halt by a loud toot and both girls knew who it was without looking. It was the brash young farmer's son from Pear Tree Farm. He had given

144

the girls a lift from town on a couple of occasions when they had been grateful to accept his offer to avoid the five mile walk back to camp. It was OK when they were in pairs, but on one occasion when it had been raining, Lucy had foolishly accepted a lift on her own and it was all she could do to keep the filthy man's hands from lifting her skirt and reaching right up to her secret parts.

'They usually like it,' he had sneered as she had shied away, pushing herself as far into the door as she could, just out of his reach. It was amazing that he had been able to control the car with one hand. Fortunately, on that occasion, he had shrugged and left her alone, letting her out at the park gate before speeding off towards his farm. 'You'll come round. You'll see,' he had called out with a laugh, his voice trailing back towards her. From that moment on he had never left her alone and though each time she had refused his advances, he did not give up.

'I'm going into Bedford later,' he called out, 'if either of you beautiful girls would care to have a lift.' He lifted his hat to wave as he sped off up the track, one which crossed the park grounds and on to his farm near the woods.

'Not flipping likely,' Maggie giggled, not noticing Lucy shudder as they turned towards the laundry.

'You coming with me this afternoon, Maggie?'

'No I don't think so Lucy. It wouldn't be much fun playing gooseberry with you and your officer friend and anyway I'd like to get my letters written home and have a rest. Me feet have just had it for the day and if, like we often do, we miss the truck and have to walk back from Bedford, I think me feet'd drop off in protest. You going to be all right on your own though?' Maggie added with genuine concern.

'You know me Maggie; tough as you like under my weak as a wimp looking face.'

'I certainly wouldn't describe you as a wimp Lucy. You know your mind, that's all, and your face is, well ... attractive, I'd call it.'

'Thanks for the flattery,' replied Lucy. She knew full well that she was not beautiful, but she also recognised that certain men seemed to find her looks appealing. There'd only been a couple she might have encouraged over the years, but this was the first time a stirring of something special had caught her unawares. Most of the time she knew that she was quite capable of rebuffing unwanted advances.

There was that man in Bedford a month ago. She had several chance encounters and at first found it amusing, but after a while it got a bit irritating. He was a chap with an American accent, as far as she could tell, and thought he was God's gift; worked over at Shortstown at the aircraft factory, working on the engines for those huge airships. Lucille remembered the flights of the R31 last July and again in October where it had cast an eerie shadow over Haynes Park. She had heard it had been damaged on its flight in November, though. Anyway, this American chap had bumped into her, literally, near the bridge on the Embankment. She had looked over her shoulder at a couple who were rowing along the river, thinking she had recognised them and was not looking where she was going.

Whether it was by design, or a complete accident, suddenly she was jolted to a halt and her bonnet was knocked off her head.

'May I do the honours?' the young man had asked gallantly, retrieving and passing Lucille's hat to her.

'That's very kind of you sir. Thank you.'

'Anything for a lovely lady.'

'Are you American?' Lucille asked, unable to hide her curiosity.

'Yes I am. My family live in America. I was wounded in the Battle of Amiens under General Pershing.'

'I'm sorry to hear that but what brought you to here in Bedfordshire?'

'I was sent to a place near here called Wrest Park to recover. One day I saw the R31 fly overhead and I thought, that's for me and ended up working at Cardington.' He did not add that he deserted to do so. 'And you? Are you local?'

'No I'm not,' replied Lucille, not wanting to divulge too much personal information, 'but I'm in the Women's Auxiliary and I'm serving up at Haynes Park Camp.'

They had been walking side by side along the river and had just reached the pleasure boats when the young man asked,

'Would you like to take a boat on the river with me?'

'No, I'm sorry sir, but I don't have time to join you today,' Lucille hoped her rebuff would be accepted without quibble.

'But it would only be for half an hour and it would certainly be a pleasure to have your company.'

'I'm afraid I must get to the market square to pick up the truck back to our camp.'

'I could walk you home afterwards, if you like. Make sure you get back safely.'

I'm sure you would, thought Lucy, but kept her sarcasm to herself.

'That's very kind of you sir, but I must be going now. Good day to you but thank you for your company.'

As Lucy had turned to head back towards the town the man had grabbed her arm, but, to her surprise an officer she recognised from the camp had come up behind him and placed his hand on the American's shoulder and restrained him.

'Is this man bothering you?' Sergeant Major Regmund had asked.

'I'm fine thank you,' replied Lucille, shaken but relieved to leave them both and head towards the Town Hall, where the truck should have been waiting. Unfortunately, as she ran towards Bedford Bridge, she was just in time to see the back of it driving away from the town.

'Bother,' Lucy had exclaimed as she began to follow in the same direction. She was usually happy to walk, as she had often done in the past, but this time she would have appreciated to have put Bedford and the unfortunate incident far behind her. All the same she enjoyed the exercise and was soon striding along the main road, fields on either side of her. Her thoughts had turned to the officer who had rescued her, a quiet good looking man who had often smiled warmly at her, but never spoken. He's bit of a mystery, Lucy thought, although appealing in his own way.

After a little while Lucy was aware of footsteps close behind her. Not wanting to look over her shoulder, she quickened her pace. The footsteps had also quickened and Lucy, knowing that soon she would be taking an isolated path away from the main road and through Wilshamstead Woods, was getting increasingly irritated and just a little nervous.

Just as she was trying to decide whether to continue the much longer route and stay on the main road, there was a toot behind her. It was the farmer's son and, since he was a familiar face and was heading her way, she had accepted the lift

148

willingly. Glancing over her shoulder she noticed that the person who had been following her had headed off the road and on to the path and so maybe it was just a coincidence that he had been heading in the same direction as her. She had sighed, cross with herself for being so scared.

'Thank you,' she had said as the car sped away and she had enjoyed the few moments of relative luxury until she realised that this young man had not taken her previous refusal seriously either. Talk about escaping one enemy only to be cornered by another!

'Can't you take no for an answer?' Lucy snapped as she shied away to stop his hands wandering where they should not. He had just laughed.

Lucy had been so relieved when she had finally been dropped off at the drive to Haynes Park.

'I'm beginning to get a trifle impatient. They're usually not as stubborn as you, but I'm up for the challenge.'

Lucy watched his car speeding in the direction of his farm, tooting his horn.

Lucy shook her head vigorously as if to dispel the unbidden memories of a few weeks previously. She and Maggie headed for the hut where the women were housed, unlike the men who were living in tents. She did her best to get ready as quickly as she could, teased by Maggie who lounged on her make shift bed, making the occasional amusing comment at Lucy's expense.

'You'll miss the truck if you don't go soon,' Maggie urged, 'I've never seen you make so much fuss of your hair. Come here and I'll give it a final brush.' Lucy perched on the edge of Maggie's mattress while Maggie began brushing with long even strokes, removing every tangle before pinning it back for her.

149

'Bye!' Maggie had called after her friend. 'Enjoy yourself.'

Unfortunately Lucy walked out just as the truck disappeared from view on to Church End Road. Undeterred by this lack of good fortune Lucy resolved to walk. She was sure to catch up with the officer in town, if she kept a look out.

She strode purposefully out of the park grounds and on towards the woods, singing to herself as she went. It was at the edge of Wilshamstead Woods, when she was about to take the track down to the main road, that she heard the car behind her and as quickly as she could she jumped behind an old elm and crept back into the relative safety of the dense woodland. For a few moments she stood holding her breath but then, thinking the track was clear, she made her way back to the clearing.

Just then she heard a noise behind her and she stopped still, her heart pounding with fear.

'Oh it's you,' she said as nonchalantly as she could. 'Good afternoon sir.'

Since there was no other way, Lucy brushed past the man hoping to reach the relative safety of the road.

'Not so fast miss. I thought I'd bump into you again sooner or later. A bit foolish of you to be walking here on your own aren't you?' As he spoke the man rushed after Lucy and caught hold of her.

'Unhand me please sir,' exclaimed Lucy as she struggled, twisting and turning to set herself free.

'Not so fast,' the man replied as he grabbed her shoulder, bringing Lucille to her knees. 'You're asking for it, I'd say,' his eyes narrowed as he leant over her and brushed his mouth against her ear.

'If you stop struggling and come to me willingly, I'll let go of you.' the man whispered as he moved to cover Lucy's mouth

to stop her from screaming, digging his knees into her back, holding her firmly.

Suddenly Lucy was aware of the glint of a blade in his free hand and she went limp, slowly nodding her head.

'That's a good girl,' he leered and slackened his grip, his hand slowly moving to her breast.

Lucy tried to turn her head towards him.

'Please sir, don't touch me. I'm not like that. I implore you to let me go on my way.'

'Why should I?'

'If you let me go I promise I won't tell a soul.'

At that point they heard voices on the edge of the woods and Lucy could see panic in the man's eyes. She was just about to yell for help when he grabbed her hair and covered her mouth once more. Suddenly she felt an excruciating pain and her body fell limply into the undergrowth.

PART 6
BEDFORD POLICE STATION
2019

CHAPTER 12

Thursday May 9th 2019 ~ Morning   Bedford
Police Station

Joanna was in a daze as she was led into an interview room. DC Cathy Peterson smiled encouragingly at her. Joanna felt reassured by the presence of this young officer, a petite lady in her late twenties with short bobbed black hair and sharp Mary Quant fringe in contrast to her pale oval face. Cathy had been sitting with Joanna on the journey to the police station in Bedford and could not believe that this woman was a murderer. Still, it took all sorts and who knows what her husband had been like.

As DI Norton started his questioning it was obvious to Cathy that he had made up his mind that she was guilty. All he needed was a neat confession, a few questions with the family and in the village to establish a motive and then he could move on to the quieter life of planning his retirement in a month's time. He could not wait.

DI Norton sat down opposite Joanna, stretched up, clicked his fingers and motioned DS Brown to take the empty seat beside him. A red light flickered as the sight-sound recording equipment was activated. Cathy stood by the door.

'Interview commences at 10.15 am on the ninth of May two thousand and nineteen. Present are myself, Detective Inspector Norton,' at which his chest seemed to puff out imperceptibly before he continued, 'DS Brown, DC Peterson and Mrs Joanna Thomas of Pear Tree Farm, Haynes,

Bedfordshire.' DI Norton nodded towards his fellow officers as if making formal introductions.

Joanna's brain switched off and she closed her eyes. All she could see was Bob slumped on the kitchen table; a place that had known only laughter and the day to day frustrations of running a farm. She could not comprehend her situation.

'Please can we confirm that you are Mrs Joanna Thomas of Pear Tree Farm, Haynes?'

Joanna nodded her head and whispered, 'Yes,' in a rasping voice, her tongue sticking to the top of her mouth and lips barely moving.

DI Norton continued, 'Mrs Thomas, we know this is hard for you but please concentrate and try to tell us from the beginning what happened this morning.'

There was a long pause as DI Norton tried hard not to sound impatient. He could murder a cup of coffee and, smiling at his unfortunate pun, clicked his fingers and the whirring ceased.

Turning to the Cathy he barked, 'Fetch me a strong black coffee. Two sugars and make it quick.'

Seeing Cathy's hesitation he snapped, 'What the hell are you waiting for? You'll only be gone a minute or two.'

Knowing that Mrs Thomas was so vulnerable and shouldn't be left alone without another female present Cathy glanced nervously at the frightened lady before she left the room. When she returned Cathy was even more concerned.

'So, when you came down this morning you lost your temper and stabbed your husband, didn't you Mrs Thomas. Tell me the truth.' And he thumped his fist on the table just as Cathy placed the steaming coffee in front of him. Startled momentarily, since he had not realised that she had returned, air hissed through his teeth before his voice softened,

'Let's go over the facts again, shall we?'

With Cathy's presence in the room, Joanna took a deep breath and with all the dignity she could muster, she whispered,

'I did not kill my husband, Sergeant, Inspector, or whatever you are, and I would really like you to find the person who did.' And with that she sighed and could say no more.

In sheer frustration DI Norton got up and left the room, motioning for Cathy to take his place.

DS Brown, who had by this time not said a word, raised his eyebrows at Cathy as his superior departed. He looked over at Joanna, who had closed her eyes once more, cutting out the reality she did not wish to perceive. He spoke for the first time,

'DI Norton leaves the room at 10.15 am and the interview is terminated,' and then he clicked his fingers and the room was silent.

'Have some tea Mrs Thomas. I've made it nice and sweet to help you with the shock. I'm afraid we're not allowed alcohol otherwise a touch of brandy wouldn't go amiss, I'm sure,' encouraged Cathy.

Joanna opened her eyes, her expression showing obvious relief that the obnoxious man had left her in peace. She sipped the sugary tea, her fingers tightly gripping the warm mug, her eyes never leaving the brown liquid until she had drained the last dregs. Then she looked up.

'Why doesn't he believe me?' she implored, looking straight into Cathy's eyes.

'We'll find out the truth,' were the only non committal words of comfort Cathy could offer before she led Joanna back down to the cell, where she curled up under a blanket and sank into a fitful sleep, from which she did not wish to wake.

DS Tony Brown was an officer in his early 30's, with good looking features in a boy-next-door sort of way, but married to his job. Always had been. After the disastrous, in his opinion, interview with Joanna Thomas he went straight out to the lobby and fetched John, the herdsman, leading him to the interview room, where he waited patiently for DI Norton to return so that questioning could commence.

'Tell me Mr Cookham, what happened this morning,' DI Norton asked, in a tone far more pleasant than the one he had used on Mrs Thomas. Tony suppressed a frown, remaining stony faced as he had been trained to do. He was there to listen and observe; to make a note of any expression, tone of voice or non verbal clue.

'Well, officer; Inspector; it was a pretty normal morning. I went straight to the winter shelter in the field at 4.30 am to lead the Friesians to the milking parlour where Bob was getting the equipment ready. That was at about 4.45. Always is. Or at least it's been that early since Bob bought the Jerseys.

We worked together, as usual, until the last few cows needed to be milked, when Bob went to have a cup of tea before checking his Jerseys. I finished off and led the cows safely over the track and into their winter shelter, shut the gate and strolled home to grab a cuppa. I was just feeding Bengie, my dog when my pager bleeped to tell me that there was a problem with the Jerseys. It comes directly from their computer, you see. I thought it was odd because Bob should have been there by then to sort it out. It was probably a blocked pipe or something. As I walked up the track I saw Sally's van and went up to say hello, but she was beside herself. She told me what she had seen and

I rushed to see if I could help. I thought there must be some mistake. An accident or something.'

'And how was Mr Thomas this morning? Was he agitated in any way? Does he confide in you at all while you're working?'

John realised that the inspector's questions were hinting that Joanna rather than himself was the suspect at his stage, so he was guarded with his answers.

'Bob was fine this morning. We only ever talk about the farm. He moans about the price he gets for milk. Anyone would, the way we work such long hours to get it to the public, but otherwise he was his usual quiet cheerful self.'

'And you heard or saw nothing when you left Mr Thomas to finish clearing away.'

'No, like I said, I was focused on the cows and getting them safely back to their shelter. I use the entrance on the other side of the barn that leads over the track to their shelter. I didn't come into the farmyard at all until I saw Sally, the post-woman.

'So you saw no one else enter the farmyard after you left Mr Thomas.'

'No I didn't, but I'm sure Mrs Thomas didn't do it. She couldn't have. She's such a gentle person.'

'Excuse me, but we'll get to Mrs Thomas in a moment. So when you walked up the track to your cottage you saw no one.'

John paused for a moment. There was something, but it escaped his memory. Everything was a blur in his mind before he had found Sally. He thought of Fiona the milk lady, but dismissed it since she did not call on a Thursday. Helen? No, it was much too early for Helen's visit. It was so frustrating because he knew there was something important, stuck in the crevices of his mind. He sighed.

'No, I just met Sally in the lane and went in to find...

'About Mr and Mrs Thomas. Do you socialize with them at all?'

'Every now and then we meet in The Greyhound in the village; casual like. We don't make an arrangement.'

'And do they ever argue, as far as you know?'

'I know there was a big argument before Christmas about a shower. Joanna wanted one and Bob didn't see the point. Mind you it was all a ruse to tease her. He had organised for one to be put in as a surprise just after Christmas. You should have seen her face the following day. That satisfied look like getting in the harvest just before a storm. Smug like.'

'So he was a bit tight fisted, your boss then?'

'No, I wouldn't say that. He was a farmer. Farmers always watch their pennies don't they? Never had any cash on him. Used to amuse everyone that Joanna would always be the one to pay, even when they had a meal for her birthday. It's just the way he was.'

'So there was nothing, no rift or anything since Christmas?'

'They were devoted to each other, as far as I could see; proud of their two children; gone off their separate ways now of course.'

'Where have the children gone then?'

'Well, Paul is usually at University in the West Country but he's home on holiday at present. Bob would have liked him to stay to help run the farm, but Paul's not really suited to it. Never has been. Emily has married and is living Bromham way.'

'Paul and his dad have a row over it, then?'

'No, inspector. You're blowing things out of all proportion. I think it's a bit like the shower thing. Bob makes a big thing of it to test Paul's resolve.'

'So can you give me any reason why Mrs Thomas would murder her husband; any rumours of either of them having an affair maybe?'

At this point John got quite cross. 'I can assure you officer, Joanna didn't kill her husband and that, as far as I know, she had absolutely no reason to do so.'

'You'd better start thinking of your own excuses then, because, if **she** didn't murder her husband, then I'm afraid the finger is likely to point at you next. After all, as it stands at the moment you were the last person to see Mr Thomas alive. Think about it.'

DI Norton left the interview with a suppressed chuckle at his masterly interview techniques. It would only be a matter of time. The self preservation instinct would click in and John Cookham would come up with some believable motive or other for Joanna to have murdered Mr Thomas. With that thought he headed to the incident room to give out some orders to the gathered team.

'Items and finger prints have been taken at the crime scene and sent to forensics but we still haven't located the murder weapon. I need a couple of you to organise a team of uniformed to carry out a door to door and speak to people in the village. We're searching for a motive here. I'm sure we'll soon have ample evidence for Mrs Thomas to stand trial. We'll have a briefing this afternoon at 5 pm so have your reports ready. I hope to have enough information by then to charge Mrs Thomas. She may be a mild mannered lady but it is surprising what someone can do if they are riled.' In the pause there was a sound of someone drawing breath in disbelief. 'Any questions?' he added.

There was no response and he was too tired of the business of police work to recognise the dissent and deal with it.

'Don't forget The Greyhound. You can uncover a great deal of gossip in a village pub. Wish I could go there myself,' he chuckled. The officers before him smiled politely. It was well known that he liked a tipple. 'Right then, I'll have a break and then continue with the interview of the cowman. DS Brown, you take over here and allocate areas to the team for the foot work. We should get it covered in no time.'

DI Norton headed to the canteen to have some lunch then back to Interview Room 2 where John Cookham had been brought back for him. It had a glass partition so he observed Mr Cookham for a while. The man was slumped in his chair but his expression was of concern, rather than guilt or fear. He looked a compassionate sort of man, mind you, one who deals with animals everyday would have to be.

On entering the room he went through the usual procedures before continuing the interview,

'Now Mr Cookham. I can see you want to return to your duties on the farm but since you have worked closely with Mr Thomas for a few years now.' He lifted his eye brows making the unspoken question clear.

'Eight years, sir.'

'Well, in eight years you've worked alongside your boss seven days a week, twice a day. Surely, you must have heard or seen something to make you suspicious or concerned things were not quite right.'

While John had been on his own he had racked his memory for something. What was it? He shook his head.

'There's nothing Inspector. They appeared to everyone to be devoted to each other and Bob wasn't one to make enemies.'

'This tiff over the shower and the argument about their son Paul's future on the farm must have caused bad feeling, but there was something else wasn't there? Something you're concealing from us. Who are you trying to protect and why, that's what interests me Mr Cookham?'

John remained resolutely loyal to the family who had given him his livelihood. He just shook his head in disbelief but when he heard the following accusation it riled him to the point of almost losing his self control.

'So the only other explanation is that you're having an affair with Mrs Thomas,' the Inspector spat out. DS Brown winced.

'That's total, utter rubbish. How dare you make such accusations?' John cried, standing up, as if tempted to punch the policeman.

'Why are you trying to protect her? You're only stitching yourself up and what might be **your** motive for murder?' The inspector glared into John's eyes, defying him to strike.

It was at that moment John remembered what was bothering him. He sat down with a bump, all energy drained from him, and the inspector, feeling pretty sure that he was about to hear the nugget of 'truth' which would nail Mrs Thomas, sat back down with a self assured grin.

'Spit it out then. What is it that you've remembered?'

John paused, collecting his thoughts along with his dispersed temper, 'Well, just as I was turning into the track toward the farm to see to the Jerseys I saw a bicycle disappear from view.'

DI Norton was incredulous. 'A bicycle,' he repeated with a sneer. 'Where did you suddenly dream that one up from?'

'I saw it heading pretty fast towards Church End.'

There were a few moments of quiet as the Inspector summed up the situation.

'Well, that'll be all for now. You'd better go home and look after those cows hadn't you, but we haven't finished with you yet. Interview terminates at 2.00 pm.'

John got up slowly and headed for the door, glancing over his shoulder just in case the inspector suddenly changed his mind. Relieved, he accepted a drive home in a police car.

Although numb with shock his primary concern was the welfare of the animals. He went straight to the Jerseys. Some were eating hay, oblivious to the change in routine, but several were restlessly vying for position for milking or nudging the machinery in sheer frustration. He unblocked the system, which took a matter of moments, stood watching and soothing the animals before heading for the winter shelter where he was not surprised to find old Mr Thomas waiting for him.

They said little as they went through the familiar motions of bringing the cows in together. John had to get the equipment ready because Bob's father, Peter Thomas, was not familiar with it. Instead he did a good job reassuring the animals, impatiently waiting to be milked. Like their masters, the cows did not like the pattern of their day disturbed. It surprised John that Peter Thomas could behave so calmly, when his own son had been murdered that very morning. Nevertheless the proximity of the animals and the routine was strangely comforting for them both.

CHAPTER 13

9th May 2019 ~ Midday

Back at the police station DI Norton had called a small team who gathered for the briefing. Some sat on their chairs and others perched on the corners of desks, all waiting impatiently for the inspector to arrive. Although he still enjoyed the respect of the force after forty years of successful service, many were restless for change and could see that he had lost his way; that ability to look beyond the obvious. For some this led to a hunger to prove their worth for future promotion, but there was also one young officer DS Saima Akhtar, new to Bedford, who was different. She was incessantly teased by the more experienced officers because she had a pure desire for justice and she felt instinctively that there was more to this case than a domestic incident. Mind you, the last thing she wanted to do was make a fool of herself. All the mumblings came to an abrupt silence as Inspector Norton cleared his voice.

'Let me sum up the case. A normal day in the life of the farm as far as I can see. Mr Bob Thomas got up at 4.30 am to milk his Friesians as usual. The cowman John Cookham brought the cows in to the milking parlour to be milked at approximately 4.45. At about 5.40 Bob Thomas returned to the farmhouse for a quick cup of tea when the murder must have taken place. The murderer must have known their schedule. Meanwhile John Cookham finished the milking and returned the cows to the shelter across the track.

At 6.15 am the post lady Sally heard sobbing and saw Mrs Thomas slumped over her husband and the blood splattered floor. No murder weapon was found. Not long after that John Cookham also witnessed the scene from the kitchen door. Both claim that they did not enter the kitchen. By this time Mrs Thomas is sitting opposite her husband, talking to him, covered in blood.

The post lady said that she normally calls at about that time and waves to Mrs Thomas through the kitchen window on her way to the front door. It was only because she heard the noise that she went around to the kitchen door, at the left hand side of the house, and she said that the door was wide open. She ran back to her van and dialled 999. A few minutes later she talked to Mr Cookham.

Their son, typical student type, computer still on, curtains closed, empty cans of lager all over the floor was found in a drunken stupor upstairs. Being the only other person in the house at the time, as far as we know, he was dragged, no sorry, encouraged to get up from a deep alcohol induced sleep and we brought him in for questioning. It was no good questioning him in that state and so he was left sleeping it off in a cell. I expect he's awake by now and angry to be waiting.

The murder must have taken place between 5.45 and 6 am, which should be confirmed by forensics. The finger prints on the door handle are muddled and smudged as you can imagine, but there are certainly Mr & Mrs Thomas's, the others are indistinguishable. Nevertheless, I believe that Mrs Thomas murdered her husband, but for now she claims her innocence, backed up by John Cookham. He was the only other person who saw Mr Thomas that morning, as far as we know, but I would have thought the fact that he had been responsible for taking the cows back over to their shelter safely was alibi enough. We need to check his pager and Bob Thomas's too. That must happen on site so I've sent an expert over to the farm.

An officer has checked Mr Cookham's house just in case and found nothing, and he hardly had time to change or get rid of the evidence of blood stained clothes. Anyway he's not the type. I can tell. Any questions before I hand it to you all to report any of your findings?'

'Well sir. The door being wide open does seem a little odd so early in the morning and the fact that there were no other distinguishable finger prints on the handle is not strange since the killer would almost certainly be wearing gloves to carry out his crime, don't you think,' DS Akhtar interjected.

Irritated by this enthusiastic upstart the inspector dismissed it with a brush of his hand, showing that the remark was not important enough to comment upon. A couple of men gave knowing looks as the Inspector continued. 'Over to the rest of you. What incriminating facts have you gleaned about the Thomas family?'

'What about the bicycle, sir? John Cookham mentioned it at the end of his interview. Should be easy to track down, someone on a bicycle at that time of the morning,' prompted DS Brown.

'Just a distraction to throw us off the scent more than likely, but certainly look into it. If a person **was** on a bicycle in the area at that time, then we may have another useful witness. I'll leave it to you to follow it up.'

Yes, sir,' replied DS Brown, feeling as if he had been dismissed by an over-powering headmaster.

'Well sir, most people said that both Mr and Mrs Thomas were pillars of the local community,' offered DC O'Toole. Thomas O'Toole, a stocky good hearted man, third generation of a family of Irish descent who had settled in Bedford in the heyday of the brickworks back in the 50's. He had been carrying out a door to door enquiry at Haynes Church End and nearby farms for the last two hours with DS Akhtar.

The inspector frowned.

Unperturbed, DC O'Toole continued, 'some villagers said that arguments between the Thomases were common knowledge down at The Greyhound when Mrs Thomas wanted something and Mr Thomas didn't want to pay for it.'

'I thought as much. Anything in particular recently?' Inspector Norton smiled at DC O'Toole, a family man in his later thirties, dull, set in his ways and always looking for a quiet life.

'The biggest row they had was over having a new shower installed just before Christmas, but Mr Thomas surprised...'

'Oh I know all about the shower thank you,' interrupted Inspector Norton impatiently. 'Anyone else?' DC O'Toole was the second person to redden at the feeling of being dismissed.

'I heard they had had a heated discussion over which charity to support for the Tractor Rally just last week,' another brave officer piped up and several smirked behind their hands.

'Is there no scandal you've uncovered in the village or in the family? Is there nothing more incriminating than a mild tiff in the local? Are you investigative officers or would it be better if I returned you to traffic duty?' Inspector Norton boomed in frustration as the meeting came to an unsuccessful end. 'I don't think you need a doctorate to come to the conclusion that she killed her husband, so get off your back sides and go out and dig up the evidence to prove it!'

Saima felt a personal jab here. Yes, she had a Doctorate in Criminology and was far more qualified than the inspector who was old school, and she had heard his argument over and over. No, she also had the experience and proven record behind her. She lifted her shoulders and DC Cathy Peterson caught her eye and smiled at her.

The inspector stormed out of the room and back to his office. There he sank into his chair, reaching down to remove a hip flask from his locked bottom drawer and stared at the framed picture of his wife Beth. His eyes watered. Six weeks and he and Beth would have been enjoying the luxury of retirement together. For forty years she had stood by him, patient, understanding, never once complaining about his ridiculously long hours and his perpetually stressed state of mind. They had enjoyed three weeks away every year. Always the same, renting an apartment on the Algarve where they had planned to spend their retirement, away from damp old England, until... DI Norton let out an involuntary sob. Until Beth had died of a brain haemorrhage just six months ago. The irony of it. Years she had worked as a nurse, latterly for Macmillan; giving every hour of her time and energy to people who were dying or suffering, supporting the families and helping them to cope.

His thoughts wavered between anger at the injustice of life and cynicism. It saved the Government another pension, and the way he was going, he knew he wouldn't last long, alone and without the adrenaline of the Force. In so many ways he longed for retirement but in others he dreaded it. He put Beth's picture back on his desk; the tidiness of which he knew irritated his colleagues. He hated loose ends and if he had to stay longer to see this case completely solved he would, but he hoped to leave on a high. His sense of well being depended on it. As his phone rang he snapped his desk drawer shut and locked it with one hand as he pressed the call speaker button with another.

'Detective Inspector Norton,' he barked.

'Good afternoon. My name is Reverend Morrison. My house keeper explained that two of your officers called this morning but I was out on a house call. The lady officer, DC Peterson I think Mrs Hammond said her name was, left your card for me to call you with information. I have noticed some unusual happenings here at the churchyard in Haynes over the past year and thought I'd better inform you.'

'Thank you Reverend Morrison. What is it you are trying to tell me?'

'Well, it's about the grave of a young woman who died in 1919.'

Trying hard to quell his impatient temper, which he had only experienced in the six months since Beth had died, DI Norton interrupted, 'And what has a death back in 1919 got to do with our current enquiry, might I ask?'

'I know this sounds incredible Detective, but the lady in question was murdered too, and there **have** certainly been some strange things happening.'

Trying to get rid of this time waster as quickly as possible, but determined to be polite, DI Norton concluded the conversation with, 'I'll send someone around this afternoon, if that's convenient.'

'Yes, I'll be here,' replied the Reverend.

DI Norton put the phone down and sighed. He never used to be this short tempered. He was always enthusiastic to the point of obsession to follow up any leads, however obscure they were, because it was often these threads that turned into ropes to trap the murderer. He got up and strode back to the briefing

168

room where DS Brown had taken over and had started to allocate tasks.

'I'll take over here if I may,' DI Norton's words were of a request but everyone present recognised them as a command.

'DC O'Toole, I'd like you to remain here this afternoon for the interviews of Emily Dewer, Mrs Thomas's daughter, who should be arriving shortly, and the son Paul. Then we'll interview Mrs Thomas once more before we decide whether we have grounds to charge her or whether she can go, probably to her daughter's since she can't return home.

DC Peterson and DS Brown. Please can you go and check on Mrs Thomas first and then I've just had a Reverend Morrison on the phone? He lives up in the village. He sounds a bit unhinged to me, muttering something about a murder in 1919, but we'd better follow it up. Can you go to see him and then interview the victim's parents at their bungalow? No need to bring them in at this time, after all, they've got a farm to run, but I do need a volunteer to get up early and check the timings of the milking in the morning.'

'I'm happy to do that sir, but what about the bicycle?' DS Brown replied.

'Thank you for the offer. You can follow that one up too,' DI Norton retorted, 'while you're over in the area today. See if you can track the person down. Heading over towards Clophill, by all accounts, if Mr Cookham was telling the truth. DS Akhtar, I'd like you to continue looking though the videos and organise a search into the background of the family; bank records, medical records, that sort of thing. DC O'Toole will join you when he's finished with me. In fact I'd like you to stand in on the interviews with Emily Dewer and Mrs Thomas, for the female presence, but also to have a female perspective.'

'OK, sir,' DS Akhtar replied, rather wishing she was going out rather than doing desk work, however important.

'That's all for now. Catch a short lunch break but I want you to resume your tasks in half an hour. Any questions?' There was a short pause before everyone started to move and the briefing was closed. Most headed towards the canteen but DC O'Toole waited behind.

'Let's get the son over with first shall we?' remarked DI Norton.

They requested that Paul Thomas be brought down to Interview Room 2 and a few minutes later the lad arrived, pulling his fingers through his greasy hair and rubbing his eyes, his face ashen.

Having sympathy with the lad's drink induced symptoms, DI Norton gestured with his hand, 'Sit down lad. We've just got a few questions to ask you and then you can go.'

'What's happened, officer?' asked Paul slumping in the chair opposite the detective. 'I've done nothing. Why on earth did you drag me here?'

'All in good time Paul, isn't it? Paul Thomas, son of Bob and Joanna Thomas?'

'Yes that's right but..' DI Norton put up a hand which instantly silenced the young man.

'Please can you describe your whereabouts over the last twelve hours?'

'Why do you want to know?' Paul glared at the inspector defiantly, but after a pause continued anyway. 'I went to The Stone Jug for a quick one. You know, half of lager,' he reddened at the obvious fib, since he remembered driving home along Great Lane after two pints. Would old George down the pub back him up he wondered, or drop him in it. He looked up and the inspector was obviously waiting for him to continue.

'Yes, I was a bit annoyed really. My Dad and I had had a bit of a barney. Nothing serious but when I came home I didn't care to speak to them, so I went straight up to my room. I'm home to revise for my exams you see, so I switched on my computer and got on.'

'And what time would you say that was?' DI Norton asked.

'Not late. I came in at about 11pm I think.'

'And then?' encouraged the inspector.

'And then I had a couple of Red Bulls to stay alert and worked through the night, but towards the early hours I turned back to lager. It switches off the mind again, otherwise I wouldn't sleep. Then I went to sleep and you lot woke me up. Now what's this all about? I have a right to know why I'm here.'

'All in good time, but what did you and your dad have an argument about?'

'Same old thing really, like milking a cow and just as boring. Dad still wants me to come back, when I've completed my degree, to take over the farm when he gets past it. He knows it's the last thing I'd want to do, and anyway, it's a done deal that John'd do a far better job. Jolly good thing really. He was born to it. Em and me, neither of us were ever interested in farming. I don't know why Dad still goes on so. A habit of his I suppose.'

DI Norton nodded at DS Akhtar, confirming their mutual realisation that Paul clearly had no idea that his father was dead.

'What have I said now?' Paul massaged his neck and stretched his head back so as to soothe his irritation. 'It's not fair. I've done nothing wrong.'

The officer cleared his throat. 'What time do you think you settled down to sleep then?'

'It must have been at about quarter to six I pulled the curtains. I'd switched off my PC at five thirty.'

'So you didn't see or hear anything unusual between five thirty and six thirty?'

Paul screwed his eyes up in a frown, dredging his aching brain for something and then he suddenly reddened at the memory.

You can read this one's thoughts like subtitles on his face, thought Saima.

'What was it Son?' the inspector asked.

'Well, I was about to draw the curtains but I glanced out over the fields. It always looks its best in the early morning light. Then I noticed something moving in the trees. Nothing unusual in that. It's usually a muntjac deer or maybe a badger. They can be a real nuisance, the muntjacs especially - there are loads around here, but then a girl appeared and she was looking towards the farm. I grabbed my binoculars but she must have done the same.' Paul blushed again. 'You see I didn't have a stitch on, so I stepped back into the shadows, closing the curtains and jumped into bed.'

'And had you ever seen this young lady before?'

'Yes I have; a few times. Once at the Haynes 100 and another evening on Great Lane. I stopped and offered the girl a lift to the pub, since I knew she was staying near there.'

'Do you know this young lady personally?'

'No, Inspector I don't.'

'Well, thank you Paul for answering all of my questions. That's all for now. DS Akhtar has something quite difficult to tell you and then you'll be given a lift home. We think it's best that you stay at your grandparents for a while.' And with that said he left the room, DS Brown coming in to take his place, explaining the change to the microphone before taking his seat.

Saima cleared her voice. It was just like Norton to leave her with this difficult task.

'I'm afraid to tell you this Paul, but your father was brutally murdered this morning. Your mother is in custody at the moment because she was the only person on the scene of the crime when we were notified.'

'What!' exclaimed Paul, his eyes opening wide for the first time, startled with shock. There was a second's pause as he attempted to digest the policewoman's words. 'That's bloody ridiculous, blaming my mother. She would never do a thing like that. They are inseparable, my mum and dad. Can I see her?'

Saima noted that Paul was still using the present tense. 'No I'm afraid you can't at the moment, since you were both at the scene of the crime. We're not saying your mother's guilty Paul, but that she's here helping us with our enquiries. Now, would you like a cup of tea or something?'

'No, I just want to go home.' Paul slumped further down in his chair, his shoulders and head hunched forward in dejection, his eyes clouded with disbelief.

'I'm afraid that you'll not be allowed to stay at the farmhouse. You can either stay with your grandparents or your sister, who will be here shortly.'

'I'll stay with my gramps,' was all Paul would say and there was silence for a moment or two. Then his eyes glared open. 'What about that girl? You don't think she did it, do you?'

'I can assure you that we'll be following up that lead shortly, Paul.'

'What about my lap top? I need it to study.'

173

'We're just checking that it corroborates with what you have told us and then we'll deliver it to you.'

'But...'

'No buts I'm afraid,' replied DS Akhtar. 'Now, if you'd follow me and come and wait in the lobby then an officer will take you back to the farm.' As they walked, Saima noted that Paul seemed more concerned about his lap top than either of his parents. She sighed.

CHAPTER 14

9th May 2019 ~ Afternoon   Bedford   Police
Station

Joanna sat bolt upright on the hard bed and stared at the grey breeze-blocked wall in front of her. Initially her mind had been completely blank, unable to register reality or to acknowledge her grief. It was all too overwhelming. It was like a pain seeping from her temples, all the way down her bent spine. It circled her inner organs; stomach cramp, heart burn and a tingling sensation across her chest. At one moment of panic Joanna's hand had inadvertently flown to her throat as her breathing became erratic. She had gulped some stale air from this enclosed cell, unable to imagine all those inmates whose smells and presence still haunted the room, with all their secrets and lies. That's how DC Cathy Peterson had found her half an hour later when Joanna had barely registered her presence in the room.

Cathy could sense the aura of deep pain like barbed wire, surrounding Mrs Thomas as she entered the room.

'You'd be better to rest,' Cathy encouraged as she gently took Joanna's arm, who, like an obedient child after a grilling from her father for some misdemeanour, automatically lifted her legs to curl around herself as Cathy pulled the blanket over her shoulders.

'You believe me don't you,' Joanna whispered as she closed her eyes, almost expecting Cathy to put out the light. Cathy stood there a moment or two listening to Joanna's laboured breathing. The atmosphere was far from peaceful as doors slammed and footsteps moved along the stark corridor.

Cathy stood outside the cell for a few moments just to make sure that Mrs Thomas had settled down. Occasionally she heard raised voices from above and could imagine a heated interview taking place with that young thief they had picked up in the early hours of the morning or the drunk they had found sprawled around the foot of the statue near Debenhams in town. Seeing the approaching officer he had even had the audacity to pee on the statue just to make sure that he had been taken into a cell for a rest. Sometimes it was just because he fancied a change, a sandwich and a hot cup of tea or even a cooked meal if his luck was in. Not this time though. Cathy knew he would be given short shrift and sent on his way after a few hours to dry out.

Later, up in the canteen Cathy's friend Saima had confided in her over a cup of tea, 'He even winked at the constable as they bundled him into the car.'

'That figures,' replied Cathy who remembered with fondness her times on the beat. The girls had laughed.

'Share the joke,' a fellow officer had called from the other side of the canteen. 'We could all do with cheering up.' Saima had shut him up by just placing her index finger on her nose and smiling at him. This made Cathy laugh even more, admiring her friend's ability to silence a man with just a look. She wished she could do that sometimes. For the remainder of their break the ladies whispered to each other over their mugs, Cathy describing the scene at the farmhouse and the possible suspects.

'So, do you think she did it? Killed her husband with a knife that is,' Saima asked.

'I'm almost sure she's innocent, Saima, but the difficulty is proving it,' Cathy replied in an only just audible voice. 'But where's the murder weapon?'

'And we need to find the murderer. That would help.'

'Yes I know, but the DI is so determined to have a quick result before he retires; to bow for his final accolade as it were.'

'It's not like you to take any notice of that but I'd better get back to my desk,' Saima's intake of breath and slightly upward shifted eyebrows left words unspoken. 'Good luck anyway.'

'Thanks Saima. You too. You don't know what your sleuthing skills will uncover. Keep a close eye on Mrs Thomas, will you?' Cathy asked. 'I'm worried about her.'

At that moment the Duty Officer paced over to interrupt their conversation.

'Cathy, Mrs Dewer is in the lobby, that's Joanna Thomas's daughter. Norton's asked if you could escort her to see her mother.'

'OK thanks Robert. Shall we take her together?' She looked at Saima who nodded.

A quarter of an hour ago Joanna's daughter Emily had arrived at Bedford Police Station. She was still pale from the numbing shock of being visited by a constable knocking on her door to tell his grave news. They had stopped up the road to drop off Emily's baby daughter Kiran at her mother-in-law's, whose look of anguish was far from comforting. The surreal drive in the back of a police car into Bedford had done nothing to bring her to her senses either. When she called her husband's number she was almost relieved that no one answered. She had heard the reassuring anonymity of the answer-phone and waited what seemed like an eternity for the bleep.

'Brian. Give me a call as soon as you can. Terrible emergency. Can't explain on the phone.'

With the enormity of the situation, she managed to gulp back an involuntary sob and quickly pressed the 'end' button before the tears started to flow. By the time the police officer who had brought her in had explained who she was to the duty officer in reception, Emily had calmed down and had been asked to sit in the lobby and wait.

'I'll only be a few moments. I'll fetch someone who can tell you if it's possible to see your mother now,' the Duty Officer reassured her before he disappeared through some swing doors.

Emily sat with reluctance, just in time to see the drunk removed from the premises rather unceremoniously. Her mind was blank.

A few moments later she was led down a corridor of cells by two women police officers and, glancing through the small grilled opening in the door, she first caught sight of the huddled figure of her mother beneath a blanket, with her back to the door, curled around a pillow.

Emily pulled her shoulders back as if to prepare for a great burden. She had to be strong for her mother. She would not allow any nagging doubt that her mother might be guilty to enter her soul. The kindly policewomen let her into the cell and one of them called to her mother,

'Wake up Mrs Thomas. Your daughter's here.'

Bleary eyed, Joanna came to with a start and seeing Emily over the shoulder of the police woman she stood up as if to go to her daughter.

'Sit down Mrs Thomas,' Cathy said in a voice that was kind but firm and she pulled a grey plastic seat for Emily to sit opposite her mother. 'This is DS Akhtar,' Cathy gestured towards the other policewoman who was standing by the door. 'If you want to ask anything then she will answer your questions. Would you like tea?'

'Yes please,' replied Emily sitting down and stretching her hand out to her mother. For the first time in her life she was at a loss as to what to say. 'White with no sugar for both of us please.' Emily was numb with the news of the brutal death of her father but was equally shocked by her mother, who looked vacant, dazed, like a stunned animal in pain but unable to express what was amiss, trusting no one. She realised that if it was hard for her, it must be several times more traumatic for her mother. Cathy went off to find someone to fetch the tea before heading back up to meet DS Brown in the lobby, leaving DS Akhtar with the suspect and her daughter.

Joanna looked up and shivered. 'It was awful, Em. You can't imagine.'

There was silence as Emily tried to find words of comfort but none existed. She held her mother's hand across the divide between them.

'I didn't do it Em. You believe me, don't you?'

With anger welling up inside her that her mother was being treated like a criminal Emily exploded, 'Of course I do Mum. We'll get you out of here soon.'

At that moment memories of their farmhouse home flooded back to Joanna and she sobbed. Reading her mind Emily exclaimed, 'I'll take you home with me as soon as I can. It'll be OK.' Then wishing she could eat her meaningless platitudes she was relieved that the tea arrived.

Of course it wouldn't be OK. It was not an accident from which someone could recover or a bit of bad luck with business;

temporary, difficult at the time, but manageable. Her dad was dead. Murdered!

They drank their tea in silence after which DC O'Toole came to fetch Emily to be questioned.

'I'll be back to fetch you soon,' Emily tried to reassure her mother.

Joanna just stared at the closing cell door.

CHAPTER 15

May 9th 2019 ~ Afternoon   Haynes

The vicar opened the door of his modest detached house in Silver End Haynes the moment Cathy knocked. 'I'm sorry I wasn't in when you called earlier, and it's probably nothing, but I've noticed something very unusual happening in the graveyard over recent months.'

The Reverend Morrison was a white collared vicar in his seventies, his eyes shone with warmth. He was obviously single but his demeanour was of a man well looked after. He led them into his office. His desk was littered with papers and books; as was his table and some of the floor. He frowned.

'Helen, the lady who was here when your officers called earlier today, comes in to clean for me twice a week, but she leaves my office well alone.' He looked shamefaced and almost boyish for a moment. 'It's fanciful of me to imagine this has anything to do with your enquiry, but all of a sudden flowers have started appearing at a gravestone. At first it didn't strike me as odd, you know, relations finally taking an interest after years of neglect and all that, usually when they're thinking of their own mortality.'

The Reverend Morrison paused, looking apologetically at his guests who tried to return his gaze in a benevolent manner, as if they had all the time in the world. To DS Brown, Tony, any piece of information in a case like this, however trivial, might be the missing link in a chain of events which still made little sense to him.

'Go on Reverend,' he said.

'Would you like my house keeper to make a cup of tea Sergeant? It'd be no trouble.'

'That's kind of you, but we'd rather listen to your information.'

'Oh yes, yes, let me think. Where was I?' The ageing vicar reminded DS Brown of his grandfather; friendly, forgetful but certainly no fool.

'Take your time, Reverend. Your information may be just what we need.'

'Well, one day I was walking through the churchyard and curiosity got the better of me. I walked over to take a closer look at this grave and was surprised to see that it was a military grave, back from WW1. A young girl who was in the Women's Auxiliaries and worked at Haynes Park Military Camp right through until after the war. She was only 21 when she died.'

'And who do you think has suddenly taken an interest in this grave, Reverend?'

'That's the funny thing about it. I asked the verger, who lives in a cottage near Haynes church, to watch out. As you can see, I live a mile or so away up in the village now. The grand rectory was far too old and expensive to maintain and too far away from the main village, so the church moved the rectory up here back in the 1990's. Well, my verger said that he had noticed flowers appearing from last May but had no idea of the source until an unusual sight caught his eye; A Mark 2 white Jaguar, 1965 I think, parked next to the church on three occasions, each time with different occupants. On each occasion the driver guided his passengers to this grave where they laid some flowers or a wreath.'

'Just as a matter of interest, how was your verger so sure of the age of the old Jag?' This question, so in character for a man renowned for noticing the slightest detail in his questioning, was really due to his own passionate interest in Jaguars, which he tried not to discuss too often in the climate of stringent fuel economies and environmental constraints.

'That's an easy one to answer. Each year in June we hold The Haynes 100 Rally, a glorified village fete really, but more of an excuse for all those vehicle enthusiasts to give their old classics a dust off and drive in style in a convoy around the village. I saw the car at the last rally and talked with the owner.'

'Sounds excellent, Reverend! I'm fairly new to the force in Bedford but I must make a note on the calendar for next year.'

Cathy coughed politely.

'Now, getting back to the case, why do you think we might be interested in your observations, however strange they might be?'

'When you left a message with my house keeper earlier, I just thought I ought to let you know.' The Reverend's voice trailed off rather lamely. 'I'm sorry if I've wasted your time Sergeant. I shouldn't have bothered you because I know you're busy. Silly of me.' The vicar stood up as if to end the interview, keen to get on with preparation for Sunday's sermon and already feeling more than a little foolish.

'Not at all, Reverend. Any lead is vital for a complete picture of the case. I'll get one of my officers to follow it up and let you know. Thank you for getting in touch with us.'

DS Brown shook The Reverend by the hand and smiled.

'Pease don't hesitate to contact us if you think of anything else. Oh, by the way, have you any idea where the white Jag comes from?'

'Yes I do as a matter of fact. It belongs to a chap in the next village who set up a company called 'Wayback Classic

Tours' several years ago; In 2012 I think, same year as The Olympics. Don't know his name though. He and his wife come to church occasionally; at Christmas, Remembrance Sunday and Easter, that sort of thing. He takes folks on tours in his cars on special occasions; weddings of course but much more than that. He does interesting variations on a theme of military tours of Bedfordshire too. You'll have to ask him.'

'Thank you again, Reverend, and your verger lives in Haynes Church End, near the church you said.'

'That's right, Sergeant; Mr Downer's his name.'

DS Brown smiled at DC Peterson before striding purposefully to their unmarked police car waiting just outside the rectory gate.

'We need to go to Pear Tree Farm soon and so Mr Downer's on the way. What do you think?' Tony Brown asked.

'I think it's important to go to see the parents first then let's see what time we have left.'

Tony manoeuvred their Ford Rapide, a sporty electric saloon, out of the cul-de-sac and headed in the direction of Church End. Soon they were pulling into the yard of Pear Tree Farm in front of the bungalow, the home of Peter and Madelyn Thomas, the deceased's parents. Mr and Mrs Thomas were obviously stunned by their son's unfortunate death, and were barely able to speak. After ten minutes Tony and Cathy left them and sitting back in their car, they were drained by the experience. It was always harrowing talking with the bereaved and yet they always had to be alert to any signs, however small, that the situation was not as it seemed.

Next they decided to stop off at the churchyard, firstly out of curiosity and secondly to see if it gave them some fresh clues. They parked up and strolled under the lych-gate, passing the ancient ironstone porch of St Mary's Church on their right. It was not difficult to find the grave of Lucille Vardon. Tony had an interest in anything of a military nature and, although worn, the stone cross still bore the military insignia of a World War One memorial. There were an assortment of flowers and a wreath at the foot of the grave. Strange, both officers thought simultaneously, although neither spoke. Each was deep in their own thoughts.

Cathy glanced across the churchyard towards the large manor house on the hill. She felt a shiver of a connection. Could the death of this young woman bear any relevance to this case? DI Norton would dismiss her as insane if she even suggested it. She could imagine his sarcasm already. It was too far-fetched, surely? Mind you, in her early days on the team he always encouraged her to rely on her first instincts.

'Trust your intuition,' he had always reminded her. 'It's surprising how the brain processes what seem to be irrelevant and illogical thoughts and makes sense out of them. It's a bit like a jigsaw piece that looks distinctly like the angry sky but turns out to be part of the restless sea; still part of the whole picture but not in the way you predicted it.' Not long after that DI Norton seemed to lose his way, almost certainly when his wife died. Sad really, he was a great detective in his day. The best!

'What do **you** think?' Tony asked as their Rapide moved out into the lane.

'I think it's worth following up, Tony. I know what Norton will say, but maybe we need to be selective as to what we report back for now.'

'I agree with you. I don't know why but I do.' He smiled at Cathy. 'How about tracking down this Jag man next?'

185

'That sounds like a good plan.'

Tony's eyes gave away his enthusiasm for the visit.

'In your dreams!' joked Cathy.

Unfortunately the Jag man was out on one of his trips so they told his wife that they would be in touch and headed back to the police station.

CHAPTER 16

9th May 2019 ~ Evening

By 6pm the team were gathered at Bedford police station where DI Norton held the first full debriefing. The new leads had been populated7 on a large screen, compiled automatically from each officer's report. He stared at it without much conviction and once each officer had reported back their findings he summed up.

'Since none of you have come up with any motive, and no evidence has come back from forensics to nail Mrs Thomas to the case as yet, I suggest that, DC Peterson and DS Brown, you follow up this lead by talking to the verger in the morning and then tracking down this man in Clophill. The rest of you continue to find that evidence we're searching for. It should be a *cut and dried case*,' he smiled, quite please with his well worn cliché of a pun. 'I'm still sure she's guilty. DC O'Toole, you come with me to interview Mrs Thomas once more to try to find any discrepancies in her story. Perhaps we've been too soft so far. Maybe a day in the cell will have done the trick, but then we have to let her go. DS Akhtar, please go and fetch her from the cell.'

Privately Cathy Peterson cringed. If her boss could only stop and hear himself speaking. If Joanna was innocent, then she would be in such a state of shock by now. She had just lost her husband following a brutal, and what appeared to be an unprovoked murder.

'Her daughter has already arrived, sir. She's sitting in the lobby and wants to take Mrs Thomas to her home north of Bedford. Have you any objections, after she's been interviewed again that is?' Cathy asked.

'On no account must Mrs Thomas go back to the proximity of the farm for now. If we get nothing from her tonight then she must be released, and to her daughter's sounds like the best option.' He paused again making sure he had everyone's attention. 'You've got just over three weeks, is that clear? So act sharpish. I don't want to leave behind an unsolved murder case. That would be most unsatisfactory.'

'What happened to innocent until proved guilty,' Tony mouthed to Cathy.

'What was that, officer? Speak up, if you have anything relevant for the case, otherwise hold your tongue.' There was another pregnant pause. 'OK then. What are you all waiting for, Christmas?'

Dismissed, Tony scrabbled to his feet and headed to the door whilst DC O'Toole, Bernard, downed his mug of coffee, shrugged and followed DI Norton, the others glanced at their disappearing backs before returning to their desks to update their reports before leaving.

'Just a minute. I'll follow you down,' Cathy called to Tony as she paused to wait for DS Akhtar to come out of the briefing room. The two women police officers walked together along the corridor towards the cells.

'What do you think of her Saima?' Cathy asked.

'If you ask me, I feel sorry for the woman.' Saima looked over her shoulder nervously. 'I think he's lost the plot, to be quite honest with you.'

'I know what you mean. There was nothing Mrs Thomas said this morning which gave me a glimmer of a reason to doubt that she was telling the truth. I may be talking out of turn here, but I don't believe she's guilty.'

'I've read the interview transcript and I quite agree with you,' replied Saima equally quietly. 'And if we're right, then the poor woman has gone through enough of an ordeal already, to be treated like a common criminal. I'm relieved that you think the same as me.'

'Just one thing. In the morning can you try to see if you can find out anything about Lucille Vardon, but keep it quiet?'

'No problem Cathy,' Saima replied before she headed back down to the cell to fetch Joanna Thomas.

Cathy found Tony waiting in the car park beside her Harley Davidson.

'I'm bushed,' he said, before she had a chance to speak. 'Let's call it a day and meet here early tomorrow.'

'Say 8am?' asked Cathy as she popped on her helmet, her dark hair flicking outwards under the pressure, then she climbed on to her pride and joy.

'Fine by me. I've got to visit the farm to time the milking remember.'

Cathy grinned before speeding off. Tony watched her, half wishing he had had the courage to ask her to have a drink with him. Another time, he sighed.

Back inside Saima found Mrs Thomas sitting bolt upright staring at the walls.

'We'll soon have you out of here, Mrs Thomas. DI Norton wants another word with you and then your daughter's waiting upstairs to take you away.'

Joanna's shoulders dropped a fraction at the news as she followed Saima up the black tiled stairs and into the interview room.

'Sit down Mrs Thomas. I hope that you're rested now and are ready to tell us what really happened,' DI Norton's smooth voice fell into the quite room and Saima noticed Joanna's shoulders hunch up once more. Leaning forward she wrapped her arms around herself as if chilled.

'Are you cold, Mrs Thomas?' Saima asked with concern, but Joanna's head nodded in more of a flinch, as she watched the inspector click his fingers and a red light indicated that the conversation was being taped. Her mind glazed as first he went through the preliminaries.

'So,' he said, leaning slightly forward towards the table and Joanna's back straightened to even the distance between them. 'Would you like to start again from the beginning?'

Joanna sighed, longing to see her daughter's reassuring face again. 'I told you Inspector. I was taking my usual shower and I'd dressed to go down to cook Bob's breakfast and I found him slumped...'

Distraught, Joanna burst into tears and through her gasps she choked, 'I didn't do it inspector. Please find my husband's murderer. He didn't deserve to die.' And with that she had no will power to say any more.

The inspector terminated the interview and left, deep rifts furrowing his brow, leaving Saima to encourage Joanna to follow her to her waiting daughter. Saima gulped back emotion at the scene of mother and daughter being reunited, hugging each other tightly before walking out into the evening.

7 populated: In computing to automatically add information

CHAPTER 17

Friday 10th May 2019

The following morning at 8 am Cathy arrived to find Tony already seated in the car waiting for her.

'How did it go this morning?' Cathy grinned as she settled in the driver's seat.

'Just confirms that the cows are Mr Cookham's alibi, in my opinion.' Tony yawned. 'Where to first, Cathy?' He asked. On days like today Tony liked to give Cathy, the opportunity of taking the lead, even though he was her superior.

'Shall we start with the Jag man? His wife said that he would be at home this morning doing paperwork.'

They pulled up a long drive in Clophill to find a man in a scruffy old oil stained maroon jumper and equally shabby trousers cleaning a beautiful white Jaguar. These cars were frowned upon by so many people as gas guzzlers, harmful to the environment, but in Tony's opinion it was just as well that there were some enthusiasts willing to weather the scorn of the masses to keep some of these old beauties on the road. The car was nearly sixty years old. Tony's school boy eyes shone with excitement. Cathy nudged him, but realised the likelihood of Tony saying anything sensible was inconceivable, so she asked, 'We're looking for the owner of the company Wayback Classics. Can you tell us where he is please?'

The man straightened, looking this officious woman in the eye and wondered if he had filled in his tax form incorrectly, or if the 'Environmental Police' had caught up with him at last. He was sure he had been careful not to use more than his allocated allowance of petrol for the Jags last year, the new environmental law passed in 2017. Then he saw the awe in the face of the gentleman and relaxed, knowing at least he had the attention of one kindred spirit.

'I'm the owner of Wayback Classics,' he replied, pleased to see the look of incredulity on the young woman's face. 'David Webb, how can I help you?'

'Great car,' replied Tony, unable to hide his admiration.

Cathy glanced sideways at Tony with impatience,

'Mr Webb, we are police detectives here to talk about the tours you've recently given when you visited the grave of a young woman, Lucille Vardon, in Haynes Churchyard.'

'My word, you people must be desperate for work if you're opening up that case. The young lady died one hundred years ago,' David Webb smiled.

Not to be deterred Cathy continued, 'This is DS Brown and I am DC Peterson. We are investigating the recent murder of a farmer in Haynes and the vicar mentioned unusual goings on in the churchyard recently.'

'You've got the wrong church for unusual goings on,' David chuckled, but realising the serious nature of their call he replaced his grin with a frown. 'Sorry, that was unhelpful. The old church at Clophill was turned into a centre for walkers a few years back and it seems to have stopped ghost hunters. Yes, I heard about that murder. Terrible thing. It was the wife wasn't it?'

'What makes you say that?' asked DS Brown, alert now.

'That's what they all say. I don't know much about the people of Haynes to tell you the truth. I think it was the post woman who found the farmer. She was talking in The Stone Jug yesterday. Terrible state she was in too.'

'We were asking about the grave in Haynes,' Cathy prompted patiently.

'Oh, I see,' said David Webb, more than a little confused.

'Why did you visit the grave of a young girl, Lucille Vardon, with at least three of your clients?'

David frowned. 'I don't understand your drift, but anyway, someone got in touch with me via Futurenet; some web site or other all about Lucille Vardon. I read up on her for interest's sake. Strange story. Anyway, I was asked to do three quite different tours, but each of them visited this grave. Weird wasn't it? It was very secretive and I wasn't allowed to use my usual banter whilst driving.' David paused and laughed nervously. 'Who knows? Maybe it was better that way. The clients had won prizes, you see. Anyway, the correct amount of money was transferred directly into my account. You can see the paperwork if you like.' David had his fingers crossed behind his back, hoping that he could lay his hands on the documents and wishing that he had done his office work, as he had promised his wife, instead of cleaning his beloved cars.

'We'd like to do that, but have you got the details of the clients?'

'No, as a matter of fact. If I arrange the tours myself I keep all those sorts of details. My wife sends out an invitation for another tour on special offer and we often get repeat bookings that way. In this case the people from the website arranged it all. I only had to turn up and send them the bill via Pay Pal. They might have records for you guys of course, but we don't. All was paid on the day of each tour and so there was no problem.'

'Can you tell us anything about the clients and the name of the website?' Cathy asked.

'Shall we go into the office?' David asked.

They walked around the back of the house, through a pleasant farmhouse type kitchen and into a cramped office. It was a bit like the vicar's room. There was hardly a space on the floor or on the desk that was not covered with paper.

'The paperless office,' David joked to hide his embarrassment. He scrabbled around in the pile behind his desk. 'Ah,' he said. 'It's all here,' obvious relief on his face. He looked around at the two chairs which were also piled with boxes, books and papers. 'My wife is always nagging me to tidy up. Maybe we should go into the lounge.'

In contrast, the front room was spotless, not a grain of dust or item out of place. It was verging on what they used to call minimalist back in the 90's. David motioned for the two officers to sit down.

'Would you like to look through these while I make a cup of coffee? Tea or coffee?' he added as an afterthought.

'That would be great,' Cathy agreed. 'Two white coffees with milk and no sugar thanks.'

Cathy and Tony leafed through the information. Apart from the itinerary of the tour, including pick up points, which would certainly be of help, there were no names or addresses; only this reference to a web site.

'We'll keep these if we may,' Tony said as David Webb came back into the room with a tray of coffees. 'Would you like to make a copy for your records first though?' He smiled his thanks.

'You don't have any names here,' Cathy remarked. 'Any ideas?'

'Well, there was a young lady and man. What was it now? I'm sure her name was Anna and she called her boyfriend Nick. She talked about Jersey a few times and also, ah yes, Cambridge. I think they are studying at Cambridge University. You may get more information from Mrs Broom at Broom Cottage where they were staying. She's stayed there a few times. Seen out on Mrs Broom's bicycle quite often. A bird watcher so the rumour goes.'

'That's interesting,' remarked Cathy, thinking of the son Paul's statement about seeing a young woman in the woods and also John Cookham's memory of a girl on a bicycle. 'Go on.'

'Then there was the American or maybe Canadian couple; in their late forties, I would say. Trudy and James I think. They were staying at The Swan Hotel in Bedford. Shouldn't be too difficult to get details from there. The other people were certainly English. Military type. Don't know his name but his son was called Toby. Of course Toby called his father Dad, so that's not much help is it? I picked them up in Woburn from The Inn on the Green. Interesting tour. Yes, definitely military. You see, each tour seemed to be tailor made with the client in mind. I'll go and get those copied if I may, before you take them. My wife fills in the final tax return and she's a stickler for detail. She'd be in a right mood if I couldn't find the documentation.'

'I understand,' smiled Tony, encouragingly. 'You've been most helpful.'

As Tony and Cathy were leaving David Webb asked, 'So you're not opening up the old case again then; you know, the girl Lucille Vardon. She was murdered too.'

'Now that **is** interesting,' Cathy paused. 'We might just do that,' she added, leaving David Webb looking more puzzled than ever.

On the way back to the station they dropped in on Mrs Broom.

'Yes, lovely lass. Shoulder length fair hair. Slim and fit looking. She was a bird watcher; twitchers they call themselves. She's stayed here three times in all but I didn't much like the boyfriend. She was too good for him. A perfect guest you could say.'

'Can you give us her name please?' Cathy asked.

'Yes of course. Unusual name, a bit French you see, since she comes from Jersey. Anna Beret, yes that was it.' Tony glanced at Cathy but said nothing.

'Did she have the use of a bicycle while she was here?' Cathy continued.

'Oh yes. She asked if she could borrow my old thing. She went out quite early in the morning I noticed, before I was up, but she would you see, being a twitcher and all. That's what they do.'

'Do you have any personal details of Anna Beret so that we can contact her?'

'The young lady always paid in cash and so did her boyfriend but I do have her mobile number if that would help. Cambridge, she's studying at. Now what was the college? Oh dear, my memory. Ummm, I don't know.'

'Well, if we could have the number, we'll also give you ours and if you remember anything else then give us a call. When did she leave you?'

'She caught the bus back to Cambridge only yesterday afternoon to finish her final dissertation. Pembroke - that's the name of her college, I'm sure of it. She's not in any trouble is she?'

'We are investigating a murder over near Church End Haynes. A young girl of her description was spotted twice in the area and we'd just like to ask her some questions. Just in case she saw anything suspicious. Did she go out on your bike yesterday morning?'

'Yes she did as a matter of fact. Very early. I didn't hear her go out but I heard her come back in at about, oooh, quarter to seven. I'd just got up you see.' Mrs Broom paused. 'I'll fetch her number for you.' Mrs Broom rummaged in a drawer for a little notebook and showed Cathy the number, who wrote it down, speaking aloud to have a record on her dictaphone.

Cathy thanked Mrs Broom and they left Clophill taking the route to Haynes along Great Lane.

'What do you make of that?' Tony asked. 'The link with Jersey, is certainly a coincidence?'

'Nothing in police work....'

'Is a coincidence,' Tony finished Cathy's sentence.

'But she doesn't sound the type for premeditated murder does she?'

'It takes all types. She might have a motive. It could be revenge. I bet you she's related to this Lucille Vardon.' Tony paused and each sat with their own thoughts for a few minutes. They headed back toward Haynes, seeing Haynes Park in its resplendence on the hill beside the church, before turning down towards Church End.

'Different world to our typical cases in Bedford isn't it,' Cathy remarked.

'A bit like 'Midsomer Murders!''

'You've put the words into my mouth, I only hope this one's not followed hot on the heels by several more before the inspector logs off for good.'

'Me too. Did you ever watch the series? A bit like a busman's holiday for us. Too far-fetched by half,' Tony said.

'I watched it regularly when I was in my teens. Even catch a nostalgic episode on Channel 3 occasionally. I'm half expecting to find the verger sprawled on his kitchen floor covered in blood too!'

'Don't let your imagination get carried away with you!' Tony said as they pulled to a halt.

They opened the gate which led into a beautiful cottage style garden, befitting of the quaint rural setting. The sergeant had to bend his head slightly to enter the tiny porch before tapping the door with its ancient, brass knocker in the shape of a woodpecker. They heard a rustle behind the door and the sound of bolts being drawn and expected to see a wizened old man when the dark oak door finally opened. To their surprise a business like man in his mid forties, dressed in a shirt and suit trousers, welcomed them. A back door banged shut.

'The vicar warned me to expect you,' the verger said, but seeing their puzzled looks he explained. 'I work as an architect in my office at the back of the cottage in the mornings and it's rare for people to disturb me here. I often leave the front door locked, even during the day.'

'Very wise. You can't be too careful though, with a murder taking place up the lane from you. May we come in, Mr Downer?'

'Of course. Come into the front room, or maybe it would be nice to sit in the garden. Would you like some tea or coffee?'

'Coffee would be nice, thank you.'

Mr Downer pointed towards the back door, a stable split-level contraption with only the bottom part bolted, the top open wide allowing the spring air to filter though the house.

Outside there was a small patio area, surrounded by tall shrubs and perennials, delphiniums in various blue hues intermingled with pink and yellow lupins and multi-coloured aquilegia. The patio was a sheltered suntrap, the warmth reflected off the old red brick wall and the limestone paving beneath their feet.

'How can I help you?' he asked as he sat down next to them with yet another tray of coffee. I'm going to have to ask to use the facilities, thought Cathy as she politely thanked the verger and began her fourth coffee of the morning.

'We gather you've noticed some strange happenings in the churchyard. We'd like you to tell us about them,' encouraged DS Brown. 'We know about the flowers appearing at a young lady's grave in the last six months, Lucille Vardon, isn't it? Can you add anything to the Reverend's information?'

The verger's account agreed with that of the vicar's until he reached the last couple of days.

'I thought that would be the end of it, but yesterday morning, yes, the morning of the murder, I heard some noises over at the churchyard at first light. I looked out over towards the church and a taxi had pulled up and a man was wandering around. About half an hour later I heard a small motorbike with a faulty exhaust. Not electric I'm sure. I put on some clothes to go and investigate. After all, that's my other job to keep an eye on the church, and I could see that there were two bicycles leaning against the fence too. I crept through the lych-gate and stood and watched. There was a small gathering of people around Lucille Vardon's grave. They stood there for a few moments and, as far as I could see, only laid some flowers and a wreath before moving off.'

'Did you recognise anyone?' asked Cathy.

'The back of one of the ladies looked vaguely familiar. She had a large hood up but I'm sure I've seen that red coat before but I just can't place it at the moment. I recognised the two lads from the Post Office. Nice lads. The others I didn't know at all. I'm sorry,' he paused, 'I'm not being much help am I?'

'What time would you say that was?'

'I went out just after 6 am. The church bell had just chimed. It's quiet through the night but starts up again at six. Some of the neighbours, city types, complained you see.'

'What happened next?'

'Well, not wanting to interfere, since they didn't seem to be doing anything untoward; just paying their respects, I crept back here and closed the door. I tried to watch through the front room window but the hedge is too high, so I went upstairs and was just in time to see the back of a bicycle disappearing towards the A6, a car following behind. I walked back over to the churchyard about half an hour later. It was deserted by now but I looked down at the grave. There were two vases of flowers and a wreath but also some rosemary planted around the edge. You know, rosemary for remembrance. Anyway I peered closely at the grave and it was exactly one hundred years since the death of the girl Lucille Vardon. An odd coincidence don't you think?'

Cathy felt a second shiver of recognition. Could the deaths really be linked?

'Did you know Mr and Mrs Thomas personally Mr Downer?'

Tony watched the man's face cloud over in obvious sadness. 'Yes, we all know the couple quite well. Farmers are busy people though, and have little time to socialise, but if there was ever a fund raising or charity event you could certainly rely on their generosity, in money if not in time, though Mrs Thomas would certainly attend if she could. She's in the WI. We're lucky to still have one. A small but merry band of village ladies who are willing to get involved in anything in the village, fund raising mainly. Ethiopia has been their recent project. Her daughter went out there in her gap year about four years ago. Joanna, Mrs Thomas, organised the village dance only three months back for St Valentine's Night. Good evening by all accounts. Old fashioned dancing, with everyone dressed up in their finery and women with dance cards. Some men took dance cards too in deference to equality. Joanna even persuaded Bob to go. It was quite a laugh and Joanna and Bob led the first dance in true style. Stunning couple they looked too. I've got some photos somewhere but I suppose you wouldn't be interested in that.'

'We would as a matter of fact,' Cathy smiled. 'Anything which helps us to piece together a full picture of Mr and Mrs Thomas and their life together is useful.'

'So there's no truth in the farmer, Mr Thomas being tight fisted?' Tony asked, trying to guide the interview in a more productive direction.

Mr Downer laughed. 'That's an urban myth in my opinion. It's true that Bob rarely had any cash on him. That's not unusual. With his hours he has no time to go into town or to a bank machine. He'd just leave all that to Joanna.'

'So you can't think of any reason why Mrs Thomas would kill her husband?' Tony asked.

Mr Downer's face darkened over with obvious anger at this point.

'It's bad enough that Joanna's just lost her husband, but for you to accuse her of murder. That's absurd. You'd be better spending the time finding the real killer, and I reckon most of the rest of the village would say the same!'

'Yes, they have, Mr Downer,' Cathy said looking into his eyes in the hopes that he would understand that she agreed with him, even though she was unable to say those comforting words. With no more to be said for the present they thanked the verger for his time before finding their way to the farm where they found Bob's mother alone in her bungalow staring out towards the farmhouse and the yellow crime scene tape, which cordoned off the main farmhouse.

The door was wide open, leading through a porch straight into the kitchen where Mrs Thomas senior stood at the window, gripping the side of the sink. She was a slight woman with fairly short layered ash blonde hair, in contrast to her reddened eyes. In her mid to late sixties, Cathy guessed, slightly rounded by a good healthy diet over the years wearing a similarly long cable knit maroon cardigan that Cathy had seen on Joanna when they took her in.

Madelyn Thomas turned her startled face towards them as if she had not heard their approach,

'My husband's over at the farm,' she said, as if by way of an excuse.

A bit defensive, Joanna thought, but so wouldn't you be if your son had just been murdered and your daughter-in-law been taken in as a suspect.

'We're sorry to trouble you again Mrs Thomas but may we come in?' Tony asked. They stood hesitant in the porch, not wishing to intrude on the poor woman's grief and yet knowing full well that it was imperative that they interview key people in the case as soon as possible before time had elapsed, and subdued their instinctive reactions. The mind begins to play tricks, often inadvertently trying to ease the pain or grief, or rationalise the unfathomable.

'I'd rather wait 'til...' Mrs Thomas's voice trailed off.

'We just want to ask you a few questions Mrs Thomas. It won't take long,' Cathy tried to reassure the woman. Tony just watched her reactions with sharp eyes.

'Oh, yes, yes of course. Come in. How silly of me. It's the shock. I just can't believe what's happening,' and she sat down on the nearest chair, a Windsor which spoke of traditional farmhouse kitchens, and started to weep with quiet dignity, her husband's handkerchief already quite sodden.

Cathy put a hand gently on her shoulder before instinctively moving the kettle on to the hottest part of the hob. Her parents had a range in their old cottage north of Bedford. Tony sat down opposite Mrs Thomas and waited. They were experienced enough in their partnership for him to know not to plough in with questions and let Cathy do the leading.

'Where is your husband now?' Tony asked as Cathy poured the already boiling water into a mug, reaching for the sugar. This poor lady needed something sweet.

'He's just popped out to one of the fields, over there behind the farmhouse. Just checking on the state of the barley. He always does that before lunch.' She's lying thought Tony, watching even more carefully.

Cathy placed the mug of tea in front of her. 'Here you are,' she said, her voice kind and gentle.

Mrs Thomas took a gulp of the tea and grimaced.

'The sugar'll do you good. Help with the shock,' explained Cathy.

The lady looked alert for the first time and looked straight at Cathy, 'It'll take more than a spoonful of sugar,' she replied, putting her mug down, folding her arms and looking directly at the two officers.

'You can't have any idea what it's like.'

All the signs were there, Tony thought. Her arms as barriers between them, her shoulders now upright, defiantly pretending to be in control. They would gain little from this interview.

'Please can you tell us again, just what happened yesterday morning? Anything you say could help us find the killer of your son,' Cathy continued.

'We saw nothing, officers. Since my husband retired from the milking we sleep in late. A farmer never really retires you know, but the milking everyday is relentless. My husband only stands in when Bob...' and at this point Mrs Thomas stifled more tears before taking a deep breath, determined to control herself.

'We stand in when Joanna and Bob have a well deserved holiday once or sometimes twice a year. Apart from that we now have the luxury of getting up at 7 o'clock. The first thing we were aware of was your police vehicles turning up in the drive at 6.30. Peter shot out of bed to see who it was, since we never have visitors at that time of the morning and there was such a commotion. You see, we hear little traffic, only the distant sound of the A6 which your mind blanks out. It's a haven of peace in a busy world. That's what my cousin always says when she comes to stay.'

At that point they heard heavy footsteps at the door as Peter Thomas strode in, pulling off his boots with the help of an iron gadget in the porch, as he placed a large spade with several other tools in a wooden rack, which most homes would use for umbrellas. He slid his feet into his worn out moleskin slippers, straightening his back to reveal the distinguished, still handsome figure and features of a man used to life outdoors and the regular rhythm of farming to the seasons. His mannerisms were open but his eyes glared, an unspoken message - don't upset my wife any more than she is already.

Madelyn Thomas instinctively moved to stand up and make her husband a cup of tea.

'I'll do it,' reassured Cathy.

'We're sorry to bother you Mr Thomas but can you tell us anything else which would help us to find your son's murderer?' Tony asked.

It was obvious that the phrasing of his question had surprised the old farmer, who by now had sat down at the large oak table, placing his tweed cap absentmindedly on the uneven wooden surface.

'I don't know what Madelyn has told you but we don't know anything. It's such a shock. We heard nothing until your lot came and arrested Joanna yesterday. I looked out of the window and rushed out into the yard just as you were piling her into the police car. That's the first we knew of anything.' Tony watched him carefully. It appeared that he was telling the truth and yet his instincts told him that something was not as it appeared.

'Can you think of any reason why Mrs Thomas, Joanna that is, would have murdered your son?' Tony asked directly as Cathy placed a mug of tea in front of the man.

The old farmer shrugged his broad shoulders, his tweed jacket rising and revealing his brushed cotton chequered shirt, mud marks splattered on the front. As he picked up his mug, Cathy noticed his finger nails were also full of dirt.

'They were happy I guess. They certainly appeared happy. Apart from the odd spat on insignificant things, they never argued.'

'I'm sorry to ask you this, knowing the loss you have suffered, but was Joanna or your son having an affair, as far as you know?'

Did Cathy imagine it or did Madelyn Thomas have a quick intake of breath and glance at her husband. Of course it could be indignation at the question.

'Certainly not!' she hesitated. 'As far as we are aware, that is. After all, do you truly know anyone?'

It was obvious to Tony that this answer was deliberately leaving a shadow of doubt. Why?

'And you, Mr Thomas? Did either your daughter-in-law or your son ever give you any reason to think they were unhappy or have you heard any village gossip?' Tony asked.

'I can think of nothing officer. There has never been any gossip about either Joanna or Bob, as far as I am aware and neither of them have ever said anything.'

'I'm sure she is innocent,' joined in Madelyn Thomas. 'She was a devoted wife and mother in a way only another farmer's wife can understand.' She stopped quite abruptly. There was another glance between the pair - or was it just reassurance?

'What do you mean by that exactly?' asked Tony.

'What my wife means is the long antisocial hours, seven days a week, little or no time to themselves, few holidays, twice a year if they were lucky. If you marry a farmer you marry the

206

farm too. Isn't that right dear?' Peter Thomas looked over to his wife for confirmation and she just nodded in agreement and said no more.

'Well, that will be all for now, but remember that the farmhouse is out of bounds, even to both of you, for the time being. The forensics team are still in there today, but please can you ensure that Paul keeps out too, however tempting it might be to pick up some of his things. Where is he by the way?'

'He's with a friend up in the village. He'll be back tonight. And Joanna? You let her go then?'

'Joanna helped us with our enquiries but it is important that she, especially, stays away from the crime scene and stays with your granddaughter for the foreseeable future.'

Was it relief Tony noted in Mr Thomas's expression or did he imagine it?

'So she's not going to be charged for the murder of my son?' asked Peter Thomas.

'No. We are still fully investigating the crime but we promise we'll find your son's murderer,' Tony answered as he noticed Cathy crossing her fingers behind her back. He could hear his mother's truism, '*don't make promises you can't keep.*'

'There's not enough evidence as yet to charge anyone and as your wife said, there appears to be no motive. We need to keep an open mind at the moment and gather the facts of the case. As soon as we know anything we'll let you know. Are you happy for Paul to remain here, meanwhile?'

'Of course Paul can stay here, officer, as long as he likes' said Madelyn Thomas. 'That goes without saying, but I'm surprised he doesn't want to go to his sister's.'

'I'd have thought so too, but he seems adamant that he needs to continue with his studies here before he goes back to uni next week. That is, if we allow him to go,' Tony said.

Did Cathy see a shiftiness in Peter Thomas's eyes for a moment? What was that all about? Madelyn Thomas glanced towards the door.

'What do you mean, allow him to go? Surely he's not a suspect too,' Peter Thomas exclaimed, his nose raised in an air of indignation.

'Everyone involved is a suspect, Mr Thomas, until we eliminate them from our enquiries with hard evidence.'

'Quite so,' replied Peter Thomas, his demeanour relaxing in resignation, signalling that he had said all that he was going to say.

'Thank you for answering our questions,' Cathy said as they headed for the door.

Once inside their unmarked car Cathy sighed. 'How strange. I can't make them out.'

'I think it's lunchtime,' Tony said pragmatically, 'and we should have a break. How about heading to The Woolpack in Wilshamstead since it's on our way back to Bedford?'

'Good idea. Then we should head back to the station to update our records on the system.' Cathy pulled out of the farmyard and turned towards the A6 and they were soon enjoying a welcome drink outside the pub. They were unable to talk openly here and so they relaxed for a few moments.

'Are you off anywhere nice for your holiday this year Cathy?'

'Nothing planned yet Tony. As you know, I'm on my own out of choice and that's no incentive for going away. I had enough singles holiday in my early twenties to last a life time. And you?'

Ignoring the question Tony continued, 'I thought your last relationship was pretty serious Cathy.'

'It depends on what you call serious. Tom met my parents and their embarrassing hints about the need for grandchildren made me squirm, but once I became a detective it was as if he didn't want to know. All that tolerance to my unsociable hours evaporated and he became a right nag if I was just a few minutes late, and if I had to cancel, well, you can imagine!'

'I certainly can. It's no surprise that half the police are married to their jobs and the other half are divorced and on the sidelines of their family life, looking wistfully in.'

'Either that or they throw in the towel and marry a policeman,' Cathy joked and then reddened.

'We've got time to take a trip to Cambridge this afternoon.' Tony changed the subject.

'How about checking through this lot first,' nodding down at her e pad. She clicked it on to see that the recording had successfully been transcribed into script, but it often made errors and so it was best to read it while the interview was fresh. 'You know Norton's a stickler for accuracy and I don't know about you, but my head's spinning.'

'OK. How about an hour to gather our thoughts, then we should still be there for half three, ample time to track down this girl and eliminate her from our enquiries.'

'How can you be so sure Tony?'

'Didn't you notice something was going on between those two back at the farm bungalow? I'm sure they know more than they are letting on. No, my hunch is that this is a family matter and the killer is closer to home. Why leave their door wide open otherwise?'

'That's true. Let's go back to the station and then confer on the drive over to Cambridge.'

CHAPTER 18

10th May 2019   Anna in Cambridge

It was nearly four o'clock when Tony and Cathy finally parked up and walked towards Pembroke College, its pristine green lawns in contrast to the red brick and sandstone arches of the diamond leaded glass windows. Cathy loved Cambridge. She did not feel jealous of those lucky enough to go there or regret the decision not to study further. She had wanted to join the police since she was ten, just like her brother had wanted to be a pilot. He had done it too. Joel, who was five years older than Cathy, had joined the RAF, and the family were so proud when he served over in Libya back in 2011, based in Cyprus, before he decided to apply for The Red Arrows. It was a pilot's dream and David was a wizard in the sky. Her parents often went to shows around the country just to watch him.

They asked at the gate about Anna Beret and explained that they were police officers. The warden showed them straight to Anna's room, up a steep staircase and along a corridor where even Cathy had to bend her head under the eaves. They thanked the lady warden and knocked on the door.

'Just a minute,' came the muffled response.

'She can't be asleep surely. Even a student is up at 4 pm surely,' whispered Tony.

'Shhh,' replied Cathy as the door opened.

A puzzled young lady with long wispy fair hair opened the door. Anna did not say anything, assuming that there was some mistake.

'We're police officers, investigating a murder in Haynes. May we come in please?'

Anna, startled now, opened the door ajar to give the officers just enough room to show their ID before squeezing into the room. She gestured for them to sit on her two seater sofa under the alcove at the window as she perched on the edge of her bed.

'You're about one hundred years too late aren't you? Surely even the police have better things to do than opening up that case,' Anna exclaimed.

'What do you mean?' asked Tony, wanting to find out what this young lady knew about the case, if anything, or whether it was just a coincidence, being in the wrong place at just the wrong time. He watched Anna closely.

'How you've tracked me down, I don't know, but you must be aware that I've been investigating a murder in Haynes. In fact it's taken up all my spare time over the past year but the murder happened to a young woman auxiliary back in 1919 at Haynes Park Camp.'

'What's Haynes Park Camp?' asked Tony, still fishing for the truth.

Anna's hair fell in a screen around her tired face as she looked down to the floor and up to the officers; almost as if she did not believe this conversation was happening.

'It was an army training camp in World War One. The girl was murdered in Wilshamstead Woods but no one was convicted of the crime.'

'Do you feel angry about that, Miss Beret?' Tony asked.

Anna laughed, which sounded more like a cough with her eyes opening wide.

'Look, I'm in the middle of proof reading my final dissertation and then I'm off home to Jersey for a while. I don't know what this is about but are you really here to discuss Lucille Vardon's death or is there something else?'

'Where were you yesterday, on the morning of 9th May **this** year?' Tony asked.

'I was staying in Clophill at Mrs Broom's B & B. What's this all about?'

'First, do you mind us asking why you were there, Miss Beret?' Tony continued.

'Not at all. My boyfriend was treating me for a birthday surprise but I was also invited to attend a memorial of Lucille Vardon's death which I found out about on Futurenet.'

'Tell us where you went exactly on the morning of May 9th,' he continued.

'I cycled to Haynes churchyard where several other people were gathered. Some laid flowers although I'd placed a seagull above the grave too, a while back. Thought it'd remind Lucille of her roots back on Jersey. She's a long lost relation you see.' She did not know why she omitted to mention her experience in the woods near the farm.

'What time would that have been exactly?'

'6 o'clock in the morning.'

'And did you go straight to the churchyard from your Bed and Breakfast?'

Both Cathy and Tony noticed Anna pause a few moments too long as if she was considering her reply.

'No. I didn't actually. I'm a twitcher,' and seeing Tony raise his eyebrows she explained, 'I watch birds, officer. I often go out at strange times, especially early in the morning and yes, I did cycle to the woods near Haynes Church to listen to the dawn chorus, or spot any nocturnal flyers returning from their night's hunt.'

'You mean owls and the like?' asked Tony, ever patient when interviewing someone for the first time.

'Yes and night jars, in fact any bird that prefers to hunt under cover of darkness.'

'And what did you see in the woods? The woods near to Pear Tree Farm, is that?'

'Yes, I think so, inspector. I was wandering around and I came across a clearing, quite by chance, that looked out towards the farmhouse. Lovely old Georgian building. I think that's its name.'

'Did you see anything odd there?' Tony continued.

Anna's cheeks glowed a touch of pink with the memory. She had to tell the truth to these officers although she found it hard to hide her embarrassment. After all, it looked as if she was spying on the farmhouse, which was far from the truth.

'Well, yes as a matter of fact. I was following a barn owl returning to the woods where I know there are some owl boxes. It was attempting to make its last kill. A magical sight as it swooped down on a young rabbit. Anyway, the owl missed the rabbit and flew towards the woods but as my binoculars tried to follow the sweeping path of the owl's flight I noticed....' At this point Anna paused, reddening at the height of her embarrassment.

'What did you notice?' prompted Tony.

'Well, the farmer's son, who I've seen out and about a few times in the area, was standing at his window gazing back at me through his binoculars and he was, uhhhhhm, he was naked.'

Cathy smiled. This was hardly the behaviour of a murderess unless she was a very good actress. It's not surprising she looked as if she had something to hide. She looked sideways out on to the roofs of the college and straightened her face, but looking back she saw that Anna was too distracted to notice.

'So what did you do then?' Tony asked.

'I fled, officer. I ran back through the woods towards my bike, but unfortunately I bumped into a tree or tripped over something and bumped my head. I had to sit down for a few minutes and I think I blanked out for a while. I'm not sure. Anyway, when I came to I found my bike, cycled down the track and past the churchyard. When a taxi turned in front of me towards the church I decided to follow and pay my respects to Lucille Vardon. It seemed the right thing to do and I was a bit disoriented to be honest with you. Then I cycled back to the B & B along Great Lane.'

'Did you at any time go near the farm on that morning or enter any of the farm buildings?'

'No, certainly not,' replied Anna, indignantly.

Cathy interjected here, thinking of one line which might prove useful in their search. 'You mentioned a message about the gathering around the grave. Do you know who it was from?'

'Not **who** exactly,' replied Anna, 'but I do know the website. I should think it was from the person who runs the website.'

'Can you show us the website?' asked Cathy.

'Certainly I can,' and she pulled her e pad from her desk beside her bed and her fingers hovered over the screen for a few seconds. 'Here it is.'

Cathy looked at the screen with interest, noting the address on her notebook to check up later.

'You can't seriously be investigating Lucille's murder surely,' Anna exclaimed, looking genuinely puzzled.

'No you're right Anna. The farmer was murdered in his kitchen less than half an hour after you were standing peering at the place with your binoculars. The farmer's son mentioned it in his statement and so we had to follow it up.'

If Anna had been standing up at the time she would surely have slumped down. As it was, sheer horror was etched on her face; her hand flew to her mouth. To Cathy this reaction was genuine, even though the circumstances sounded suspicious, but in an instant the girl's expression clouded over again. Was this yet another unfortunate coincidence?

'Is there anything else you want to tell us?' she asked quietly, jogging Anna out of her thoughts. Anna's shook her head. 'Then I think that's all for now. Thank you for your help, but we do need a contact address in Jersey, if, as you say, you will soon be leaving the mainland. We do ask you, however, not to leave the British Isles for the time being, under any circumstances.'

'Oh, of course,' was all Anna could reply, her hands shaking as she took Cathy's proffered ePad and scribbled contact details on the screen before she fumbled for the door to let the police officers out.

'We'll be in touch,' said Cathy as they left. She wanted to reassure this lady, but murder was murder and no lead could be excluded for the time being, not until the full forensic reports had come back. Cathy thought that Anna was hiding something, though she felt sure that the girl was innocent of the crime.

As they strolled across the quad, Cathy asked, 'So you don't think it's worth interviewing the boyfriend then?'

'No I don't think so. Do you? After all Mrs Broom verified what Anna said and so did Paul Thomas. Mrs Broom would have told us if Anna had acted strangely or she had found blood stained clothes in the dustbin or a dirty sink. I think Anna Beret is innocent, however strange it appears that she seemed to be in the field stalking the farm. What DI Norton will make of it I really don't know.'

'It's nearly five. How about heading back to the police station, coordinating our notes from this afternoon and then getting together to confer about leads which need to be followed up? The briefing is at eight in the morning and you've been going since four this morning. How about calling it a day?'

'Sounds good to me.' There was a moment of silent reflection when Tony was weighing up the implications of his next request. 'Would you like a drink before heading home, Cathy?'

Cathy did not take her eyes off the road but Tony felt the heaviness of her intake of breath. Her immediate reaction was reluctance to say no and yet all she really wanted right now was solitude, her own little flat, a glass of wine and maybe a Chinese take away from around the corner.

Tony continued, 'We could pop to The Greyhound for a bite to eat and listen to the local gossip at the same time. After all, they haven't seen our faces yet.'

Cathy groaned. Her vision of a take away and evening with a choice movie evaporating. Once a cop always a cop. That's probably why she was still alone at the age of thirty one. Shame really. In a different life she might have been tempted by the possibility of a liaison with Tony. He was just the right height and build for her. Fit and yet obviously did not have time for a daily routine of weight training and the ego that usually attached to a person like that. No, he was just her type. Kind features, yet manly, good looking in an unassuming sort of way. She sighed.

'I'll take that as a yes then, on the condition that you let me drive.'

'Just as well, unless you fancy risking life and limb on the back of my Harley,' Cathy smiled, relaxing now she knew where she stood. This was business after all and not really a date.

'Oh, I don't know. The feel of vibrating leather and clinging on to an attractive young lady. How could I resist?' He grinned sideways at Cathy and was pleased to see her shoulders relax. 'No. It's only fair,' he said. 'You've been doing all the driving today. I'll pick you up at seven outside your place, OK?'

'If I stand on the side of my street at night I might look as if I'm touting for business,' Cathy laughed.

'Maybe you are!' joked Tony, receiving a playful punch in the arm. 'Hey, both hands on the wheel please!' he protested.

At seven thirty they were pulling up in The Greyhound car-park. It was quite full for a Tuesday night so Cathy was glad she had had the forethought to phone for a table asking for one in the bar area for eight, giving them half an hour to have a drink in the corner unnoticed and eavesdrop on local gossip.

They talked quietly about something and nothing.

'If you did go on holiday where would you like to go?' Tony asked.

'Somewhere quiet. Ideally where I can relax, walk and forget about the world. And you?'

'Me too. My ideal spot has to include water though. Sea or lake, I'm not fussy but it just calms me down.'

'I know what you mean and we couldn't be further away from the sea here. I don't even find time to walk along the embankment in Bedford. I should really, rather than putting on the TV.'

'Not so nice to walk on your own though. Maybe we should meet up sometime?' Tony looked sideways at his date. There was definitely an attraction there. He loved her sense of fun and really would like a ride on the back of her bike one day. He began to daydream of the effect it might have, their close proximity as he hung on as Cathy opened the throttle...

'Hey charmer, wake up. You asked me on this date remember,' Cathy teased although her trained ear was also listening, tuning in on the different conversations at the bar. It was much like being a simultaneous translator, listening and speaking at the same time, focusing ninety percent of the time on what she was hearing, allowing her own words to tumble out of their own accord. Suddenly both were alert.

'It doesn't seem possible. They were both in here just last Saturday night,' one man mused as he balanced on the bar stool, his pint of real ale held tight in his hand; 'family occasion with their son and the old man I think. Seemed to be having quite a good time.'

'It makes no sense. There must have been someone else involved. I'd lay my life to say she didn't do it. Don't mind what that post woman says.'

'Hard for Old Peter though. He was starting to take it easy. Do you think he'll be able to persuade Paul to stay around to help him?'

'Not a chance. That lad hasn't got an ounce of country ways in him. He wouldn't know which end of the cow to milk!'

'That's true.' The two men laughed but within moments stifled their nervous laughter to leave a moment of awkward silence between them. In fact the whole bar had gone quiet all of a sudden. Then one of the men started whispering, 'Do you think there's any truth in ...' but neither Cathy nor Tony could hear anymore because one of the young waitresses came up to them with their meals. Despite this setback they were pleased to be positioned in the lounge bar, a table for two next to the inglenook fireplace. Cathy went to the ladies and made a note of the description of the two men for future reference. It would be worth chasing up. Returning to their table she noticed that a candle had been lit.

'Very romantic,' Cathy mentioned wryly.

'Quite so,' remarked Tony, ever the gentleman, holding Cathy's seat for her. They continued their banal conversation. Their patience soon rewarded by another couple who had arrived at the bar. The lady was soon sipping a gin and tonic, sitting on a bar stool in the corner, and the man was standing beside her, his shoulders sharp and his eyes glaring. They seemed to be having an argument.

'I'm telling you, I was with Joanna the evening before. We were deciding whether to go ahead with this new venture; an arts weekend. We've so many talented people in the village, artists, writers, musicians, actors; Joanna was really keen to put on an event to raise money for Helen's leukaemia charity.'

'You don't know what goes on behind closed doors. That's all I'm trying to say,' her husband countered.

'I don't know how you of all people could say that. We've known Joanna and Bob almost since they got married. I know we're not close, though farmers never have a great deal of time to socialise on a regular basis, but you can't possibly think Joanna might be guilty! I've had enough of this.'

The lady slipped down from her stool and headed for the door.

The barman looked as if he was about to say something to the husband, but looking over towards Cathy and Tony he must have changed his mind.

You have to be a bit of a diplomat in their trade, thought Cathy. A successful barman, especially the owner of the establishment, must forever span a tightrope between neutrality and conviviality.

'Another one, Jeff?' was all he asked.

'Better not. I'll be in even more trouble if I don't go home now. What do you think of this business, Bill? After all you must have seen a different side to Joanna and Bob over the years.'

'Not my place to say Jeff,' Bill smiled with the unspoken reassurance that he was a man of honour and that confidentiality was the key to his success. 'Terrible business though,' he added.

'It is too,' replied Jeff as he headed for the door.

It was obvious that on the table next to Cathy and Tony's were a group of strangers to the village and they would get nothing from listening in to their conversation and so they began to focus on their food and each other. Tony had chosen plaice and chips, to which Cathy raised her eyebrows as she tucked into her salad.

'Do you think we might wangle a trip to Jersey on this one Tony?' Cathy asked with a smile.

'Not a chance. Have you ever been there?'

'I went on a day trip there from Guernsey when I was a child. Didn't like it much; too much traffic, much like home, if my memory serves me correctly. I loved Guernsey though.'

'I think you're being too harsh to judge Jersey on a day trip. I stayed there for a week once and it's very beautiful. Stayed at St Brelade's Bay. Would love to go back.'

'I believe you, but I'm really not sure what Norton's gonna make of all this,' Cathy whispered, looking over Tony's shoulder to check that nobody was listening. She paused and then continued in a light-hearted tone. 'We spent the summer on Guernsey in little coves, rock pooling and swimming in the sea. A delightful holiday. I'm so glad my parents avoided trips to theme parks, and we learnt to love walking from a very young age.'

'I know what you mean. Jersey was similar; a memorable holiday for all good reasons. Think we'd better make tracks now, don't you? I'm shattered.'

Tony paid by card, acknowledging the barman with a nod of thanks before guiding Cathy towards the door, his hand resting in the small of her back. Cathy liked the sensation and smiled noticing a sign beside the door on their way out:

"10p to say you've just left
50p to telephone to say that you've been delayed
£1 to say you're not here" [8]

'Wouldn't do in our trade,' she nodded to the barman and left.

Later when Tony dropped Cathy off at her flat she resisted the temptation to ask him in for coffee. Make life far too complicated, she thought. She raised her hand in a wave as he sped off up the street.

8. Quotation may not be entirely accurate

CHAPTER 19

Saturday 11th May 2019

The following morning Cathy acknowledged Tony with a nod as he rushed in for the emergency debriefing session of the day. After half an hour, as each person present gave an account of their enquiries, the screen in front of them was filling up. It was obvious that DI Norton was frustrated by the lack of motive uncovered for anyone, let alone the wife, to kill the poor farmer. He finished with a summary.

'Forensics have confirmed that the victim was killed by a single stab in the back by a long, rather large blade. It could be a kitchen knife but Mrs Thomas senior was taken to the farmhouse kitchen and she assured us that none were missing. Of course that's not conclusive. There were footprints in the blood and bloodied prints at the door where they stopped. Grey fibres were also found, but Mr Cookham notified us last night that he had noticed Bob Thomas's grey overalls were missing, as were a pair of trainers Bob Thomas used in an outside office near his Jersey cows. Traces of Bob Thomas's blood were also found in the sink there. We need to find those overalls and trainers as soon as possible.

Mr Cookham has given us his own overalls, which were bought at the same time, and they have gone to forensics. Does this point back to Mr Cookham? Why would he incriminate himself and anyway, DS Brown verified the timings of the milking.

A thorough search of the area has shown very few clues. There were lots of tyre marks in the mud around the farmhouse, the most recent being a tractor, the post-van, bicycle tracks and almost certainly a milk float, but Mrs Thomas Senior assures us that the milk lady does not visit on a Thursday morning. There were also different bicycle tracks from the path near the wood. Nothing more was found and since the door was wide open it doesn't give us a clue as to whether the murderer came from inside or outside the house or what weapon was used.' Norton looked around briefly before returning his attention to the array of information posted before them.

'Let's go through the list of names next. We have the chief suspect Joanna, who was at the scene of the crime, but we have no motive other than that her husband didn't often put his hand in his wallet,' he paused as if hoping for someone to pipe up with the missing nugget of evidence. Since nobody spoke up he continued, 'John the cowman has a barn of cows and a computerised automatic pager. Both convincing alibis, don't you think?' Silence.

'Then there's the son who was in a drunken stupor upstairs and I believe his shock of hearing the news of his father's demise was genuine, as was him talking of his father in the present tense. Nevertheless he did seem more concerned about his laptop than his parents. It is taking a bit longer than anticipated to try to check his machine since he was a computer buff. He was certainly none too pleased when we asked him to copy the files he needed on to a memory device and leave it with us.'

'Then we have a crowd of nutters gathering at the churchyard to pay their respects to a girl murdered exactly one hundred years ago. An odd coincidence or more?' he added, in no way attempting to disguise the sarcasm in his voice. 'One of those we now know was also a bird watching stalker in the woods next to the farm. From the accounts of your interview you seem sure of her innocence but there are still a few loose ends to convince me. After all, she was closest to the scene of the crime as far as we know. She was still in the vicinity an hour or so later and one coincidence in a quiet backwater like that is strange enough, but two of them sets alarm bells ringing in my head.

Finally we have the victim's mother and father acting a little oddly. Mind you, with due respect, I think that's quite understandable under the circumstances. Any parent would be out of their minds with grief.' DI Norton looked up for confirmation but continued without giving a chance for the assembled officers to speak.

'There has been a door to door in both Church End and Silver End and longer interviews with the verger and the vicar, so where do we go from here? Well, a couple of you have mentioned the cleaning lady but have not as yet interviewed her. Helen Carter, you said her name was. She'd know about the family scandals if anyone does. Then there were the people speaking in the pub but they were probably covered in the door to door.' He nodded towards Cathy at this point. 'Next we need to track down every one of those nutters in the churchyard and interview each of them. Who else was at the churchyard? The verger mentioned another lady on a bicycle, Anna Beret I assume, and two young lads, one in a car and one on a motorcycle. Also there were two men the Jag man described. One of them might have witnessed something, even if their activities, however dubious, were entirely innocent. Were they the same men at The Gathering? Maybe it was a ritual killing, a bit like Murder on the Orient Express,' he chuckled, but seeing that no one joined him in his mirth he began to issue orders, ignoring DS Akhtar's hand, signalling that she had something to add. Each officer present left the room with tasks to follow through and Cathy and Tony booked out a vehicle once more.

'Howdy pardner,' joked Tony. 'Seems like you're stuck with me again today.'

'I can think of worse fates,' replied Cathy, reaching for the keys, taking it for granted that she would do the driving.

'I'll take that as a compliment. First let's go to find the elusive Helen Carter, I think.'

'I agree. We should have interviewed her on the first day. After all she was at the vicar's, then later the verger's and then I'm sure someone was at the farm bungalow too and it may have been her. Each time she disappeared. She must know something which might even lead us to the killer.' Cathy frowned. 'But first can I nip back to see Saima for a mo? I've just thought of something. Do you think you could bring the car round to the front and I'll meet you there?'

Cathy thrust the keys into Tony's hand. His eyebrows lifted and he thought of a tart response, but Tony had worked with Cathy a great deal and trusted her judgment so he let her lack of respect for a senior officer pass. One day, he thought, I'll show her who's in charge. Or one night maybe and he chuckled as he turned the car around.

Cathy found Saima Akhtar staring furiously at her computer screen and knew her instincts had been correct. She pulled up a chair so that they could talk quietly, out of earshot. 'Any news, Saima?'

Saima's look spoke volumes of her frustration at being ignored by DI Norton. 'It's all here,' she remarked dejectedly. 'He doesn't want to know but every detail is here.'

'What details?' asked Cathy, getting her e pad out to take notes.

'You don't need an e pad at all. Even from reading the web site we can trace the lead up to the murder let alone the details in the forum archive.'

'Which murder are we talking about?' asked Cathy, in a voice she hoped was devoid of scepticism.

'Both,' replied Saima in a matter of fact manner, looking into Cathy's surprised face.

'You have a girl from Jersey in 1919 and again in 2019 and I've checked. They are related.' Saima paused and looked at Cathy who nodded before she continued. 'Both murders took place near Haynes Church End; this one at a farm and the other in the woods nearby. In 1919 there were two possible suspects. One from Canada and a Sergeant Major. Well, we know there was a man from Canada here at the church and I would bet my life that the Sergeant Major is a distant relation to the army chap the Jag man mentioned. That's from the website alone but look at the forum too. I believe this is a conversation from Anna, the Jersey girl stalker. She mentions a farmer, his son and an old car. Look at this photo on the website. That's the car she's talking about.'

Cathy was lost in thought. She tried to rationalise this information, to sieve through it to some sort of logical conclusion, relevant to the case they were now dealing with. She could see that Saima was bewitched by this story of the unsolved murder back in 1919. Was she reading too much into it?

'But that was in 1919 Saima. Are you sure it has any relevance to the case today?' She added, trying hard to keep an open mind.

Saima looked sharply up from her screen. 'The discussions on the forum may be about 1919, whether their relations were guilty or innocent or who else might be involved, but surely you can see now that the 1919 murder is linked to the farm murder. The fact that the gathering on the anniversary of Lucille Vardon's death was close to the time of our current murder points towards revenge, doesn't it Cathy? Then you have your motive,' she added in a flourish, a couple of officers looking up as she raised her voice.

'If you're right, then Joanna Thomas is in the clear.' Cathy looked relieved but then frowned, 'But Anna is back in the frame. Have you tracked down the webmaster yet?'

'No, that's proving a bit tricky. It must be someone with the most up to date encryption facilities, way beyond my abilities. I need to ask permission to contact HQ but I'm too nervous about asking Norton, especially after he ignored me this morning.' At that point they noticed that the Commissioner had arrived and had been shown into Norton's office.

'You know the Police Commissioner personally, Saima. He recommended you for this job. Maybe you could catch him before he leaves and ask for his advice on your findings and having some IT expert look into it. These people at *The Gathering* would have to be tracked down and interviewed.'

'I might just do that,' replied Saima. 'Thanks Cathy. I feel so frustrated. You do think I've got something don't you? I'd hate to make a total fool of myself.'

'It looks pretty convincing to me, Saima, and anyway, *"Each lead is a silk thread of opportunity,"* as my last boss used to say. *"Silk may look flimsy but, my word it's strong,"* he used to add, but I must be off, otherwise Tony'll go without me.'

Saima gave Cathy a lopsided grin as she dashed for the door.

As Cathy drove off Tony cleared his throat. 'Well?' he said.

She briefly outlined her conversation with Saima.

'That sounds bizarre. I suggest we focus on finding Helen Carter and discuss it later.'

'She usually starts the day at the farmhouse apparently but, since that's still out of bounds I guess that she'll be at the bungalow.'

They pulled up in the yard and looked over at the Georgian farmhouse, which looked dejectedly silent. One of the side barns was ajar, not the milking parlour, but instead they headed for the bungalow. The front door was open so they paused.

Madelyn Thomas looked startled. She had been staring at a book which seemed to hold various accounts, written in long hand in an enormous ledger, the likes of which Cathy had only seen in a museum.

'My husband's over at the barn,' she stated by way of an apology.

'We haven't actually come to see you or your husband, but we had hoped to find Helen Carter here.'

Cathy noticed Madelyn's eyes mist over but it vanished in a moment, leaving just her normal empty expression. 'Oh. She should be here in about fifteen minutes.' Madelyn hesitated. 'Would you like to have a cup of tea while you wait?'

'No that's all right thanks. We'll just have a look around while we're waiting,' replied Tony, eager to get out of the claustrophobic atmosphere.

Cathy and Tony wandered around the farm yard, looking down at the tyre prints and in the shrubbery beside the farmhouse door. Tony looked around the door and frame for any clues they might have missed and then both headed towards the barn.

Cathy saw it first. Her eyes wide at the sight of the Austin 7hp in front of them and it looked very like the car she had seen earlier on the website Saima had shown her. Her brain registered pictures in her head, like an old fashioned slide show her great grandfather had shown her when she had been very little. Single images flashed before her eyes, Haynes Camp, soldiers at the mess, Haynes Park and finally two young girls standing at the end of the long drive next to a car, this car. She was sure of it, although the picture had been a little blurred with age.

She listened to Tony and Mr Thomas.

'Yes, she's still in full working order, 'Peter Thomas chuckled. 'Albeit a bit cantankerous. Just like any old lady really.'

'Remarkable,' replied Tony. 'Have you had it for long?'

'We've had it in the family since nearly new actually. It was left to my great grandfather in a will from a rich relative in Birmingham. That was in 1913, just before the war. Farmers have never been that rich. I believe it was mothballed during both wars but it's been running almost all the time since then. Give or take...you know.'

Cathy barely heard them. She was transported back to 1919 and she was walking down the lane towards the car and the two girls. There was a young man in the car but she could not make out what he was saying. She looked down at her long skirts, surprised as they swished on the ground. She heard laughter and the sound of the young man as he sped off, leaving the girls shaking their heads, but the vision faded when she saw a bicycle pull up.

'Tony,' she interrupted shaking off her weird vision. 'Helen Carter's here. Please can we use your lounge to talk with her?' she said, turning to the farmer.

'Of course,' he said. 'Just ask the wife,' and he nodded over to Helen before disappearing back into the barn, Tony glancing over his shoulder with longing before following Cathy.

They arrived back at the bungalow porch in time to hear Mrs Thomas warning Helen that the two police officers were on their way over to speak with her. They both looked around as Cathy and Tony entered.

'Your husband said that it would be possible to use your front room for the interview if you agree Mrs Thomas. It shouldn't take long,' Cathy explained. Helen led them through and waited until they sat down before sitting opposite them.

'Do you mind us asking you a few questions, Mrs Carter?' Tony asked.

'Miss Carter, actually. You are only doing your job. How shocking all this is.'

'Can you think of any reason why Mr Thomas, that's Bob Thomas, was murdered?'

Cathy noticed Miss Carter frown.

'Well,' began Helen, taking a deep breath. 'No, not really.'

'You sound hesitant. Miss Carter. Anything you can tell us, however insignificant, might help us find Bob Thomas's killer.'

'I can't think of any reason why anyone should want to murder Bob at all. He was such a good and honest man. No, I can't,' answered Helen decisively.

'Then can you tell us what you were doing between 5.30 am and 7am on 9th May, Miss Carter.'

Helen hesitated, but then decided that it was better to tell the truth, however odd that truth might sound.

'I went up to the churchyard. There were a group of us gathered in memory of girl called Lucille Vardon. It was 100 years since Lucille Vardon died and we wanted to pay our respects.'

'And what is your connection to this Lucille Vardon, Miss Carter, may we ask?' It was Cathy who spoke this time.

Helen's shoulders hunched up and her eyes narrowed. Cathy wondered if she was angry or if she was going to cry. When she reached into her bag for a tissue and put it to her eyes Cathy softened. 'We know you've been through a lot in the last year, so take your time.'

'You know nothing!' spat out Helen, thrusting her tissue, unused, back into her bag. 'You don't know what it's like to lose your only daughter,' she continued in no more than a whisper. 'I noticed her grave you see, Lucille's that is, when tending Kirsty's, and I was shocked that they died at the same age. Only twenty-one,' at which point she did burst into tears, the tissue retrieved once more.

'We may not understand,' Cathy continued gently, 'but we do try to be understanding. After all you must know Mrs Thomas, Joanna, better than most in the village. We'll come back on another day, but if you think of anything then please let us know.' Cathy and Tony stood up to leave but Cathy turned back at the door and asked, 'Did you know that there is a website all about Lucille Vardon?' she asked noticing Helen wince imperceptibly at her question. Helen just nodded yes in reply and they walked out, thanking Madelyn Thomas as they left.

CHAPTER 20

Tuesday 14th May 2019   Godalming   Police Station

It did not take long for Saima to get permission from the police commissioner for her theory to be pursued, and a team was allocated the task to track down the people on the relevant forum discussion. This did not prove to be insurmountable, with so much written on Futurenet about the Lucille Vardon case in 1919, genealogy and notes from the interviews, including door-to-doors.

Once Colonel Regmund had been identified the commissioner approved, even if it meant annoying the military and interviewing one of their own. In fact, the commissioner decided that it was important enough to send DI Norton down to Surrey to carry out the interview, much to Norton's annoyance at being out ranked. Saima knew now that Norton would ensure that she continued in more of a desk research role for as long as he had the authority. He was both angry but also embarrassed about wasting this gentleman's time, so before he started the official interview he apologised,

'I'd just like to say that this was not my idea to come and interview you today, but I was ordered to do so,' his face donning a sickly smile.

'You're just doing your job, Inspector,' replied the Colonel as DI Norton clicked a switch to record the conversation.

'Can you confirm that your full name is Keith Robert Regmund?' he asked.

'Yes, that is correct.'

'Your occupation, Colonel Regmund?'

'I'm bound under the Official Secrets Act I'm afraid. I'm not at liberty to say.' Inspector Norton glanced at Cathy, who he had decided would accompany him.

'Where were you, sir, between 5.30 and 7 am on the morning of 9th May 2019?'

Keith Regmund drew breath before replying. He was hardly officially bound on this occasion, but nevertheless he was reluctant to divulge his whereabouts for personal reasons. He weighed up the risks of an untruth, knowing full well that his skill would allow him to mask the lie to all but the most sophisticated of equipment. In that split second of hesitation he decided to tell snippets of the truth.

'I was in St Mary's churchyard, Haynes, Bedfordshire at 6 am and then drove home at about 6.30 am.'

'Why were you in Haynes on that particular morning, Colonel Regmund?'

'It was,' and he paused. 'It was personal business and I'm not sure I wish to say.'

'Are you implying that you were on an intelligence mission and that you cannot tell us, sir?'

'No, I didn't say that, officer.'

'So, why were you in Haynes that morning?' DI Norton was beginning to run out of patience. He felt he was on a fool's errand and was tired after the journey to Surrey. He'd had so little sleep either. They sat in an airless interview room at Godalming Police Station, both gentlemen resenting the intrusion into their lives.

'Do you mind me asking on what grounds I have been dragged in here Inspector, because I'm sure you understand that I've got better things to do with my time?'

'We are actually investigating a murder Colonel.' DI Norton resisted the temptation of thumping the table, but his face was grim. 'If we are to eliminate you from our enquiries,' he continued in a more controlled tone, 'then we need to know exactly where and what you were doing and if anyone can corroborate your story.'

'You are saying that there was a murder near Haynes churchyard on May 9th 2019?'

DI Norton watched the man carefully. His eye brows were raised imperceptibly, a sign that he was processing information as he spoke, but he could also see a man of training, whose calculated mask was drawn.

'Yes, sometime between 5.00 and 6.30 on the morning in question, sir.'

'I see, Inspector,' paused Keith Regmund, gathering his thoughts whilst deciding to tell as much truth as he felt was prudent. 'At 6 am I joined a gathering at the church to commemorate the death of a young woman, Lucille Vardon, exactly one hundred years ago in 1919. My son was doing some research about family history and my family had links with Haynes Park during World War One. I left at 6.30 and drove home.'

'And what time did you arrive at the churchyard, sir?'

'At precisely 5.59 am. I stopped at the motorway services at Toddington to have a coffee at 5.20 and left there at 5.35 arriving at exactly a minute before the due time.'

DI Norton did not doubt the accuracy of this timing, considering the man before him.

'Is there anyone who can verify this?'

Keith Regmund swore silently that he had resisted messaging his wife when he had stopped, but he replied,

'There is as a matter of fact. I gave this Canadian guy a lift to Flitwick Station and I'm sure he saw me arrive too.'

'And have you any contact details for him and do you know if this man is still in the UK?'

'No and yes. We didn't exchange details but I do know he was catching a flight home from Heathrow that afternoon.'

'So, if we can track down this chap it will help to verify your story. Did you at any time drive to or near Pear Tree Farm on your way to the churchyard?'

'I have no idea where Pear Tree Farm is, Inspector. I've never heard of the place.' This was true. He had heard of a farm and the farmer's son on the forum but not the name of the farm, and anyway, that was back in 1919 damn it. He forced his expression to remain blank.

As Cathy listened she felt more and more irritated. She wanted to know why and how this man was linked to Lucille Vardon's death and was frustrated that she was not allowed to ask. Surely Norton could see that Lucille Vardon's murder exactly one hundred years before that of Bob Thomas's was relevant? The fact that so many people were in the area at the time of the murder, at an hour when usually there were hardly any signs of life, must mean something. Even if they were a diversion tactic or maybe it was a group murder of revenge, as Saima had flippantly suggested.

While the pointless interview droned on, Cathy let her imagination soar, knowing instinctively that there was a connection. She just had to prove it.

DI Norton sighed and trying to regain his lost sense of professionalism he asked, 'I really apologise for taking up your valuable time but have you any further information to give us, sir, which might help us with our enquiries?'

Taking care not to divulge anything about his family's possible involvement with Lucille Vardon's death, Keith Regmund replied,

'I know that the Canadian chap was staying at The Swan Hotel in Bedford. I'm sure they would have a forwarding address and contact details Inspector.'

'Thank you for helping us with our enquiries Colonel. I'm really sorry to have inconvenienced you in any way but here is my card if you think of anything else. Would you like a lift anywhere? In an unmarked car, I can assure you.'

'Yes Inspector. I would very much like to be taken home.'

That night Keith dreamed of bayonet charges and muddy trenches.

He shouted, 'Charge!'

Waking up with a start with sweat pouring from him, he wondered if he had shouted aloud. The clock said 2am. He went to his office, tempted to search for more evidence but paralysed with uncertainty for the first time in his life. His privacy had been violated but how much more did they know about his work.

'Enough,' he said aloud. His position could be compromised no longer. Tomorrow he would set in motion his retreat and withdraw for a while, not only for his personal safety but for his family's too, and the organisation he worked for. He closed the screen down almost as soon as it had booted up.

Feeling calmer now he slept well waking before 5 am, when he crept into Toby's room one last time before disappearing into the new day and by 10 am he was out of the country.

CHAPTER 21

Thursday 16th May 2019   Canada

'Hey Honey, come quick! There's a policeman from England wanting to speak to you. He's on the big screen now. Something about a murder!' Trudy frowned at her husband James as he rushed into their office.

A little out of breath from rushing up the stairs James stared puzzled at the large screen on the wall. 'I'm James Bouchard. How can I help you officer?'

'Detective Inspector Norton actually, of Bedford Police. Is it convenient for you to talk, sir, because we need you to answer some questions to assist us with our enquiries into a recent murder?'

'Fire away inspector. I'll do what I can but I can't see that I can be much help to you.'

'Were you in the vicinity of Haynes Church, in Bedfordshire, or anywhere near Pear Tree Farm on the morning of 9th May, Mr Bouchard?'

James reddened, very aware of Trudy's face scrutinizing his every expression.

'As a matter of fact I was there briefly, Inspector. Why do you ask?'

'What time would that have been, sir?'

James paused. Whatever he said now he would still be in big trouble with his wife. It's not that he had lied outright, but he certainly had omitted to tell the whole truth. He took a deep breath.

'I must have been dropped off by the taxi at around 5.30.'

Trudy gasped and James hoped that she was not in the inspector's line of vision. He had nothing to hide, damn it. Why shouldn't he tell the truth?

'Please can you account for the next hour, Mr Bouchard? Please tell us exactly what you did and when you left the area.'

'Well Inspector. After I was dropped off I had about half an hour to kill. Nnnno!' he stumbled on his words. 'I didn't mean that, Inspector.' His face reddened further and he gulped. 'I went for a bit of a walk and then went to the churchyard just before 6 am where there was this sort of gathering. I don't know whether you know Inspector.'

'Yes, Mr Bouchard, you don't need to explain why you were in the churchyard. However incredible it may seem to us, we understand that you were commemorating the death, a murder in fact, of a Lucille Vardon in 1919.'

James suddenly looked relieved, 'You haven't reopened the case after all these years, surely inspector?'

Inspector Norton ignored this remark. In truth he was fed up with the whole thing. 'No of course we haven't, but did you go anywhere near Pear Tree Farm between 5.30 and 6?'

'No inspector. I can assure you that I didn't. I'm not very good where mud and animals are concerned. I like to keep my shoes clean, as it were.' Realising he had made another comment which could be misconstrued he opened his mouth again, but the inspector interrupted,

'Did you, by any chance see a chap arrive, an army type?'

'Yes, Inspector. He came just before 6 am and laid a wreath. He gave me a lift to Flitwick Station afterwards.'

'Well, that's all for now, sir, but we may need to contact you again on this matter.'

'Please may I ask what it is you *are* investigating then, Inspector?'

'There was a murder, sir, at Pear Tree Farm, we estimate soon after 5.30 am. Since you were in the vicinity and do not appear to be able to account for all of your time, you are in the frame as it were, but don't worry about it now, sir. I'm sure we know who the murderer was.'

'That's a relief,' replied James quietly before the screen went dead. The silence in the room was deafening before Trudy stormed out and slammed the door. He could hear a frenzy of activity coming from their dressing room but he could not bear to go and look. This was unbelievable, after all, he was innocent, but then he remembered his great grandfather.

Suddenly he felt used, manipulated, framed but above all he felt grubby for lying to his wife and he knew that he had absolutely no excuse. He put his head in his hands and groaned.

Cathy, who had listened in on the conversation was frustrated yet again by burning questions she was not allowed to ask. Why was James Bouchard at the gathering and what connection did he have with Lucille Vardon?

James went to work, not knowing what else he could do, but at home that night the silent house filled him with dread. Could those people trace him here, he wondered? Where could he go and more importantly where had Trudy gone? She had a short vacation due so he guessed where she might head to think things through. Within moments he had made the decision to follow her but he knew he could not risk taking the car.

Their house had a back gate in an area full of trees and shady paths. As the sun was sinking he took a drink out and ambled to the wooden love seat in this secluded spot, a jacket slipped casually over his free arm, inside out. He and Trudy used to sit there a lot when they were first married. He sighed with relief. If he was being watched somehow from the house he was almost sure he could not be seen now and anyway he tried to act normally.

When it was quite dark he slipped behind the seat and felt his way through the trees to the back gate. He slipped on his Tiger Cats jacket and felt for the scarf and hat in the pockets, each with the logo of his favourite team stamped clearly on them. Taking the key out of his pocket he was soon outside, locking the gate behind him. Within two blocks he was mingling with people heading for the game but instead of continuing with the crowds he got on a nearby bus, as supporters poured off through the other door. He paid by cash and was taken to the bus station. There he caught another bus and within half an hour he was heading for the lakes. He put his cap away and folded his denim jacket in his lap once more, pulling it inside out as he took it off. Close up it would look a bit strange when he put it back on but from a distance it would be OK.

CHAPTER 22

Friday 17th May 2019   Helen in Bedfordshire

Cathy and Tony left it a few days before tracking down Helen Carter again. She was just heading home to her cottage from the vicarage.

'We're really sorry to bother you again Miss Carter but we need to ask you some more questions. Is it a convenient time?'

Helen Carter looked startled to see them but nevertheless she invited them into her house.

'Can you tell us any more about the Thomases?' DS Tony Brown asked as they sat down on the ageing sofa.

'What do you want to know?' Helen replied.

'Were they good employers for a start?'

'They were farmers. Part of village life. She found it a bit hard at first but with our help she settled in.'

'You're talking about when Joanna and Bob first got married. That must have been over twenty years ago.'

'Yes of course. They always treated me well and my Kirsty too. Always good to us they were.'

'Were you aware of any marital disharmony?'

'No, they were extremely happy, as far as I could tell. We never discussed anything too personal mind, but no, I can't think of anyone less likely to murder her husband than Joanna.'

'Do you go up to the farm most days?' Tony asked.

'Well, yes, either to help out at the main farmhouse or the bungalow. It's my job. Housekeeper, like with the vicar and the verger. Keeps me busy and pays the bills. They've asked me to move into the farmhouse, to keep an eye on things in fact; Peter and Madelyn that is. They don't want to move there themselves and they don't like the place empty. I'll be going there in a couple of days' time.'

Cathy noted that Helen Carter was wearing a designer dress and that she had some rather expensive jewellery on too, but she did not comment on it.

'Can you think of anyone who might want to kill Mr Thomas, Miss Carter? Any rumours or local gossip that you think we should know about?'

Helen, still perching on the arm of a chair fidgeted, looking as if she wanted the interview over quickly.

'No, there's really nothing I can say to help you, officers.'

'You told us the other day that you were in Haynes churchyard on the morning of 9th May. Please can you tell us what you did before and after this strange gathering?'

'I was tending the graves, like I always do, before the group arrived and then afterwards I cycled home.'

'So you didn't go anywhere near the farmhouse that morning?' Tony continued to probe.

Did Cathy perceive a second's hesitation before Helen answered?

'I spent some time with my girl. Is that a crime?'

'Now, tell us a bit about this gathering. Do you know who organised it and any of the other people there?' Cathy noted another hesitation. Only slight but it was certainly there.

'There's this website. I became interested in the girl Lucille when I found her grave one day. She died the same age as my daughter, you see. As I was telling you the other day, I took the time to tidy up her grave too. I found it therapeutic. Something to focus on.'

'Did you recognise anyone else at the gathering?'

'I knew the young man Jake Foster and his mum. They arrived in their car and then two boys from the village, lads the same age as my Kirsty. They were all at school together.'

'Can you give us their names please?'

'Yes of course - Afzal and Sadiq, the sons of the people at the Post Office. Both IT wizards. They've helped me out enough times. Jake's the best though.'

'And where does this Jake live?'

'7 Stacey Avenue, just opposite the Post Office. Kirsty was a good friend of his, so I knew him well. He's been to Iran in the army. You can't help but get to know the youngsters when you have children of your own, officer.'

Tony looked over at Cathy and she nodded.

'We'll leave it for now Miss Carter, but if you think of anything else please call us. We're really sorry to have troubled you, but you knew that we needed to speak to you and it appeared that you seemed to be avoiding us.'

'Not intentionally I assure you,' Helen replied, visibly relaxing, the muscles on her face making less of a frown.

'We'd best get on then but I expect we'll see you tomorrow,' Cathy said as she switched off her recording device.

Helen paused and then suddenly remembered.

'Oh,' she said, 'at Bob's funeral. I'll be there to support the family, of course.'

As they drove away they were aware of a shadow watching their departure from behind the curtains.

'What did you make of that, Cathy?' Tony asked.

'Odd lady, but grief does terrible things. Looks like we've got a bunch of people but none of them have true alibis, do they, or a clear motive?'

'None of them are likely suspects either,' Tony mused.

'I'm not so sure. Something's not quite right Tony.'

'Let's just drop in on those lads before heading back to the station,' said Tony.

They interviewed Afzal and Sadiq; polite, quiet lads who did not know very much. Just that they had helped Helen Carter when she first went to IT classes. Jake's mother said that Jake was out, so they had to leave it for another day.

CHAPTER 23

Monday 20th May 2019 2 pm

Cathy and Tony sat at the back of Haynes Church. It was packed but after the funeral service only the family walked towards the family grave where Robert Thomas was to be buried. Nothing unusual happened to alert their attention throughout the proceedings, except that Helen stood behind Bob's dad Peter throughout. She even sat behind him in a pew in church.

Understandably the wake was not to be held at the farmhouse but at the church hall, and they saw Helen slipping away early, before the coffin was finally lowered; probably to make sure that everything was ready. The hall was a drive away, up in the main village and so they noticed that she was given a lift by the verger.

Half the village were there by the time Cathy and Tony arrived at the village hall, all offering platitudes of sympathy towards the family as everyone mingled. Helen was serving teas behind the counter. Joanna sat in the corner, protected from the crowding guests by Emily.

22nd May 1919 2pm

*People lined the lane outside the church to watch the coffin
process by, a Union Flag was draped over it and guards flagged
it on either side of the hearse. The horse walked slowly on and
there was a guard of honour waiting at the entrance to Church
Lane.*

*Following behind the military was a line of personnel from
the camp including Lucille Vardon's best friend Margaret, and
many who had walked from the village. Quite a crowd had
gathered, although only one of Lucille's uncles was able to
attend, since he was on the mainland at the time. This lack was
made up by her numerous friends from the camp who had
ordered a huge cross of flowers which rested on the coffin lid.
It was certainly a fitting tribute for one so popular. Lucille
Vardon was given full honours having died in service in the
Queen Mary's Army Auxiliary Corps and a gravestone was
erected with a military insignia, paid for by her friends and
fellow workers.*

Bedfordshire Times 1919 ~ paraphrased and names changed

CHAPTER 24

Wednesday 22nd May 2019 5pm Bedford   police station

The electronic screen in front of them was covered in virtual post its and it filled almost a wall. DI Norton opened the proceedings,

'Let's update the facts before we discuss the new issues, but I must say that I find the whole investigation thoroughly frustrating. It should be solved and going to court by now in my opinion.'

It took half an hour clarifying the new information then DI Norton pointed to the orange posts on the left of the screen with Joanna in the centre.

'You have the wife, who I still feel is guilty, but no one has come up with any motive or the murder weapon.' He glared his disapproval around the room.

'We've discounted John the cowman. He seems to be the only one in the whole bunch with some sort of an alibi,' he paused. 'Then there's the victim's parents and son too. Who would murder their own son? My gut feeling is that the son Paul isn't in the frame either, but you feel there's something odd going on at the bungalow, am I right?'

Cathy nodded in affirmation.

'There's the housekeeper Helen next. She seems a bit shifty too, but what would her motive be?'

Then he pointed to the right of the screen to a picture of Lucille Vardon, surrounded by six yellow 'post its' one of which was Helen who was the only one in both groups.

'This 1919 murder, I believe, is one of two things, pure coincidence or just an elaborate smoke screen? Very clever if it's the second. Each one of these six *was* in the vicinity at the time of the murder. Only the two lads back up each other's story about leaving home together, otherwise none of them seem to be able to account for exactly what they were doing before the 'gathering.' Even those two boys could have made up a plot and be lying to us. Are they all guilty?' He paused.

'NO!' the inspector boomed out, waking his audience to sudden alertness.

'No,' he repeated firmly but not quite so loudly. 'I truly believe this,' and he waved over the yellow half of the screen, 'has absolutely nothing to do with our murder.' Here he turned to face his captive audience. 'This,' he paused, 'shows your complete failure as a force to find the truth,' and he glared at Saima at this point.

'You are more than happy to waste our time going down this cul de sac, dragging us all in your wake, while the murderer is still free. I now have just over one week left in this post before I retire. I want Joanna Thomas nailed for this murder and I'll bring her back in myself and interview her again personally. While you,' and he waved his hand at his audience, 'go out and find the evidence. You haven't even come up with the murder weapon and forensics said we're looking for a large sharp instrument. Shouldn't be too difficult to find. I know the area's been scoured. Well, search it again!' and he banged his hand on the desk making everyone leap to their feet.

On 6th June they celebrated DI Norton's departure from the force but the atmosphere was subdued and full of suppressed frustration. The case was hardly any further forward, much of this was due to a chasm between the perceptions of the two main investigative officers, DI Norton's and DS Akhtar. To everyone's surprise the Commissioner made the decision to put DS Akhtar in charge of the case on a temporary basis.

There had been another enormous and costly search for the murder weapon with no success and Cathy and Tony were exhausted. They wanted to talk to Anna Beret again but knew that she had returned to Jersey so Tony persuaded Cathy to come with him on a long weekend break; not in any official capacity, although his argument was that it could be a bit of a busman's holiday.

CHAPTER 25

Friday 7th June 2019   Jersey

The Flybe plane touched down at Jersey airport at 11.50 am and Cathy and Tony grabbed their carry-ons and soon they were heading out to the taxi rank.

'Sea View B & B at St Aubin please,' Tony instructed the driver as they made themselves comfortable.

'Just a weekend break?' remarked the driver.

'You might call it that,' replied Tony evasively. 'Yes, we needed a bit of a break,' Tony continued with more conviction, smiling conspiratorially at Cathy.

'Perfect spot for an early summer holiday, St Aubin. Plenty of cafes and restaurants open in the evenings and a lovely place to stroll around. Some of the other areas are a bit quiet at this time of year. Not hiring a car then?'

'We thought we could catch the bus to St Helier but we're visiting someone in Millbrook off St Brelade's Road and thought we could possibly walk.'

'You can walk, jog, cycle or even roller skate along the front. In fact you could hire a couple of bikes and even get over to St Brelade's Bay and St Quen, if the weather's nice. The Smugglers is worth a visit for a good meal but you'd have a few steep hills on the way.'

'Hey, that's a good idea. We hadn't thought of bikes.'

'Not that sort of bike anyway,' grimaced Cathy, thinking of her Harley at home and how good it would have been to explore on it.

'Looks like a fine weekend. Cool but perfect for some exercise,' chuckled the driver. 'Or you could always phone me.'

He had pulled up a cobbled back street outside an awning fronted door. He leaned over and took Tony's fare in one hand and offered him his card in return.

'Thanks,' said Tony. 'We might just do that, but we'll book a time for our trip back to the airport now if that's OK.'

Tony and Cathy took their bags and thanked the driver before ringing the front door. A middle aged lady welcomed them, ushered them in, pointing out the lounge and dining room before leading them up two flights of stairs to their adjoining rooms.

'If there's anything else you need then there's a bell near the lounge, but I won't be there between one and three. Breakfast's between seven thirty and nine,' she said before leaving them on the landing.

There was a moment's pause of embarrassment, as they did not know what to say to each other before Cathy broke the silence.

'Let's just drop these and walk down to the harbour for some lunch. Then over lunch we can plan our strategy. After all we've only three days and lots to fit in.'

Once outside again they ambled towards the water's edge where they found The Boat House overlooking the harbour. Both ordered pizzas and they began to relax over a glass of Italian red as they nibbled on garlic bread to stem their hunger. Reluctantly Cathy got out her ephone.

'Let's list what we have to achieve first. There's visiting Anna of course.'

'That may be a telling interview. She'll be pretty shocked that we've followed her to Jersey.'

'We'll have to step carefully though. After all, we're here in an unofficial capacity.'

'She doesn't know that though, does she,' added Tony.

'How about meeting her somewhere neutral? For a drink or something. If she's innocent I'm sure she'd be happy to help.'

'I think I'll have to leave that to your diplomatic feminine wiles.'

'I don't know though. Your masculine charms might be more successful, but I think we should do our research first. Get our facts right.'

'OK, then,' paused Tony. 'How about we walk down to Millbrook this afternoon and try to find the house where Lucille Vardon lived back in 1919. Her family that is. Anna lives near there too. Tomorrow, I think we should go into St Helier to the library and see how much we can find in their archives.'

'Then in the afternoon we'll ring Anna and try to meet the following day. We could hire those bikes. She's a bird watcher and I was reading that the place to go to is over at St Quen. We could try to arrange to meet her over there.'

'OK, then. We have a plan,' said Tony just as their meal arrived and there was a mutual unspoken decision to talk of other things and enjoy their lunch.

'Where to now, pardner,' exclaimed Tony as they headed for the door, 'my, that was good.'

They left the harbour heading northwards along the front, with the castle ahead of them and the bay sweeping along towards St Helier. 'Sure beats Bedfordshire,' he added with satisfaction.

After much searching they found the impressive Georgian town house which Lucille Vardon's family had lived in a century ago and Cathy surreptitiously took a photo with her ephone. They also headed up some side streets, following a map they had picked up at the airport, and found where Anna lived now, a fairly ordinary 1970's house. Not wanting to draw attention to themselves they made a loop and headed back down to the front where they sat on a bench and stared out to sea.

Cathy sighed. 'Are we mad?' she asked. 'DI Norton would put us on a disciplinary.'

'Look at it logically Cathy. What were we taught at college? There's no such thing as a string of coincidences in this game. Anyway this is our own time.'

Just then a familiar looking cyclist sped along behind them, slowed down a little behind their seat and then cycled off in the direction of St Aubin. It was Cathy who caught sight of her, but not wanting to turn around she stood up and moved to the rail. Tony followed.

'Don't make it obvious but I'm sure that cyclist was Anna. She wore a helmet and sun glasses but I'm sure it was her.' Cathy glanced along the bay back towards The Boat House and sure enough the cyclist had stopped and was looking towards them through binoculars. Of course, she could be looking out along the bay. It was as if she sensed Cathy watching her because the cyclist moved her line of vision to some sea birds flying over. Cathy dared not stare but as she glanced back she could just see the bicycle disappearing through a car park along the front.

'She must have seen us outside her house,' Cathy exclaimed in annoyance, realising the element of surprise had vanished.

'Not to worry,' replied Tony pragmatically. 'By tomorrow, when she's not heard from us, she'll begin to relax and wonder if she'd imagined it.'

Not wanting to bump into Anna, they strolled further along the bay and decided to take a back road up to the B & B. Both agreed to have a freshen-up and rest before supper and Cathy was glad to read for a while. Once Tony's head hit his pillow he was asleep, enjoying a catnap for an hour or so.

That evening they ate at a little Indian restaurant.

'I only want one course Tony. I'm still quite full after lunch.'

'Me too. Shall we have a Cobra beer or stick to wine.'

'No, a bottle of Cobra would suit me fine. More refreshing.'

There was a moment's pause. Tony looked over at Cathy's familiar face. They had spent a great deal of time together in the last year, on a purely professional basis, of course. DI Norton did not pair people off for good. He liked to mix and match to keep his officers on their toes, but Tony had shared more cases with Cathy than with anyone else and he was warming to her company. He had booked single rooms but asked that they be next to each other. After all. Who knows? He cleared his throat.

'So, do you ever wish you weren't alone Cathy?'

'Where did that come from?' Cathy grinned. 'Don't let the sea, sand and scenery give you any romantic notions, Tony. It'll take more than a bottle of Cobra to do that.'

'Maybe we should've had a bottle of wine,' Tony replied, his eyes laughing at her.

'Maybe not!' Cathy replied. 'Relationships and police-work go together like oysters and beef burgers. They just don't from my experience. Let's not even go there.'

'Do you like Jersey any more this visit?' Tony changed tack as they tucked into their meal, not noticing someone peering at them through the restaurant window.

'I'm warming to it. I like this area and the bay but I can still see St Helier in the distance so I'll reserve judgment until after tomorrow.'

'I won't ask you again until the flight home then, after we've been over the headland to the other bays.'

'That's if I get over those hills on a bicycle and don't give up and cycle back,' Cathy chuckled. 'I left my cycling days behind me when I was 21 and got the motor bike. Far more civilised.'

After supper they walked along the harbour's edge, enjoying the ambience of the gentle night life, and then returned to their B & B.

'See you at 8 o'clock for breakfast then,' Cathy smiled, already grasping her door handle for a quick escape.

'Night cap?' Tony's eyes pleaded.

'Not tonight,' replied Cathy, catching his hand and giving it a quick squeeze.

'Promises,' winked Tony as she closed the door in his face and he sighed. 'Maybe tomorrow,' he whispered to the closed door.

The next day, Saturday, they followed the taxi driver's advice and hired a couple of bikes. The two miles along the sea front to St Helier was flat and would be a gentle introduction to their jaunt the following day.

Time in the archives and the library sped by as they scrolled though old newspapers to get a picture of Lucille Vardon and what happened to her. They checked out the more recent news archives for anything about Anna and her family, and as these were all on computer they were easier to track down. They discovered little new but it was late afternoon before they reclaimed their bikes and headed back along the bay. Twice during the day Cathy got the feeling they were being watched. Once in the library she glanced over her shoulder but there was no one there. About half way along the bay she looked back and about half a mile away she was convinced she could see the same cyclist, but she did not say anything to Tony. In fact, when they stopped to ring Anna to arrange to meet, Cathy noticed that the cyclist stopped to answer her phone at the same time. Coincidence? She did not think so.

That night they found a little sea food restaurant and Tony ordered oysters for them for a starter.

'You know what they say about oysters,' he grinned at her.

'What do they say about oysters?' Cathy asked in mock ignorance.

'Ah well. That would be telling.' And he topped up her glass with a light cool Chablis.

'Umm French wine and seafood. I'm in heaven!' exclaimed Cathy.

'To Jersey,' she toasted.

'To us,' replied Tony, his fingers brushing hers as their glasses chinked.

The wine had its effect because by the time they left the restaurant they were giggling their way up the slope arm in arm.

'Night cap?' Tony's ever hopeful plea as they stumbled up the stairs.

'Just a little one then,' replied Cathy, following Tony into his room.

He looked back over his shoulder raising his eyebrows as he turned the key in the lock.

'Can't play hard to get forever,' he said.

Their need for each other was so great that they were removing each other's clothes in a frenzy of excitement.

'Damn,' exclaimed Tony in the dark, as he got his arm stuck in his sweatshirt.

Cathy giggled as she eased his broad bare shoulders free.

'Calm down, we have all night,' she whispered huskily as she stroked his bare torso.

Tony relaxed under the spell of her finger tips, no longer afraid that Cathy might change her mind. He bent down and as he sucked her nipples she cried out.

'Shhh,' he said. 'You'll wake the other guests,' as he reached down and pulled off her panties and searched for the place which would please her more. Soon they were both naked under the covers and he slipped into her willing and waiting body.

It was daylight when Cathy woke up and feeling disorientated, she sat up. Tony was standing naked by the kettle pouring out two cups of tea. She pulled the covers around her neck.

'There's no need to go all shy on me now m'lady. How would you like your tea? Milk and no sugar I believe.'

He put her cup of tea down and sitting on the edge of the bed stroked a stray hair out of her eyes.

'I've wanted to do that for a very long time,' he said.

'Is that really why you brought me away?' she asked defensively.

'Partly; but I really think we'd be good together, you and I.'

'Don't you think it'll get in the way? Compromise our work in some way. Be awkward at the station.' Cathy paused. 'Shouldn't we just forget it happened and I'll slip back to my room?' She started to move away.

Tony said nothing but leaned forward and kissed her on the lips. They sank into each others' arms, answering the questions in a way that only their bodies could.

They had a leisurely breakfast before setting off on a more strenuous cycle ride towards the cafe where they had arranged to meet Anna at St Quen. Pausing by the harbour Tony unfolded the map.

'Let's take a detour to Portelet Common and St Brelade,' suggested Cathy.

'We could call in at The Smugglers for an early lunch then.'

'You and your food! We've only just had an enormous breakfast.'

'You've got to keep a man's strength up after all this activity.'

'And I imagine you're not just talking about the cycling.' Cathy nudged Tony and he clowned around, pretending to fall off his bike. A car tooted behind them.

'Watch here, you. Catch me if you can.' Then he sped off leaving the harbour and Cathy behind him. He took a narrow lane, with two hair-pin bends at a pace before a steep incline straightened out. By the time he had reached the lane at the top he was out of breath and Cathy passed him at the junction without a second glance, holding her hand up behind her in a victory salute.

'What kept you?' she grinned as Tony came to a halt beside her.

'Just admiring the view,' laughed Tony.

They left their bikes chained together and took the stroll across the common.

'Wow,' exclaimed Cathy looking out towards St Brelade's Bay. 'I wish we were here for longer.'

'The history of the place shouts at you doesn't it, though the reminders of war blend in somehow. They don't spoil it as you'd think they might.'

Cathy sat down on the concrete edge of one of the defences of Noirmont Point and took a deep breath. 'I can imagine this is paradise for an ornithologist but for Anna to have anything to do with the murder just doesn't stack up to me, despite the coincidences. How did she sound when you spoke to her?'

'A bit annoyed to be truthful. But then, so would I be if I knew I'd been followed all the way to Jersey.'

Cathy looked across the bay and she was sure she could see the cyclist she saw yesterday looking in their direction through some binoculars.

'Tony, look over there.'

Just then the cyclist disappeared behind the sea wall. Her bike must have been leaning there because seconds later they could just see the girl cycling off through the car park but then the hotel buildings hid her from view.

'Do you think we should involve the local police in the interview?'

'I don't think there's much point at this stage. Let's just see what she says. Come on. We've got quite a way to go yet.'

Their bikes flew down to the bay with the wind behind them and did not stop until they had cycled over the next headland and down to Le Braye. They did not notice a bike in the far distance as it veered right over the brow of another hill.

Cathy and Tony were relieved to reach the cafe at St Quen's Bay, where they had arranged to meet Anna, and they ordered a coffee and crab sandwiches and waited expectantly.

By the time they had finished their lunch Anna was over half an hour late so they ordered two ice creams. Another twenty minutes went by and Tony reached for his phone and redialled the number but there was no reply.

'Phone her home,' Cathy prompted.

As Tony was obviously speaking to Anna's mum his frown spread between his forehead and his chin, in a scrunched up empty crisp packet sort of way.

'She's gone,' he said flatly as he turned off his phone. 'She left an apology for us but there was an emergency and she had to get over to Alderney a week early.'

'Why's she going to Alderney?'

'Something about puffins. I'm not quite sure to be honest.'

'Talk about wild geese. What do we do now?'

'We could try to fly home via Alderney. Not sure how though.'

The following evening Tony met Cathy at Southampton Airport. They had decided that only Cathy would do the detour via Alderney since it meant changing at Guernsey.

She slumped into the car seat, leaning back on the head rest and sighed.

'How did you get on?' he asked.

'I arrived on the island about midday. It's like going back in time, cobbled streets, Georgian houses. Pretty though. I thought I'd have plenty of time to locate Anna since the whole island is only three miles long, so I asked for the taxi driver to drop me off at the town. Town! Pouf! It's just a large village really. Anyway, I asked in the Alderney Centre if they could help me.

"Oh yes" the helpful man said. "We know who you mean. The Anna Beret you're talking about was dropped off on the island of Burhou a couple of hours ago."

Well, I knew Alderney was small, but didn't expect to find her so quickly, so I asked how I could get over to Burhou to speak to her. "You can't," the helpful gentleman told me. "Only designated people are allowed on the island when the puffins are in residence. The lady who was doing the Puffin Watch over there until yesterday was taken sick and so they asked Anna to step in early." So I asked how I could get in touch with her, since she didn't seem to answer her mobile.

"She won't," the man explained gently, as if I was a slow learner. "She only puts her phone on in emergencies. There's no electricity out there you see, so she needs to conserve the battery. Also, it might disturb the birds. Life has to be as natural as it can be."

He must have seen the incredulous expression on my face. "Don't worry," he said. "She'll be in touch at the weekend to let us know if there's anything she needs and that she's OK. Who shall I say called?" This was said as if I'd just popped to the next village back home, rather than do a detour which had required two extra flights!

Anyway, I thanked the man and wrote my name and number on the slip of paper he proffered.

Then he suggested I saw a bit of Alderney and go on a nature walk towards Burhou. Since I had nothing else to do before my evening flight I joined the small group. Beautiful it was, although a bit surreal. A few minutes out of the town and we were heading down a lane passing an enormous fort on the hill, Fort Tourgis, I think the guide said, not pronouncing the 's.' They've restored some of the fort so that you can visit it but part of the building has been turned into some kind of holiday complex too, but it still holds most of its original features. Across from here we could see the island of Burhou quite close. I made my excuses not to continue with the group tour and sat on a bench for a while just looking out. I thought I could just make out a figure looking back towards me through binoculars, but maybe that's my overactive imagination.'

'We're no further forward then?' Tony asked.

'Indeed we're not,' Cathy replied. 'Anna's going to be out of contact for at least four weeks so unless we have firm evidence to bring her in, then there's nothing we can do about it.'

'What's your instinct on Anna, Cathy?'

'Well, I think she's is innocent. She could be trying to avoid us on purpose but I don't think so. She appears nervous about something and I wonder what it is?'

'What a life though? Out there I mean, incommunicado for four weeks without even electricity.'

'Indeed, Tony - it is.' She paused. 'Do you mind if I have a cat nap while you drive us home? I'm exhausted.'

'Be my guest.'

Occasionally he glanced over at Cathy's sleeping form wondering whether their fling had meant anything to her. If it did not, how could they retrieve a good working relationship? He had certainly missed her, he knew that, but what was she thinking?

That night, on Burhou, Anna breathed a sigh of relief. She listened to the comforting sound of the wind and the sea crashing on the rocks. She breathed in deeply and could smell the salt in the air and that fresh seaweed scent of a new high tide. She thought of the puffins, her main companions on this little island and smiled as she attempted to count them in her mind's eye. She could not be further from her nightmares of late of desert sands, drab uniforms, intensive battle and vultures circling overhead. She knew little of World War One but did not want to know either.

No one can reach me now, she thought.

CHAPTER 26

June 2019   Joanna decides to go home to the farm

It was just over a month since Joanna had set eyes on her home. Emily had tried every tactic to stall this moment, preferring her mother to remain with her, retreating from a reality which could only reawaken her nightmares.

'I must go home Em. I don't know what I would have done without you, but I must pick up the pieces of my life.'

'But Mother,' Emily had exclaimed. She only used the formal form in sheer frustration. 'It's much too soon. Shouldn't you think about what's ahead of you first?'

'No, Em. I need to go home to see if I can face it all. I can't hide out here forever.' Joanna was insistent.

Emily's car crawled slowly over the gravel and came to a standstill. What struck Joanna most was the ever changing nature of the world she called home. She remembered the morning of her departure vividly as if reliving each moment as a still in the movie which was once her life. Her son had done that enough times; captured a moment on a video, frozen in time, maybe not as clear as an individual photograph but nonetheless unique.

Her eyes scanned over a field of wheat, the differences imperceptible to an untrained eye. It was now a blanket of soft green, almost pastel in the sunlight. In a few weeks it would be yellow like a rippling sandy shore, before it finally turned to gold. Joanna could imagine Bob brushing his palms gently over the tips as if stroking a beloved pet, smiling in reassurance at the tickling sensation of the ears against his skin. It should be a good harvest; he would come in and say, giving her a squeeze as she stood with her Marigold-gloved hands in the sink.

Today Joanna sat in the front seat of the car, unable to move, hardly aware of Emily coming around to hold the door open for her.

'We could go back home if it's too much for you,' she said with concern. She had dreaded this moment and even last night she and her husband talked well past midnight, discussing the dangers of her mother returning too soon, if at all, against their own needs for a life of their own.

They walked slowly to the farmhouse, Joanna's hand resting through Emily's arm, the yellow and black tape denoting a crime scene had long since been removed. Emily spotted a shadow at the window and felt an overwhelming sense of relief to know that Helen was there before them. Helen put up her hand and Emily knew that this was more for reassurance than a wave of welcome.

As they entered the open farmhouse door Joanna was simultaneously dismayed and relieved that her kitchen was spotlessly clean - leaving her vivid memories of the morning when she had left a distant nightmare. Spinning in that perception of reality, halfway between truth and fiction, she fainted. Emily just caught her arm before she knocked herself headlong on the farmhouse table. Helen rushed to Emily's aid and they gently laid Joanna on the farmhouse floor in the recovery position.

As Joanna regained consciousness a few moments later at first she was disorientated, unsure where she was.

'You shouldn't have brought her back here.' The unusually sharp voice of her father-in-law Peter drifted down to where she lay.

'It's only natural that she'd want to come home Peter,' soothed Helen.

'She's got nothing here,' replied Peter. 'I hope you'll take her straight home Em. She doesn't belong here.'

'I hope you're not implying Mum's guilty Grandpa. Surely you believe her don't you?'

'I've got work to do but when I come back I don't want to see her here, do you hear,' Peter pointed his finger at the figure lying in a heap and he stormed out.

'He doesn't mean it I'm sure,' said Helen, ever the diplomat. 'He's understandably upset. We thought there would be a trial to go one way or the other.' Helen glanced up and saw Emily frown. 'You know Em,' she added quickly. 'It would have cleared her name. After all, the police must have had evidence and they had Sally as a witness too. Oh what a mess they've made of things!'

Joanna groaned, making them aware that she was awake.

'Come on Mum,' Emily encouraged. 'Let's get you back home. I think that's enough for one day don't you think. Maybe when you're stronger?'

Helen handed Joanna a glass of water as she sat down opposite her at the kitchen table. Joanna shivered.

'It's the shock Mum. Drink up and we'll go.'

After a pause, when it was obvious that Joanna had no inclination to stir, Helen looked carefully at her employer and was shocked to see how Joanna had aged. Her cheeks were sunken and her long, once enviably graceful fingers fleshless and wiry.

'Have a cup of tea before you go,' she said.

As they drank tea, Joanna half listened to the conversation between Helen and Emily about her brother and other events in the village. She started to take in every detail of her surroundings as if looking at them for the first time. There was the tall dresser with plates, dishes and mugs adorned with cockerels. She could not remember its name but it was not cheap, a wedding present from her parents who had embraced her life as a farmer's wife wholeheartedly. There was that lucky charm of Chinese pigs hanging on the carved post at the end. Bob was born in the Year of the Pig, they had been told by one of her college friends.

The drawers, she knew, were stuffed full with cloth napkins they never used and table cloths, likewise. In the next one there would be a multitude of obsolete timetables, programmes, take away menus, guarantees and leaflets, from way back into the last century.

No one used them these days. Everything was carried out on Futurenet, that unseen virtual world. Why had she kept them? The drawer was closed but she knew it was all there. A tangible reminder of treats when the children were tiny, of trips to London, Indian meals delivered, instructions for the old fashioned toaster when the bread popped up in varying shades of golden to dark brown. Now they put bread in a slot above the built in cooker. It cooked the toast to perfection and remained so for several minutes until you were ready to collect it, still perfect to melt the butter. Only ever real butter was eaten in this household though. Jersey butter at that.

Next her eyes rested on the kitchen table. There was the breadboard, worn with age, along with its carved ears of corn. Slid into the side of the board was a familiar serrated bread knife, also with a carved handle. Joanna pulled it out, but suddenly her hands went cold and clammy and the blood drained from her face as she remembered. She thrust the knife back in its place.

Joanna got up, wanting desperately not to faint again. Emily had been so engrossed in the conversation she had not noticed the change in her mother's complexion.

'Ready to go?' Emily asked in surprise.

'Em, I know you mean well but I've decided to stay. I need to think through what's happened and it's only here that I can piece together what happened and try to see if there's anything I've forgotten.'

Helen looked shocked momentarily, but then regained her composure and smiled at Emily as if talking about a child,

'I'll look after you, Joanna. Peter asked me if I'd move in here just after the police arranged to have the place cleaned. It saves me paying rent in the village too, although I haven't moved all my stuff as yet.'

Emily's look of relief was instant. Maybe her mother was right. She had to face her ghosts sometime and as long as there was someone to keep an eye on her, it would be quite good for her own family to have some space, even if it was only for a few days. 'If you're sure Mum?' she asked.

'Of course. I'll be fine, especially with Helen to keep me company. I'll speak to you on the phone. That husband of yours will be pleased to have you to himself for a change.'

Emily kissed her mum on the forehead. 'Any time you change your mind, let me know and I'll come and fetch you.'

'Thanks for everything Em.'

Once Emily had left, Joanna felt consumed by tiredness.

'I'm just going up to have a lie down, Helen, and thanks for being here.'

'No problem,' Helen smiled.

Joanna had nothing in her head when she opened the bedroom door and sank down on to the familiar bed. Clean sheets, was her last thought as she drifted into a deep sleep.

When she woke up she felt for the reassurance of home. She reached over but was suddenly overwhelmed by a sense of grief that there was not even a comforting familiar smell of Bob's existence on the pillow and between the sheets. Surely a widow deserved that one luxury, like a child's comforter. What did her mother call it? 'An umm blanket,' Because Joanna had always made a humming noise when she had cuddled hers as a baby and had refused to go to sleep without it. Like a frustrated child, she wept tears of anguish, gulping air as she sobbed.

As she came to she was dreaming of one of her childhood games, Cluedo. It was Christmas and she was about six years old. She was sitting around the table with her sister, mum and dad, holding a set of cards in her hand. Miss Scarlet, Kitchen and Knife, they read.

'Miss Scarlet in the kitchen with a knife,' her sister had exclaimed triumphantly. 'You're the murderer, Joanna!'

'No, no, no,' she had screamed. 'Oh no I'm not!'

'Oh yes you are,' joined in her dad, in true pantomime style.

'I'm not,' Joanna had sobbed just as her mother had come over to comfort her.

'Shush, shush,' she had soothed. 'It's only a game.'

Joanna woke up. Helen was standing over her with a tray of tea, ham sandwiches and a piece of homemade fruit cake.

'You're an angel,' Joanna said as she pushed herself up in bed, propping a pillow behind her head.

Helen sat on the chair next to Joanna's side of the bed and talked while Joanna ate.

'It's too soon Joanna. Coming home. You've had such a shock. To be honest with you I know you'll find it almost unbearable. Unreal at times.' Helen's eyes clouded over with the memory of the anguish she too had suffered so very recently and she looked down into her lap, fiddling absentmindedly with a stray thread on the edge of her blouse. 'I know what it's like losing someone who's your whole world, but you've still got Emily and Paul and baby Jemima too of course. I should focus on them if I were you.' Helen's face contorted in a grimace. She paused for a few moments looking across at Joanna, waiting for a response but when there was none she added, 'I don't think you should be alone though.'

They both heard the sound of cows leaving the milking parlour. Half past five... Bob would be...Reality returned, pressing against Joanna's brain like a throbbing migraine.

'Drink the rest of your tea,' Helen encouraged. 'I've put some sugar in it.'

Joanna drank and soon she felt inexplicable sleepy again so Helen took the tray from her.

'Get some more rest Joanna. It's all too much for you to handle.'

The doctor came in the following morning and said much the same as Helen.

'Rest. Take your time. The body will be exhausted as the mind and spirit are trying desperately to heal. It's understandable. Nothing to worry about.'

Over the next few days Joanna did just that. One day she came down into the kitchen at midday to find Peter sat at the table with Helen, tucking in to ham and eggs.

'Madelyn's not feeling too good today so Helen's giving her a break,' he said, by way of an apology. Joanna knew that for Madelyn to be feeling under the weather was nothing new. Ever since she came into the life of the farm all those years ago, every now and again Madelyn had taken to her bed leaving Joanna to run both homes and it had been far easier for Peter to join her family for meals. Joanna would go over to the farmhouse, with two young children in tow, to tempt Madelyn with delicious homemade snacks. Often Helen would stay on at the farmhouse, bringing Kirsty with her for a few days and run the kitchen like clockwork, fitting naturally into the rhythm of farm life.

'Would you like anything?' Helen asked.

'No, don't worry Helen. I'm not hungry. I'm just popping down to the Post Office. It's time I got out into the village.' Joanna stopped in her tracks though, when she saw Bob's Wellington boots in the porch. Taking a deep breath she marched past them keeping her eyes forward and got into her car for the first time in several weeks. It felt so strange.

She drove down the familiar track to the lane and up to the village, where she parked behind the post van. As soon as she walked into the store, usually the hub of village gossip, everyone went quiet. After a second, which felt a lifetime to Joanna, Sally shrugged and, looking back at Kiram behind the counter, she walked out without giving Joanna a second glance. Joanna bought some first class stamps before she fled to the security of her car where she noticed that Sally had waited for her. Joanna pushed the window button.

'I don't know how you have the nerve to come back here as if nothing has happened. You're not wanted here,' the post woman said before striding back to her van and speeding off down Silver End Road.

Stunned, Joanna sat gazing towards the disappearing red van, then noticing two more familiar faces she pressed the ignition, turned one hundred and eighty degrees in one go without even looking to see if the road was clear and sped off in the opposite direction, Sally's words echoing in her head.

As Joanna drove she closed that page of her brain down, locking the memory away, to protect her conscious mind. What could she focus on? Could she find any purpose in life again? Could she ever begin to make sense of the inexplicable?

She was soon back at the farmhouse, determined to get back in the office to begin to sort the month's paperwork she imagined had piled up in her absence. As she opened the office door for the first time she could not hide her surprise to find Helen sat at her desk, working diligently on the computer. She experienced a flashback of Helen standing at that very door, her face gaunt and vacant, drained of spent emotions. Was that only a few weeks ago?

Helen looked up. 'Paul showed me what to do. Someone had to keep the books up to date and Madelyn wouldn't do it. I wasn't expecting you to come in here today Joanna. You don't need to worry about this for a while and I'm sure you'd rather rest.'

'That's kind of you Helen, but it's best to be busy. Time goes quicker that way.'

'Let me make a cuppa then and we'll sit down in the kitchen and have a chat.' Helen asked getting to her feet, her eyes full of concern.

Joanna was startled, remembering with shame her own glib words. She fought back tears, just resisting the temptation to flee upstairs.

'I understand how you feel, Joanna,' Helen continued after a moment. 'Just do what you feel you can cope with and I'll do the rest, but I'm always here if you'd like company.'

Joanna stepped back into the hall letting the door shut of its own accord. She stood shivering, the echoing conversation like the needling pain of a migraine - benign words said in honest concern thrown back at her. How could she have been so utterly thoughtless? She stood bereft, mourning her husband, but also her former life that had made her so insensitive to the needs of others.

'What goes around comes around,' her mother used to say.

Absentmindedly she walked across the yard to the bungalow, a place that only held happy memories of their growing family in a world cramped full of love and laughter. Over the next few days her life fell into a sort of routine. Waking late morning she would spend lunch with Madelyn in companionable silence. They enjoyed a light snack, not the meal Peter expected after a long morning's hard work and so she did not question that Peter left them alone as Helen prepared a meal for him over at the farmhouse.

They spent their afternoons making marmalade, chutney and jam for the village fete or tending the small enclosed garden out the back. It was a haven of peace surrounded by hedges high enough to hide the farm and woodland behind, but low enough so that the sun still streamed into the darkest corners at some point through the day. On wet days they even resorted to doing a jigsaw puzzle, sewing rag dolls or making quilted cushions.

It was an unspoken agreement that she would return to the farmhouse at about 5 pm, just as Peter was engrossed in the milking. Their paths rarely crossed. In the early evening at about six, Helen prepared them a simple supper but they spoke very little. It was a strange twilight world and yet even this new familiarity was oddly comforting. Soon after supper she would head for bed, on rare occasions watching the seven o'clock news first as she used to do with Bob.

She never left the vicinity of the farm. Every few days that kind policewoman Cathy would pop by with an update, usually to say that there was little new development but that they were piecing the jigsaw together, albeit slowly.

Also, once a week, Emily would call by with Jemima, although she phoned her mother most days too, remembering to ring at lunchtimes when she knew her mother would be awake. Once she called in at supper time. Her mother-in-law had asked if she could look after the baby, who was now over four months old, and her husband was going to be late.

'I don't know what we would have done without you, Helen,' she said as Helen carried the tray of coffee through to the lounge, passing her mother a mug covered in flamboyant bohemian dancing ladies. She picked up her own 'I Love France' mug, bought on a school trip years ago and passed a 'Home Sweet Home' mug to Helen.

'Yes, she's an angel,' Joanna added as she clicked on the remote control.

Ten minutes later Joanna made a move to go to bed as she had a habit of doing. It was only 7.15 pm. Emily frowned. 'Can't you stay up a few minutes longer Mum, since I'm here?'

Joanna sat back down again, but it was obviously an effort to keep awake and she only half listened to Helen and Emily chattering to each other.

'Mother,' Emily shouted. 'You nodded off. If you're that tired then maybe you should go up.'

'It's understandable Emily, after what your mother's gone through,' Helen said. 'She's still in shock you see.'

Emily's face softened, 'Oh I know. I'm sorry I snapped,' and she got up to give her mother a peck on the cheek. 'Goodnight, Mum,' she said lightly. 'See you next week.'

As Joanna walked out of the room, leaving the door ajar, she heard their whispering voices but she was too tired to be concerned. All she worried about at that moment was getting to her room, undressing and in bed before sleep engulfed her. The next thing she knew she was waking up, the light streaming through the window and the day had already long started, much like the day before and the one before that.

One day she paused on the landing, as she often had done over the years, her eyes drawn to the field of winter barley close to harvesting. The individual plants nearest to her stretched tall, each at virtually identical heights, their ears bowing slightly under the weight of the grain. As her eyes lifted upwards the image softened into a single fabric of golden brown, the ears giving the luxurious texture of a woollen garment skirting the edge of the field until it dipped away from view in the far right hand corner. Memories wrapped around Joanna.

The first time Bob had made love to her was at the edge of this very same field, but that year it had been wheat, ears bulging with ripeness. They had enjoyed a picnic, not from a posh wicker hamper but from a Woolworths carrier bag, though Bob had spread an old tartan car rug beneath them, parting stems of wheat at their secluded corner of the field, in a slight dip, an incline invisible even from the upstairs farmhouse windows. They had eaten their sandwiches in silence, both of them full of anticipation to the sweet dessert which filled Bob and Joanna's imagination. The heat of that early August afternoon only enhanced their desire until Bob could wait no longer. He took the half eaten sandwich from Joanna's hand, just as it had reached her lips and in a swoop he replaced it with his lips. Joanna had swallowed in surprise her mouth opening to his. Slowly she had felt his hand undo the minute buttons of her white broderie anglaise blouse and he laid her down with a subtlety Joanna never knew he possessed.

Joanna's eyes had closed, enjoying the sensations of his hand caressing her bra, but they opened momentarily as his free hand slid beneath her long ethnic skirt, seeking her private place within its folds, stroking gently up her leg before parting her panties. She gasped as he knew she would and all she could see above his head was the wheat swaying beneath a clear deep-blue sky.

This first occasion was so memorable, feeling the heat of the sun on his bare back, their bodies as ripe as the bulging wheat above their heads. Afterwards, it seemed the most natural thing in the world to lay flat on their backs, Adam and Eve-like staring up at the sky through the swaying wheat. After several moments of satisfied contentment Bob had reached up and picked a single stem and, leaning on one elbow staring down at her, he had stroked her body with the hair-like tip, starting on her forehead, across her nose and lips, down her throat, between her breasts, her nipples deep burgundy and full, across her tummy, flat in those days, and towards her private parts. It tickled and she giggled at first, but then she shivered as a tingling sensation filled her whole being, and all the while he watched her. Joanna made to sit up but Bob gently pushed her back.

'Shh.' Bob whispered as he pulled three more ears, expertly weaving the stem around it to make a brooch.

Fascinated she watched his fingers work, oblivious to her nakedness and her clothing strewn beside her. Next he wove three more fine stems, plaiting them together, cutting the stems with a pen knife he had retrieved from his shorts pocket and looping them almost seamlessly back into the whole to form a small loop.

Finally he stretched over to lift her left hand towards him, bringing her fingers to his lips and kissing each one. She was mesmerised as he slipped the ring on to her second finger, kissing it.

'You are my harvest bride, Joanna!' was all he had said. No proposal on bended knee. No waiting for an answer. No meeting her parents first. Bob had taken it for granted that Joanna would agree. A refusal would never have entered his head as even a possibility. He had dressed her then, almost as gently as he had undressed her, no embarrassing vibes between them, before they had strolled back through the spinney and in to the farmhouse to announce their engagement.

For years afterwards Joanna had worn that ring at any snatched moment of the day when she knew they would not be disturbed. Bob never took her back to that spot in the corner of the field, it had been a rare moment of spontaneity, but on many occasions they had raced to their bedroom and enjoyed pleasures on their king sized farmhouse antique oak bed!

On one occasion Joanna remembered forgetting to remove the ring before the children came in for tea and Paul had asked why she was wearing that 'dirty old thing.' That was just before Joanna's 30th birthday. She rarely got surprises. It was not in Bob's nature. She was usually given something functional such as a new toaster or a dress if she was lucky, but that year Bob gave her the most exquisite golden brooch of three ears of wheat entwined. Joanna was speechless as she looked up at Bob, so touched was she by his thoughtfulness after all their years together. Bob had winked at her, gesturing upstairs with his eyes and Joanna had thanked him with a long, loving kiss.

'Yuk,' Paul then eight had exclaimed.

Joanna smiled at the memory and retracing her steps up to her bedroom she searched in the top drawer of her bedside cabinet of antique pine, matching the bed head. She soon found a small green jewellery box. She owned precious few items of jewellery, but as she removed the box she smiled to see a small frayed purple handkerchief at the back of the drawer.

Joanna gently eased it out of its hiding place. It must have been at least ten years since she had done so. She held her breath, half expecting dusty broken fragments to fall out. As she carefully unfolded the layers of the hanky, matching fabric to the skirt she had been wearing that hot August day, she gasped! The straw ring and miniature sheath of wheat fell into her palm, lack lustre and greying with age but to Joanna they were perfect. A single tear fell on to the handkerchief to be absorbed almost without trace like the grief still buried inside her.

CHAPTER 27

July 2019

Unlike Emily, Paul only came home twice that summer. One morning Joanna was getting dressed when she heard talking from Paul's bedroom. As far as she knew he had not brought a girl home the previous night and usually her son would allow no one else to enter his sanctuary when he was at home. He even had a sign, 'Genius in Residence,' which he hooked on the door on the peg which used to hold the words 'Paul's Den' for years. It was a standing joke that for the first few months of his literate life Paul would always write an 's' on the end of his name with a little fish just above it. When his teacher had pointed the odd pattern of learning out to them at parents' evening, they had laughed.

Paul's door was open and he looked up when he noticed his mum.

'Helen's a whiz kid on this machine Mum. She could teach you a thing or two,' he said.

Helen glanced up at Joanna, obvious pride written in her eyes.

'I'll let you get on Paul. I know you've work to do,' said Helen winking at Paul, who laughed with an ease of two people in harmony.

Joanna tried to remain at the farmhouse while her son was home but found that she missed Madelyn's undemanding company. Peter too remained distant during this time. Paul usually went over to the bungalow if he wanted to speak with his grandparents. Joanna never questioned these things as strange. They were just part of the new order. Often when she came down Paul and Helen were deep in conversation, which stopped the moment she entered the room. It was not that she felt excluded but reasoned that she was almost marginalised of her own volition. She did not notice that she felt more alert and slept less during his visits.

On the first night after Paul had left for Exeter, Joanna was woken up at midnight and heard noises from Helen's room. At first she thought Helen was calling out but when she went to the bathroom she realised the indisputable fact that Helen must have a man in her bedroom. When she woke up the following lunchtime she threw on some clothes to go and talk to Madelyn about it, but on seeing her daughter's car outside she hesitated, hearing her mother-in-law's pleading voice,

'Take your mum home Em. She's really not well.'

'I *am* worried that she sleeps half the day but Helen says..'

'Pouf! Don't listen to what Helen says, listen to me Em. The farm isn't the right place for her at the moment.' Then Madelyn's tone softened, 'It would give your mum a chance to heal a bit. She never leaves the farm at all and it's not healthy, Em. Can't you see that?'

'She won't listen to me, Grandma. I've tried so many times. Maybe she should go for a holiday.'

At that point Joanna strolled into the kitchen,

'Maybe I *should* go away for a while. Have a holiday.'

Her mother-in-law and daughter looked at her in astonishment, but ignoring the guilty fact that Joanna had eavesdropped on their conversation. Emily warmed to the idea.

'Where would you like to go Mum?'

'Greece I think. I'll go to one of those smaller islands just off the mainland. I've always wanted to, but you know your father,' and she turned on her heels and walked quickly back over to the farmhouse.

Neither daughter nor mother-in-law had the courage to remind Joanna that the police might not take too kindly to her going out of the country. They looked at each other knowingly.

'Do you think I'd better call the police, Gran - before she books something?'

'That's a good idea. Use our phone if you like. I've got a number for that nice detective, Cathy something. I forget what her other name is. It's in the memory.'

Emily pressed the buttons on the wall pad phone and waited.

'DC Peterson here. How can I help you?'

'Yes, this is Emily, Mrs Joanna Thomas's daughter. I just wanted to let you know that my mother's thinking of taking a trip to Greece. I think it would do her good but I wasn't sure whether she was allowed...'

'Oh Emily. Thank you for letting us know. I'll check with DS Akhtar and get back to you. Can I get you on that number?'

'That's fine. You can leave a message with my grandma here and she'll pass it on.'

'Leave it with me and I'll let you know today. OK'

'OK thanks,' and Emily closed off the call. She sighed.

'I must get off now Gran. I'll ring you later.'

15th July 2019

Cathy was fearful that the trail for Robert Thomas's murder was going cold. She was niggled that they had had so many confusing, time consuming leads. That morning she was at her desk when she was surprised to have a message that Anna from Jersey was waiting to speak to them in the lobby. She led Anna to an interview room and within moments Saima had joined her.

'I came as soon as I could,' Anna started to explain. 'I'm sorry I rushed off like that but I had an emergency call. It's my dissertation, you see. If I'd missed this opportunity to go to stay on Burhou my plans would have to be kept on hold for a whole year.'

'Why didn't you let us know?' asked Cathy.

Anna blushed. 'I didn't have the time, truly.' She looked up at Cathy's quizzical expression but continued. 'It was all a bit of a rush and I was on Burhou before I thought of you. I was looking over towards Alderney in fact.'

'You saw me, didn't you?'

'Yes, I think I did. I felt a bit guilty then, realising that you'd chased after me but there was nothing I could do about it. I couldn't communicate with anyone except in an emergency.'

'We heard,' Saima attempted to keep the impatience from her voice. 'So what have you come to tell us today? I'm actually in charge of the case now.'

Anna turned her attention to DS Akhtar and continued. 'Well, it's just that on the morning of the gathering, you know,

9th May, as I was rushing through the woods back to my bike I knocked myself out. I crashed into a tree. Sounds silly now but I was confused. I can't remember anything until I came to, when I was disorientated and wondered what I was doing there. My mum says I sleep walk sometimes and I was frightened...'

'What were you frightened of? Take your time.'

'Oh, it sounds silly now but in my worst nightmare since I've wondered what I might have done... I've had such bad dreams about it. I have regular dreams about being Lucille you see. It's hard to split reality and fiction at times and I muddle the past and present too. I just wanted you to know the truth.'

'So what *is* the truth Miss Beret?'

'The truth is, I don't really know. During the day I'm fine, but at night my mind races through such visions. I have no idea what the truth is at all!'

Saima looked at Cathy. 'Well, Miss Beret. Thank you for coming in to speak to us. I think that's all for now, but we may need to contact you again. If there's anything else you remember, get straight in touch.' She did not add that she wondered what could be more of an emergency than a murder case.

Anna hesitated.

'Are you sure there's nothing else?' Saima asked, scrutinising Anna's face for clues.

'Well,' Anna paused. 'I received this threatening email but I didn't know what to do about it. Whether to show it to you or not?'

'You could be charged for withholding evidence,' snapped Saima, taking the print out from Anna's outstretched arm.

Momentarily Anna looked distraught. Saima and Cathy glanced down.

'KEEP QUIET AND YOUR LIFE WILL BE SAFE,' it said.

'Keep quiet about what, do you think Miss Beret?' Saima asked.

'I've really no idea,' replied Anna.

'Do you think you know who murdered Lucille back in 1919 Miss Beret?' Saima continued to probe.

'I think it might have been the farmer's son, but no one really knows,' replied Anna.

'You did the right thing telling us this,' said Cathy, sending a signal to Saima with her finger slightly raised. The interview was formally terminated by Saima.

'We'll look into it and get in touch with you but will you be all right?' Cathy asked as she led Anna back to the lobby.

'Yes, I'll be fine,' Anna replied, a little embarrassed as Paul, Joanna's son came forward and put an arm around her.

'We met at the pub in Clophill last night and Paul helped me to decide to come and speak to you,' Anna explained looking back at Cathy, her eyebrows raised apologetically.

'Are you staying at Broom Cottage?' Cathy asked.

'Yes, I am,' Anna replied as she turned to Paul.

Cathy looked quizzically at Paul, who also reddened, but said nothing as he ushered Anna away.

Later in the canteen Cathy was recounting events to Tony.

'Well, that **was** a surprise, especially Paul's arrival at the station. What do you make of it Tony?'

'It could be just another thing to throw us off the truth.'

'Are we talking about Paul and Anna being an item, the email or Anna's black out?'

'The email of course. Anna's personal life is no concern of ours and I don't believe Anna could murder, even in a sleep walk, but I'll get it checked out through expert psychologists.'

'But doesn't it strike you as odd that one of our suspects is now best friends or more with the victim's son.'

'Nothing surprises me in this case. It's the surprises which will hopefully solve the case.'

'Maybe we'd better get back to Canada and Surrey to ask if they've had any death threats too. If they have then it adds weight to Miss Beret's story, don't you think?'

Both gentlemen were difficult to trace. They spoke to Keith Regmund's wife who said, a little too sharply for Saima, that he could not be contacted.

James Bouchard was also missing. They got in touch with Interpol in Canada and soon the local police were able to confirm that James Bouchard had not only received a similar death threat but that someone had already tried to run him over. The Canadian police informed them that Bouchard was now in hiding.

Next they had confirmation from their contact at Aldershot that the Colonel was indeed in a place of safety but it was only a day later that Saima was called to the front desk because Mrs Regmund had arrived to talk.

'I need to speak to DI Norton,' she demanded.

'I'm afraid he has retired madam. How can we help you?'

At this point Mrs Regmund frowned and turned, about to walk away, but must have had second thoughts. She bent towards the Duty Officer and whispered, 'It's about the murder, you know, the farmer chap. They came to speak with my husband.'

'I will fetch DS Akhtar for you Madam.'

'No,' exclaimed Mrs Regmund. 'It's important that I speak to someone senior.'

'I can assure you that DS Akhtar is the detective overseeing the case at present until our new Inspector takes up the post. Shall I fetch her?'

'I suppose she'll have to do then. I've driven all the way from Surrey and can't return home without talking to someone.'

When DS Akhtar had led her to the interview room Cathy arrived.

'How can we help you Mrs Regmund?' Saima asked.

'Is there any possibility that you could keep that off under the circumstances?' she asked looking towards the recording equipment.

Saima and Cathy looked at one another and Saima nodded.

'It's my husband,' Mrs Regmund continued looking slightly less nervous, but her hands were fidgeting in her lap and her eyes kept flitting down to them. 'He's had a death threat, you see. He didn't want to tell you because of his work.'

She had known that Keith had been using her computer and when he disappeared without saying anything and so she turned it on to see if she could find out why. He would often send a coded message that only she would understand - something innocuous like, '*Don't forget to take Midge to the vet and I'll call you Friday.*' She would know then to get on with the rest of her life until he returned. This time was different. There was no message and unlike her husband's usual meticulous attention to detail, he had left his new inbox logged in. She knew that something was wrong. Sixth sense you'd call it. She clicked on the inbox and, upset by the message she read on the screen, she remembered the phone call and decided that it was time to act.

She stopped and pulled out the now familiar printed message from her large shoulder bag. 'Here, look at this,' she continued and then looking up. 'You don't look at all surprised,' she added.

'Your husband is not the only one who has received one of these,' Saima said. 'We can assure you that we will deal with the matter with the utmost urgency but,'...holding her hand up to stem a reply.... 'We will also use due discretion, considering your husband's position, of course.'

'What do **you** know about my husband's position?'

'Only what he has alluded to himself, Mrs Regmund, and we can assure you that anything either of you or he has said is in confidence.'

'I'd better get back then but.. .' she looked embarrassed momentarily. 'My husband doesn't know I'm here. You do understand?' she trailed off lamely.

'We understand Mrs Regmund. You did the right thing to tell us that your husband's life could be in danger. It will help us tremendously with bringing this case to a conclusion.'

'I couldn't use the phone ...or the Futurenet......I'm not sure it's secure,' Mrs Regmund stuttered.

'Very wise under the circumstances,' Saima smiled. 'Thank you for making the effort to come all this way,'

Saima led Mrs Regmund to the lobby and thanked her again.

Saima and Cathy returned to the case board, and with one tap it sprang to life. Saima scrolled to the Haynes Murder Case whilst Cathy scanned in the new evidence, then they stood back to stare at it.

If these three messages are genuine, then Anna Beret, Keith Regmund and James Bouchard are likely to be innocent aren't they?' She now circled each in yellow rather than orange.

'Who does that leave with no alibi?' asked Saima. 'There's the farmer's son Paul; interesting after Anna's hypothesis about Lucille. Then there's Peter and Madelyn Thomas. Surely they aren't murderers. And Helen; she doesn't seem to have any motive other than Lucille and she seems so supportive of the family too. She's said nothing to try to incriminate Mrs Thomas; in fact the opposite. There is Jake and the two lads in the village. Jake's allegedly gone to Iran and the young lads didn't seem to know anything at all. Then there's Mrs Thomas. It's still one big mystery, isn't it? Any ideas?'

'It's all so confusing,' Cathy replied. 'In some ways there's no real evidence and in others there's a plethora of connected people and facts. We're still missing something vital here. It's so frustrating.'

'I agree,' said Saima. 'Let's call it a day and sleep on it.'

19th July 2019   Joanna

It was Friday. Joanna had booked a trip to Brighton to leave the following Monday by train. The policewoman had taken her passport and said she was not to leave the country but, to be truthful, she did not feel well this morning.

She was picking up the print-out of her ticket which she had dropped when she felt her back go. It was not a sudden pain, just a steady progressive ache until she had to sit down and once down she could not get up again. She took a deep breath. This was silly. She was sure she had not lifted anything or moved in a poor way. She practiced Pilates and her posture was pretty good.

The phone rang but to reach it all Joanna could do was gingerly sink on to her hands and knees and crawl, little by little, towards it. It stopped, of course, the moment she pressed the receive button.

Using 'return call' she reached her daughter.

'Mum, there you are. I was worried about you. Are you OK?'

'Don't worry about me,' Joanna lied. 'I was in the bathroom.'

'Can you come over and stay a couple of nights Mum? It's just that Brian's called and he wants me to go to a do after work with him. It would be nice for you to spend some quality time with Jemima and then with both of us tomorrow. We miss you and we'd love to see you before your trip. Are you there Mum?'

Joanna had put the phone down on the floor in an attempt to find a position where she felt no pain but failed, but she did not want her daughter rushing over in a panic. She longed to say yes and be with Emily and Jemima, away from the farm but in her present state she was going no-where. She quickly made up an excuse.

'Look Emily, I'd love to come, but I promised Helen I'd be here tonight to go over the books. She's virtually taken them over from me, since she knows so much about computers, but she wants me to explain a few things.'

Joanna could hear Emily sigh and knew her daughter did not take no for an answer easily.

'I'm not sure about Helen taking over the farm's finances, Mum. After all, she was only your cleaner and you need a purpose in life.' What Emily did not say was that she did not trust Helen. She had seen Helen acting inappropriately with her grandfather in the barn and when she had rushed over to tell her gran, the response she had got was,

'I don't want to hear anything about it Emily, from you of all people. How dare you blame your grandfather like that after all he's done for you?'

Despite the anger in her gran's voice, Em was certain she felt more scared than indignant. When her grandfather came in a few minutes later, the look her gran gave Em over his shoulder appeared to implore her to keep quiet, rather than that of annoyance.

There was silence for a few moments until Joanna broke it, deciding to tell the truth.

'To be honest with you Em, I'm not feeling all that great and my back hurts. I'm not sure I **can** drive over to you, even if I was free.'

294

Em's voice softened, 'Have a bit of a rest Mum and an anti-inflammatory pill and I'll ring you back in an hour to see how you are. I could always come to fetch you.'

When Emily had put the phone down she rang John Cookham straight away and he promised to look in on her mother.

Half an hour later John let himself into the farmhouse kitchen and was distraught to find Joanna lying on the floor. She lifted her head and was obviously relieved to see him.

'Thanks John. Can you help me get up?' she pleaded.

She tried to stand but a sheer pain shot through her. John almost had to carry her out to his Jeep to take her to the surgery where the kindly doctor explained that her back was in spasm due to severe stress. Whatever the truth Joanna, was unable to walk and even moving was agony.

Two days later Joanna sat with her eyes closed, barely breathing. The minutes ticked by. She felt a glimmer of sun from the nearby window disappearing behind a cloud and then all she felt was cold. Oh so cold. To let go and give up on life altogether. To stop breathing. She almost felt she could. In that split second all she heard was silence.

She held her breath. Automatically, her shallow breathing resumed. She felt her chest rise and fall. The clock ticked loudly, her heart beating almost in tune with the tick. No one would really miss her, would they? Her daughter had her own family now, her son had his endless gadgets and computers. The farm? The crops would continue to grow without her. She had no part in it now. As her legs had given way, she thought, could she let the rest of her body give up too?

Her ephone made her jump, vibrating in her skirt pocket and without a second thought her hand dived for it, fumbling for the button. Then she saw it was DC Peterson, Cathy, as she asked Joanna to call her. Her finger paused over the button. In that binary decision she could remain in her reverie or hear some more news she did not wish to hear. Yes or No.

The phone sang on..... She bashed the answer button a moment too late and it went on to voice mail, so without thinking she pressed the off button and reached for the anti inflammatory her doctor had prescribed and swallowed it down.

Suddenly Joanna was breathless and nauseous. She reached for the water but could not swallow. She gulped, quick short gasps. No air. Panic.

She passed out into oblivion.

CHAPTER 29

21ˢᵗ July 2019   A break-though in the case

That Sunday, Cathy sat on the bench in the graveyard looking out towards Haynes Park. She had hoped to drop in on Joanna but there had been no reply. She was sure that the answer to the puzzle lay here.

To her left was Lucille Vardon's grave, carefully tended with three rosemary plants at its foot. Further down, nearer the hedge, was the newest grave with only a wooden cross to mark the passing of Robert Thomas, too soon for the stone mason to have completed his work. At the foot of this grave Cathy was surprised to see three small yellow clover-like plants already in place. Without thinking she took a photo before turning to Kirsty Carter's grave, in the shadow of the church tower.

'*Note every little detail,*' Cathy's training clicked in.

This third grave was surrounded by forget me knots but with small deep blue star-like flowers intermingled. Snap. Another shot. She sent the pictures to Saima and then went back to the bench.

It was sunny and the warmth soaked into her. She sighed. It wouldn't hurt to close my eyes for a few moments. She sat there in a trance and time passed. Her mind was blank. She came too with a start when her phone bleeped.

Retrieving it as she walked back to her bike, helmet under her arm, she was not surprised to see that it was Tony's number.

'Everything OK?' she said without thinking. Hardly an appropriate response for an ardent lover.

'Joanna Thomas has been rushed to hospital and is on a life support machine. I'm at Bedford General now. How soon can you meet me here?'

'Fifteen minutes,' Cathy replied, not questioning the fact that it was her day off, or that she and Tony were trying to spend some time apart to gather their thoughts. It was all too soon and confusing. After all they were both married to the force.

She enjoyed the adrenaline rush as her bike sped back along the A6 and she was soon at Tony's side.

'What's the news?' Cathy asked.

'Well, the parents are saying that she was understandably depressed and could not come to terms with her husband's death and they think she might have attempted to take her own life. The doctor's first diagnosis on the scene backed this up. He said her GP's opinion was that Joanna seemed to have given up the will to live.'

'Will she live?'

'They're not sure yet. She seems to be in a coma but they're not sure why. It wasn't anything as obvious as an overdose or anything, but lots of tests have gone to the lab.'

'And what do **you** think Tony?'

'She's been ill, one way or another, since Bob was murdered.... I just don't know.'

'Is there restricted access to her?'

'Just close family and friends.' Tony paused seeing Cathy's face. 'I know, but what can we do?'

'What do you **really** think, Tony?'

'Let's not guess shall we, or let our imagination run away with us. We'll get the lab report soon.'

At that moment Joanna's son Paul came out of the nearby lift, unshaven and dishevelled. At first he looked fearful when he saw them standing in the corridor, but then he slumped down on a chair beside them, his head in his hands. Cathy sat down next to him.

'Have you got anything to tell us?' she asked gently.

He looked as if he was about to speak when the lift door opened again and his grandfather came up to them.

'Come on Paul. Let's go and see your mother.' And with a resigned look Paul got up and followed him into the side ward and a moment later the doctor passed them too.

'What are her chances?' Tony asked, stopping the doctor in his tracks.

'Fifty fifty,' he replied. 'She needs the will to pull through and it isn't in our power to give it to her I'm afraid,' and he turned and went into Joanna's room, politely asking the relatives not to stay too long but to come back tomorrow. It was already getting late.

Once they had gone, Cathy and Tony looked at each other and Tony whispered,

'I think that one of us should stay Cathy. My instinct says that Joanna shouldn't be left unsupervised.'

'I agree Tony and since I've just arrived I'll do the first shift and maybe you could relieve me at about 2am.'

'Not the night I'd anticipated,' Tony replied, 'but I suppose, since I dragged you here, I must agree with you. Shall I get you a cup of tea first?'

'That'd be great.'

Cathy sat so that she had a clear view of Joanna Thomas's bed through the open doorway. After Tony had brought her tea he was reluctant to leave her, but she insisted, and a quarter of an hour later Paul and his grandfather left too.

'No change,' Paul said by way of an apology as they left her alone. Cathy found it hard to keep herself awake. She tried to think.

No murder weapon had been traced. The overalls and shoes had not been found. Forensics had found no tell tale evidence at the farmhouse incriminating anyone at 'The Gathering. ' What was all that about? Cathy mentally checked down the list of names she held secure in her memory. No one seemed to have any real motive. Revenge for a 100 year old murder? Surely not. The search of Paul's computer came up with nothing, though personally she felt it should be sent away and checked further. Her mind churned as the minutes passed.

She tried to think of something else. Tony? No, that was not such a good idea. Her thoughts returned to the case. What were the misgivings she had about Paul's grandparents? Helen seemed to link everyone together, didn't she? Surely not. She seemed to be holding everyone together. No motive either. Cathy was still making mental notes when Tony arrived back to take over just before 2 am.

'Go and have some shut eye and I'll see you in the morning,' he said.

'I think I better had,' and without a second glance she left him and took the lift down to the car park. 'Drive carefully,' he whispered after her. He knew that he was beginning to fall for Cathy but was also aware that she felt awkward. They had not had a moment to themselves since Jersey. Tony peered through the door into Joanna's room and saw that there was no change on the monitors. He sipped the black coffee he had picked up on his way in and then paced along the corridor to keep awake.

Did Cathy feel nothing after their liaison? It was so frustrating in more ways than one. Just as he was nodding off to sleep he was awakened by the sound of the lift. He checked his watch and it was 4.30 am. He watched the sign show the lift's ascent and decided to hide behind the gents' door, keeping it ajar. When the lift finally arrived he was surprised to see Paul, but the young man's expression was crestfallen rather than furtive. Paul hesitated in the corridor looking uncertain and then walked towards his mother's room but he was startled when Tony came out from his hiding place.

'Are you all right Paul?' Tony asked, as Paul slumped on the chair Tony had just vacated. A silly question to ask a lad whose father had just been murdered and mother was in a coma. Paul was shivering violently.

'I know what the murder weapon was,' he whispered, 'but I'm sure it wasn't Mum. I think she's been poisoned, in fact, I'm almost sure she has.'

'Wow, Paul. Slow down a minute. Why didn't you tell us about the murder weapon before?'

'Because I thought that it pointed too much to Mum, but there's this website see. I helped set it up actually.'

'Let's take one step back a bit, Paul. What makes you so sure that you know what the murder weapon is? Do you know where it is?'

'No, I don't, but that's the point. Two of great-great grandfather's World War One weapons are missing. Two bayonets or something, but I've no idea where they are.'

'Where are these weapons usually kept Paul?'

'At the farmhouse,' but seeing Tony's surprised expression he added, 'I know. It's a very old house and it has a secret room, only a cupboard really, behind a screen door in the office. It used to be a large oak book shelf cabinet but that's long gone. Now there are just shelves of files covering it.'

'Are you telling me that there is a cache of military rifles at the farm? I know for a fact that they aren't licensed to anyone, because routine checks were made as part of the investigation. I hope you realize that this is a very serious offence to own these without a licence. You say that two weapons are missing?'

'Yes, one's been missing for as long as I can remember. There have been ten Great War rifles on the rack all my life but there has always been one bayonet missing, but the other day I noticed that another had gone.'

'And the website. Tell me about it.'

'It's about a girl called Lucille Vardon, who was murdered in 1919. I helped to set it up. My friend Jake in the village did it. You know. Your officers tried to question him because he was at 'The Gathering.'

'So, do you think you know who murdered your father, Paul?'

Paul hesitated. 'I'm almost sure it was Helen and I think she's poisoning my mother, too.'

'Those are strong accusations to make Paul. After all, from what we've seen it's Helen who's supported your mum, in fact all your family, to get through this. What would she want to kill your parents for? What would be her motive?'

'She thinks my great great grandfather killed Lucille Vardon but was never brought to justice. From what I gather her great grandmother was a friend of this girl Lucille's at the camp.'

'The camp?' Tony raised his eyebrows, thinking of girl guides or boy scouts. Nothing would surprise him in this case.

'Yes, The World War One training camp at Haynes Park!' Paul sounded exasperated, raising his eyes towards his mother's room.

Tony took in a deep breath, not sure how to handle this obviously fraught young man. He replied gently, 'Even if your great grandfather did kill this young girl Lucille back in 1919, Paul, and Helen was related to her friend, don't you think it's a bit far-fetched that Helen would kill your parents as an act of revenge? And what about all the others? Why would she arrange for all those people to be involved?'

Paul sighed. 'It's a game. Several in fact. Computer games but with real people involved. It started as a bit of fun. A big joke. I thought I was helping Helen out, to take her mind off things you see. She's been like an auntie to me. Her Kirsty and I were always close.'

Tony raised his eyebrows questioningly.

'No, not like that, really. We'd grown up together. Been friends since we were toddlers. She used to play with me when her mum came over to the farm, that sort of thing.'

'So, how are **you** involved Paul?' Tony asked.

'After Kirsty died Helen started this computer course and we got talking. She was really interested in designing a website and I helped her. She's a whiz! She picked it up so fast. I was impressed. Anyway, I helped her at first and then introduced her to my two mates in the village. Jake had just come back from Iran and was a bit traumatised to tell you the truth. I thought it would be good for him too and he's better than I am at programming. After all, that was his job. A bit secretive about it though, he is.

Anyway, while I was away I got involved in the website a bit, but I had too much work to do to notice what was happening. When I came back he was so excited to show me this elaborate game, but it was part virtual and part reality. Hard to explain, but he was designing a prototype where the webmaster plays

303

the game and lures people in, real people. As they interact, a weird mixture of real and virtual people play a game on the screen and they try to get characters to do what they want them to do. It starts back in 1919 with people connected to Lucille Vardon. Like playing any computer game, really.' Paul lifted his eyes to Tony's for reassurance that he was making sense.

'Go on,' encouraged Tony.

'Well, Jake has designed at least three of these games and "Murder@HawnesPark" is the first one and it's pretty innocuous. Its whole intention is to get people hooked. In this one the characters involved are all virtual, but at the same time real people start to be lured in by the website and forum.'

'Then what?'

'Well, the second "MysteriousMurderTours@Hawnes" is pretty tame too. It's complicated though. As the punters play the first game, they don't realise that their choices give away vital information about themselves so that, by the time they're playing the second, they've won the first prize - the tour - a real tour for the folks at "The Gathering," but virtual for everyone else.

The webmaster knows so much about each of the real characters that the tour can seem fun at first, real or virtual. Then, after a while the victim begins to feel uncomfortable. How does the organiser know so much?'

'And?'

'Finally, they are left with a sinister feeling that their lives have been violated in some way - that they are being watched. That's when the webmaster strikes again and sends the real people an invitation they want to refuse but can't, to attend "The Gathering@HawnesPark" in the churchyard.'

'Let's get this straight,' Tony interrupted. 'There's this computer game. Some of the characters are real and they are lured into the game by the webmaster to take part in real situations. What's the advantage? I mean, what do the players gain?'

'Huge numbers of points. Free minutes to continue playing the game or to put towards another. It's big business. People pay for their initial minutes and either win their stake or lose it, in which case they have to pay more to continue. It's addictive like any other computer game, but more so because you know that real people are your characters. The control - the power you feel if you like - is immense. It gives you a huge ego trip.'

'OK, I get it, I think.' Tony wasn't sure he really understood, but decided he could listen to the automatically taped conversation later, and ask more questions after. For now he didn't want to stop Paul in the flow of his explanation. He continued. 'So, when all those people turned up at the graveyard, the person or people playing the game won a huge payback.'

'Virtually, yes. They never actually win anything. The poor sods who are lured in pay out in real cash, but then they just win points.'

You've got to remember that this is only one combination of people. The game's so clever that hundreds of combinations of people, (I don't say groups because they don't know each other in real life) can play simultaneously, all the others with virtual tours as prizes, tweaked for their personal choices, but the effect's the same.'

'I'm not sure I follow you, but why Hawnes and not Haynes and where does Helen fit in to all this?'

'Well, Hawnes was chosen because of the fantasy. It's an old fashioned word for Haynes. By the time they've started game number four "Revenge@HawnesPark" it's so compelling. They can't stop themselves and suddenly they've become suspects in a real murder, with no real alibi. I don't believe Helen has the intelligence to plan all of this but Jake could easily. He sees murder as an inevitable lesser of two evils. His whole brain has been fucked up - sorry officer, messed up in Iran. His whole reality is blurred as it is. He's housebound.'

'But he's never in when we call.'

'That's his mother protecting him. He's there all right. Up in his den. You should see it!'

Tony made a mental note for an urgent return visit to Jake's.

'So how do these games help us to solve your father's murder and put your mother's life in danger?'

'These coincidences and people appearing at 'The Gathering' are to confuse you and they have, haven't they? Jake's clever. Extremely intelligent on the verge of insane. And Helen? She's obsessed. She's been out of her mind since Kirsty died. You don't know what she'd do!'

'Seems a bit elaborate as a cover up, but I'll keep an open mind about it. When Cathy comes in I think we should take a trip to the farmhouse together to find those weapons and also root out this young man Jake, don't you?'

'I can't be with you. Don't you see? Helen needs to be locked up. Who knows what else she will do and I can tell grandma is scared of her too. I've never seen her like this and things...'

Paul stopped and stared at the lift as Helen walked out. She looked a trifle startled to see them both but soon regained her composure.

'I've just popped in to see how your mum is before I start work,' she explained. 'Any change?'

Paul shook his head. 'I'll come in with you. I've only just arrived myself,' and he looked pointedly at Tony who followed them and stood by the door. The monitor was still bleeping steadily. Helen pulled up a chair and to Paul's irritation held his mother's hand, but just as he was trying to decide what to say a nurse breezed in.

'I'm really sorry but Mrs Thomas is going to have some more tests in half an hour and I need to prepare her for the porters. She should be back by about 11am,' and she ushered them all from the room.

Tony watched Helen and Paul leave in the lift together, wondering about all that Paul had said. He knew he had to call in the Firearms Department but the timing of it was crucial. He knew the rifles would be impounded and he imagined helicopters, paramilitary and all manner of excitement at the farm. He must check with DS Aktar, but he wanted the scene photographed and checked by forensics first, otherwise the chances of uncovering new vital evidence in Robert Thomas's case would be slim.

He shook his head. Would Paul be safe with that woman he wondered? Nothing should surprise him by now. He looked at the notes of the conversation automatically taped and transcribed on his ePad and amended obvious errors. He had only had to tap a button on his jacket for it to be activated. A useful tool introduced to the force several years ago.

Cathy arrived not long after and they discussed how they could request 24 hour protection for Mrs Thomas. Even though the Commissioner had sympathy for Saima's theories, would he pay attention to Paul's accusations? Could he afford not to? Also, how were they going to search the farmhouse without alerting Helen or Paul's grandparents?

In the end they did not have to. Within an hour Paul had sent photos of the secret cupboard and the rack with the rifles and the missing bayonets. There was even a slight shadow on the wall where the paint was a touch darker showing that one of the weapons might have been taken fairly recently.

'I'll go back to the station to see what I can do and talk to Saima,' Tony said, where a lab report was waiting for him. He phoned Cathy.

'A uniformed officer is on his way to relieve you.'

'How did you wangle that then?'

'The lab report has come back from the hospital tests on Joanna Thomas and there are conflicting results, but she was almost certainly poisoned.'

'Oh dear!' replied Cathy. She couldn't say what was on her mind because the porters were wheeling Mrs Thomas back into her room.

'As soon as the officer arrives I'm heading to Haynes churchyard. There's something else bothering me. Shall I meet you there?'

When Cathy got to the churchyard she had had a text response from Saima:

'Rosemary - remembrance. Forget me knots-obvious but the dark blue ones I think are Gentian - not usually still in flower but mean 'death' - a lot of superstition around them. Little

yellow flowers are bird's trefoil-revenge! I trust you Cathy. Let me know what gives ASAP. Saima.'

An hour later Tony found Cathy digging around Bob's grave with a little trowel. She did not look up but pushed another trowel towards him and nodded towards Lucille's grave.

'But you need signed authority, Cathy. We can't do this!'

'I'm only tending the flowers,' Cathy glared up at him. 'Think Tony. Where would **you** hide a weapon after a murder? We've scoured the area and they had an army of people looking in 1919 too. If Helen's murdered someone in cold blood and she's poisoned another then who knows who maybe next.'

Tony joined in with bad grace, not noticing the figure watching them from the lych-gate, who crept back out and raced off on her bike.

'Look!' yelled Cathy in triumph, having the foresight to grab an evidence bag from her pocket to slide the offending article inside before having a closer look. There were still traces of blood on the heavy, deadly looking old bayonet so it certainly had not been buried for a century.

'Our murder weapon!' she called out triumphantly, 'and some gloves too!'

Tony pulled out another evidence bag and Cathy, holding each with her latex covered finger tips, dropped the bloodied brown leather gloves inside.

At that point the verger came rushing across to them, but instead of giving them a severe reprimand, as Tony had expected, he shouted,

'Helen's dashed off in the direction of the farm in such a state. She didn't stop when I called after her. I also remembered where I'd seen that red cloak with a hood before, the one I saw at the strange gathering on the morning of the murder. It was

Kirsty's, Helen's daughter.' By this time the verger had reached them. 'What on earth's the matter? What are you doing?'

Alarmed Tony looked at Cathy and they stood up in unison and started running back towards Tony's waiting car.

'The murder weapon,' Cathy called back over her shoulder, waving the bag in the air towards the verger.

'Please can you alert the vicar and not let anyone else into the churchyard for now. We'll send police back up.'

'But there's a christening this morning,' he called back to them into the empty air.

Cathy left her bike and joined Tony so that she could phone the station, but before they reached the farmyard they could see that more than the normal chimney wood smoke was billowing up. Both the bungalow and farmhouse were alight!

'They're trapped inside,' shouted John, who had already set the farmyard hose on the bungalow, leaving the farmhouse to burn. 'I've called the fire brigade.'

'Who's trapped inside?' yelled Cathy.

'Mrs Thomas Senior and Helen Carter,' John shouted back.

Cathy rushed off around the building to see if she could find a way in but all the doors and windows were locked. She could just make out two faces staring at each other through the smoke at the kitchen window. Neither was trying to escape – like silhouettes in a painting.

'Where's Mr Thomas senior?' asked Tony.

'I've no idea!' yelled John. 'There's another hose over in the corner of the barn. Attach it to the water container at the back of the bungalow.' Without thinking, Tony rushed to follow his command but soon the fire brigade arrived, followed by an ambulance.

The firemen soon had the blaze at the bungalow under control and two people had been rescued and were carried out on stretchers. Both women were alive, just, but at that moment Paul had arrived in his little Mini. He rushed towards the farmhouse.

'Stop!' shouted Tony, rushing towards him and grabbing the lad by the arm.

'My grandpa's probably in there,' he gasped as he struggled free.

'We're doing all we can Paul. We must leave it to the experts now.' Tony persuaded Paul to sit in the car, but as he did so Tony shouted to one of the fire crew,

'We think there might be a man trapped in the farmhouse.'

Once Paul was settled in the back seat he started muttering gibberish. 'There's the next computer game. I went to Jake's house. He wouldn't show me at first but then I threatened him and saw it all. I know gramps is locked inside in that little cupboard. I saw him on the screen.'

'Drink that,' Tony said, handing Paul a cup of tea from the flask attached to the back seat. 'Now what are you talking about?' He was worried about this young man.

'I saw the game on Jake's computer. There's this man trapped inside a burning house, in a small room with weapons on the wall. I know it's him!'

Tony frowned. The farmhouse was still blazing in front of them. The timbered roof had caught and it was proving difficult to tame. A fireman came to Tony's window.

'Any idea where this person might be? On what floor, back or front of the house?' he asked.

'Ground floor at the back, there's an office but you'll never find him. I know where he is.' Paul frantically scrambled

311

out of the car, tipping the tea all over Tony's arm. 'I'll show you,' he shouted, racing round the back of the house.

Once at the back he pointed to a window to the left. 'That's the office but he's trapped behind a false wall.'

The fireman looked suspicious. 'You either know too much young man or you're wasting our time. Which is it now before I decide to put one of my officers in danger trying to get to him?'

'Just believe me! I'll answer your questions after. I know where he is. Please let me go inside.'

The fire officer hesitated a moment but seeing this young man's pained face; he barked an order at one of his men who had already put on a protective suit and breathing and communications apparatus.

'You're not allowed in. Health and Safety, but if I give you this mouth piece, I'll trust you to give clear instructions. Can you do that?'

Paul just nodded as the fireman disappeared through the back door crouching down close to the floor, lights beaming from his head through the smouldering black. The fire was only just licking towards the back of the house but the whole building was filled with deadly smoke.

'There's a door to your left just inside the backdoor, that's the office.'

The officer tried the door. 'It's locked!' he shouted. 'I need back up to break it down.' The flames were already reaching the back lobby from the dining room when two more protective suited officers entered the building with ramming equipment. They had the door down in no time and retreated to safety.

'There's a wall of shelves in front of you. Take out the old box files from the fifth shelf and you'll see the door handle.'

The fireman threw the files on to the floor without a thought and reached for the handle. He turned to see the flames had reached the office door but fire fighters were now attacking the blaze from the back too.

'Are you in yet,' agonised Paul.

'Yes,' called the fireman triumphantly, relieved that this door wasn't locked. Expecting to find nothing inside he was astonished to see all the weapons on the walls but on the floor lay the lifeless figure of a man. Without hesitation he threw the body over his shoulder, uncertain whether he was alive or dead, but there was no time to check. He pulled the false door behind him to protect the array of amazing weapons.

'Got him and I'm coming out,' he yelled, and the other firemen were warned to turn the hoses away for a few seconds.

In what seemed like a life time to Paul, but can only have been a couple of minutes he saw his gramps carried out on a stretcher to the ambulance, an oxygen mask over his face. In no time Paul was back in the police car with Tony, following the ambulance out of the farmyard.

John, with blackened face, lifted his arm to him as he passed. Paul glanced over his shoulder to see that the fire at the front of the house was now under control but his home looked bleak, with smoke pouring out of every cracked window. Even the cow sheds were now flattened to the ground. Pear Tree Farm was destroyed.

Tony watched Paul through a secret mirror as he tried to get his muddled thoughts of the day's events clearer in his mind. Did he see a slight smile as Paul turned back from the sight of the destruction of his home? Surely not. He must have imagined it.

'We'll take you up to your sister's,' Tony explained, 'but you must remain there Paul. I know you want to go to the hospital but we don't think that it's a good idea for anyone to visit for the time being, and we'll have officers stationed on each of the doors of the private rooms.'

'But,' began Paul.

'No buts I'm afraid. We don't want any more deaths and for now there's only been one murder. Thanks to you a second and maybe more have been prevented.'

When Tony and Paul arrived at Emily's house Paul got out of the car.

'Don't forget,' Tony said, 'you need to remain here and we need to take any mobile device you have to the station.'

'But I've told you all I know. I need my iPad for my studies.'

'We'll only have them for 24 hours and we'll deliver them back to you if you're clear, but we'll be in touch later today. You do understand, Paul?'

'Yes officer, but I hope you'll take my warnings seriously. After all, look what's happened!'

'We'll go around to Jake Foster's house today but we'll also confiscate any of Helen Carter's equipment to have it checked, to verify your accusations and Paul.'

Paul had begun to walk away but looked over his shoulder. 'Yes,' he said.

'I hope you'll take my warning about those rifles. The Firearms Department are on their way to liaise with the Fire Service to remove them to a place of safety. Your family will have awkward questions to answer. You know that, don't you?'

Paul just nodded and as Tony moved away Paul was still standing watching him from the gate to his sister's home. After a couple of seconds Paul opened the gate and disappeared from

314

view. Tony pulled up by the side of the road at a distance away from the gate and waited five minutes. Paul did not emerge again so he paged for back up.

Within ten minutes a plain clothed policeman appeared on the other side of the street and stood obscured by a large lorry. It was only a hunch but nothing made sense in this case. Satisfied, Tony pulled away and went to pick Cathy up from the station. She had been dropped off to pick up her bike from the churchyard, where there was already a team of forensics digging around the graves.

The area was on a slope and difficult to tent, so they had put up a make shift barrier, leaving room for the christening guests to get into the church.

'Have you read my report on Paul's accusations Cathy,' he asked as they pulled away. 'Me thinks he doth protest too much,' quoted Cathy. 'Seriously, if it's true then surely he's implicated. Why didn't he come to us before? We need to check out his story.'

'I agree,' replied Tony. 'Our intuition seems to be in accord.' Tony smiled at Cathy, lifting his eye brows questioningly.

'Where to first do you think?' asked Cathy, ignoring the innuendo and staring forward.

'To Jake Foster's house and then to Helen Carter's I think. I'm told that the farmhouse is too dangerous for us to take a look, but we'll pop down there after. Meanwhile they'll be stripping down Paul's computer again.'

Cathy's mobile bleeped. She clicked on the message from Saima and read it aloud. 'They've found a second WW1 bayonet buried in Lucille Vardon's grave. It's almost unrecognisably rusty but forensics will confirm its provenance.

The interesting thing is that it's obviously been uncovered recently though and reburied. It's not been there undisturbed for 100 years, that's for sure.'

'You were right then, Cathy. Well done. Helen Carter must have discovered it when she tended Lucille Vardon's grave and then put it back where she'd found it.'

They had pulled up outside Jake's house in Haynes and Cathy walked to the door but when Jake's mother tried to deter them again, Cathy held up her search warrant and the mother reluctantly let them in and showed them up to his room. Cathy tried to open the door but it was locked.

'He always locks it when he goes away. In fact, I haven't been in the room for years. He's very private about what he does, you see, but I'm sure he's doing nothing illegal.'

'You say he's gone back to serve in Iran?'

'Yes, he was on sick leave for six months. It had affected his mind you see. He went yesterday. I've told the other officers who called.'

'But that means he *was* here on our first visit!' Tony said, his voice coming out as an authoritative rebuke.

The mother coloured.

'I know I lied to you but he wasn't well. He hates fuss and gets so mad if he's disturbed. He takes it out on the family, especially his younger brother.' She paused. 'I'm a bit scared of him to tell you the truth.'

'Stand back,' said Tony. Imagining so many detective shows he had seen as a child when they had broken down a door, he launched himself on to the door but it did not budge.

'I wouldn't even try,' his mother said. 'He's had it reinforced.'

Cathy paged for help with equipment and warned the mother that they would be back in a few minutes. Meanwhile they went across the road to Helen Carter's house, which was easier to enter because the back door was wide open.

It was in total chaos. Someone had been thorough. They searched through the debris but found nothing incriminating and all the computer equipment had obviously been taken out. They found no end of receipts though for expensive jewellery and clothes, all of which appeared to be still upstairs in Helen's bedroom. It was no ordinary thief then.

'I don't think we'll find anything here now Tony although we'll ask for it to be checked over. Let's interview the immediate neighbours to see if they've seen or heard anything and then get back to Jake's house.'

There was nobody in when they knocked on the immediate neighbours except a fifteen year old lad Joel. With head phones still hanging limply around his neck and music still throbbing from their ear pieces, they believed him when he said he had seen and heard nothing. The neighbours on the other side were out.

They arrived back at Jake's bedroom just in time to see a gap being cut out of the steel reinforced door.

'Wow, exclaimed Tony as they walked inside to see the walls full of photos of both murders, 1919 and 2019; pictures, photos, captions, all headed under the names of the different games until the final one that Paul had not mentioned. "FinalMurder@HawnesPark."

One wall was littered with icons, pictures linked to characters. One was of a falcon with a photo of Anna in a cartoon bubble from its mouth; a large airship - James Bouchard of course; what looked like a binary code breaking machine -

Keith Regmund; Bob Thomas - a Jersey cow and Joanna Thomas - a long purple cardigan. There were more Tony and Cathy did not recognise. They looked back at the title, "FinalMurder@HawnesPark."

Cathy and Tony stared at each other. 'Who?' was the word on both of their lips when Jake's mother brushed past.

'There's something I should tell you. That Paul, you know the son of the murdered farmer. He was here earlier today. He tried to break down the door too, but couldn't do it. He was that mad at me because I didn't have a key. Jake always takes it with him; keeps it on a key-ring round his neck.'

'Thank you Mrs Foster. We're sorry to have made such a mess but the men will have to remove most of the contents of this room as evidence now I'm afraid. Are you sure your son's really gone back to Iran? Is there anyone we could ring to verify it?' Tony asked.

'I have a number from the base at Aldershot to ring to pass on any messages. I've never used it because I was warned not to unless there was an emergency, but I'll find it for you.' She delved into a drawer in the kitchen and handed them a piece of paper, carefully writing down a copy.

As Cathy drove back to the farmhouse Tony called the number and left a message asking them to contact him ASAP. 'Paul lied about seeing Jake so what does that mean?' he asked as he clicked the phone off.

'I'm not sure,' Cathy replied, a worried frown on her brow as they turned the corner into the farmyard.

'It's worse than I remembered,' said Cathy. 'It was such a lovely building.'

'The back doesn't look too bad,' replied Tony as they strolled around the wreck, glancing up at the charred roof of a house which was once a home. They found that the forensics team were at work.

Tony called in through what was left of the back door, touching nothing and a man in a white protective suit looked over his shoulder at Tony.

'What have you found in there?' Tony asked. 'Are the armaments safe?'

'The armoury room was fine because it was protected by the screen. That's where the old man was strapped up.'

'You've taken photos I assume. Have you removed any of it yet? What did you find?'

'Yes of course to the first question. Yes, we've begun to remove everything,' and he nodded towards the tent erected in the back garden. 'The rack of weapons is still on the wall and, because it's enclosed, we've left them for now, but the Firearms people should be here any minute and they'll remove them tonight for safety reasons. We're working on the office itself first and we've found a minute camera, you might be interested in.'

'Yes we are, but can you confirm whether it looks as if two of the weapons are missing?' Tony held up the photo Paul had sent them.

The man paused and screwed his eyes as he peered down at the photo, then he looked up, puzzled.

'It's nearly like that, but three of the rifles appear to have missing bayonets. I know because we counted them. There are eight rifles with bayonets fixed on that picture, but we only found seven rifles complete with bayonets. There are ten rifles altogether.'

'And you found no other bayonets lying in the room, having dropped off or something?'

'Definitely not,' replied the man. 'Is that all?'

'All for now,' replied Tony frowning.

'What do you think Cathy?'

'I think we should get back to the station and think this through, is what I think.'

CHAPTER 30

Monday 22nd July 2019   Back at the Station

Back at the station an emergency meeting was called for the officers who were still involved in the case.

DS Akhtar outlined the day's events summing up:

'If it's true that Helen poisoned Mrs Thomas and murdered Mr Thomas, as Paul accuses, then both Helen and Mrs Thomas are now in hospital, safely under guard. Everyone so far is alive, even if only just, apart from the original victim.'

'Have we checked James Bouchard and Keith Regmund recently?' asked Tony.

'I've spoken to both the police in Canada and the military contact we have, and they assure me that Mr Bouchard and Colonel Regmund are well and have protection.'

'That's good.'

Saima nodded. 'Please can you sum up the situation as you see it Tony?'

'Well, there are only three people left on the loose who could have done this, that we aware of,' Tony continued, 'discounting John the cowman. There's Paul who did arrive rather promptly on the scene of the fire but he's under house arrest at his sister's. He doesn't know that of course. We know he lied to us about Jake and he could easily have gone to Helen's too, to destroy the evidence. We might have DNA evidence there but we have no finger prints.

Then there's this lad Jake Foster. His mum says he's gone to Iran but he may have gone into hiding, taking all of Helen's equipment with him.

Lastly there's Anna, who has oddly reappeared on the scene again at this crucial time. Where's she now?'

'That was odd wasn't it,' said Saima, 'Anna arriving at the station with Paul. She's gone back to Cambridge. I checked with her house warden and she was at a college lunch at the time of the fire. I really think she's in the clear. They did say that she'd left again this afternoon with a small backpack, though.'

The phone bleeped and Tony stretched over to answer it. 'Sorry to trouble you,' explained the duty officer, 'but there's someone on the line from Aldershot.'

Cathy, who had remained silent until that point, stood up to take the call.

'I see,' she replied. 'Thank you for your prompt reply.' She put down the receiver. 'Jake **has** gone back to Iran. He left on an early flight yesterday morning.' She looked worried as she stared at Tony. 'Have you checked on Paul recently?' she asked, frowning, bothered by something her brain could not quite equate but at that moment the phone buzzed again.

Tony put the phone down slowly. 'He's gone. Paul's gone.'

Suddenly there was a light in Cathy's eyes.

'We must go!' she yelled over her shoulder, pulling her jacket on as she sped out to the waiting vehicle, Tony close behind her.

'Where are we going?' asked Tony as Cathy drove with breakneck speed back towards Haynes, but instead she pulled into the village of Wilshamstead and turned left towards Shortstown, pulling up with a screech beside a little used footpath.

'Call for back up,' she shouted over her shoulder as she scrambled up the path. Tony did as he was bid and then raced after her. They reached a clearing which looked out over the valley towards Bedford and the Cardington hangars. It was quite a view. Walking slowly now, Cathy crept towards the nearby woods. The path continued but there was barbed wire in their way. She pushed at it but Tony moved forward and lifted it for her to crawl underneath.

They heard something deeper in the woods. Maybe it was just a deer. Maybe it was not. They crept in the direction of the sound and then they heard a frightened voice. Cathy and Tony froze.

'It doesn't make it right. Killing again. You know the saying "*two wrongs don't make a right*".'

'You're just the same as that Lucille was. Lead a man on and then refuse him. That's what they all do. It's the end of the game Anna, don't you see. It has to happen. The thousands of players just want to see the result. It's their ultimate prize for reaching this point. Don't try to scream - if you do I'll slash your throat before you can get a squeak out.'

'You're out of your mind Paul. It's not real. Surely killing your father was enough. How could you do this?'

'I didn't kill my father,' Paul sneered. 'It was all part of the plot. Helen did that for me. Easy really.'

'You're sick! How could you have your own father killed, have your mother accused like that and then put her in so much danger too?'

'He was a bully. With me anyway, and I was a disappointment to him all my life. He never understood me.'

'Why do I have to die Paul? At this moment they can't pin murder on you but if you kill me you'll get life. What will that achieve?'

323

'My fans will pay me a fortune. I'll be a made-man and flee the country. I've got friends everywhere. I'm going to Rio. The police don't suspect me, they suspect Jake Foster. I'm still at my sister's, remember. There's a man outside watching the house and I'll slip back in without them noticing. I'll have an alibi. I can see the headlines now. 'Another mystery murder in Wilshamstead Woods 100 years after the first!'

Cathy crept back leaving Tony eavesdropping on the conversation, to alert her if Paul made a move to carry out the deed. She was relieved to meet the officers coming up the path from Wilshamstead and they gathered around her and soon dispersed, creeping in different directions, so that by the time she stood by Tony's side once more she felt secure that back up was in place.

'No more of this,' shouted Paul. 'I've got to get going.'

At which point Cathy and Tony stormed through the undergrowth into the clearing. Before them the kneeling figure of Anna cowered as Paul stood over her, a bayonet aloft above her head.

Paul looked up startled, but before he could move two uniformed officers rushed up from behind him and grabbed him, pushing him to the floor and forcing him to drop the weapon.

A uniformed lady officer came up behind Anna and draped a blanket around her shivering body, gently encouraging her to stand and walk down the path to a waiting ambulance.

It was more of a struggle to get Paul to cooperate but soon he was bundled into an awaiting police van.

Later that day Tony and Cathy knocked on the door of Saima's temporary office. She was on the phone and signalled for them to sit down.

'That was the Stewartby Refuse Tip. They appear to have found a bin bag containing trainers and overalls covered in blood stains. It split apparently when one of their diggers was tidying a corner of the site. I'll send someone over to fetch it. If Helen used them she certainly thought the whole operation through, didn't she; the timing, Bob Thomas's clothes, The Gathering all added to the confusion. Still, forensics should be able to give us some evidence - DNA perhaps. Saima paused. 'Have you any more news?' She asked.

'We interviewed Helen in hospital this afternoon,' Tony replied. 'She had a friend with her in a wheel chair, who she'd obviously confided in, because there was no hesitation. The lady had said, "*The truth is always the best Helen,*" before she left her with us. After taking a deep breath, Helen admitted the murder of Mr Thomas but at first she said she'd done nothing wrong to Mrs Thomas.'

'The results came back from the lab that it was a mixture of a sedative and a herbal remedy made from lupins,' Saima said. 'Mrs Thomas's doctor was asked and he assured us that the latter wasn't prescribed. It's usually quite harmless, but not in the case of Mrs Thomas, who has a nut allergy, apparently. There were small traces of the drug in a bottle next to Mrs Thomas's bed which the paramedics had removed with the other medication they could find in the house when she was taken to hospital. Any ideas?'

'Yes, we'd read the doctor's report before going back to the hospital,' Tony said. 'It explains why an empty plastic container of the herbal remedy Yellow Lupin was also discovered in Lucille Vardon's grave, alongside the rusty WW1 bayonet which was almost certainly used for Lucille Vardon's murder a century ago. Helen guessed this, of course.'

'So Helen Carter confessed in the end?'

'Yes Saima. She's been giving Joanna something in her evening drink to put her to sleep for some time. Then she replaced Joanna's anti inflammatory drugs with the lupin tablets. They looked quite similar and she flushed the others down the toilet.'

'How is Mrs Thomas?'

'She's well enough to go back to her daughter's and is planning a holiday I believe,' Cathy said.

'That's two results then,' replied Saima, feeling that the threads of the case were coming together, 'but the doctor says that Helen Carter's not in a mental state fit for trial.'

Cathy frowned. 'So she's had a kind of mental breakdown and we can't touch her, is that it?'

'She was only a pawn in the game though, Cathy. She's suffered so much already, remember.'

'It also came out in statements from Paul's grandparents that Helen was having an affair with Peter Thomas which had been going on for thirty years,' Tony added.

'That probably explains the missing father of Kirsty,' said Saima.

'Almost certainly,' replied Cathy. 'She had him under her spell again recently and was also blackmailing him about keeping quiet about the death of Lucille Vardon. She believed that it was Paul's great great grandfather who had murdered Lucille.'

'Do you think there's truth in the rumour that it's all in our genes; even the potential to murder?' asked Tony.

'That's why, they say, men still get a kick out of wars,' Cathy added wryly. 'I do know the saying "*The sins of the fathers pass down to the sons unto the third and fourth generation,"* or something like that.'

'That's in the Bible,' remarked Saima. *"Visiting the iniquity of the fathers upon the children unto the third and fourth generation of them that hate me,"* is the actual quote.

'Oh yes, I'd forgotten you were a bit religious.' Cathy paused.

'And Paul?' asked Tony.

'He'll face charges of attempted murder and an accessory to the murder of his own father?'Saima took a deep breath. 'Yes, we'll throw as many charges at young Paul as we can. After all, he manipulated Helen at a time when she was so vulnerable. He seemed a bit screwed up about Helen's affair with his grandfather though, and angry that she *'was getting away with it'* in his words. I agree with him in lots of ways. Someone who is willing to blackmail is sound enough in mind, in my opinion, to face the consequences, but we can't really do anything about that. Paul will also face charges on being an accessory to illegal possession of firearms. Peter Thomas will face charges too. He seemed to think that, because the rifles had been in his family for generations, that he should be able to get away with it. Even gaol is a possibility.'

'And Jake? What will happen to him,' Cathy asked.

'The wider case has been taken over by the Cyber Crime Squad at New Scotland Yard. The Commissioner is thrilled that we uncovered Jake's activities. They've been trying to identify him for some time but we collected hard evidence for them. Hopefully young Jake will lead them to more senior cogs. They'll keep us informed though, and he may be brought back to the UK to face questioning and charges.' Saima paused.

'It's a good result, well done both of you.'

'I'm not sure that it's good but it's certainly justice,' said Cathy.

'Team work,' Saima smiled.

CHAPTER 31

A week later Tony picked Cathy up to go out to dinner. They had not seen each other socially while they were tying up the case and Cathy was extremely nervous. Their romantic interlude on Jersey seemed a bit of a dream now and she thought, in many ways, that maybe it should be left like that.

'You look lovely,' he remarked as he held the taxi door open for her.

'Thank you,' replied Cathy shyly, feeling her resolve to put a stop to their affair melting away in the July heat.

They spent the first part of the evening chatting about their family and hobbies outside work, avoiding anything controversial.

'I went to see Joanna Thomas yesterday. She's planning a trip to one of the small Greek Islands. She's renting a small villa there and her daughter and family are going with her but Joanna's staying on at the villa for at least a month.'

'That sounds like a perfect retreat for her to try to get her mind around what she's been through and think of the future.'

'Yes, thanks to your excellent detective work we prevented any more deaths, but there are always victims alive having to pick up the pieces.'

Cathy blushed, not used to such praise.

'Did you hear the rumour that Saima's keeping her promotion?' She asked, reflecting the glory on to her friend.

'Well deserved, I think,' replied Tony.

'The other good news is that Anna passed with a distinction and has gone to work for a year on the Farne Islands.'

'That's excellent for her. A perfect place after the trauma she's been through.' Tony paused before continuing. 'Cathy. I feel a lot for you. You know that don't you, but we both know that police-work and relationships don't really mix.'

'I know what you're going to say Tony and I agree with you. Our relationship should return to being just professional.'

'That wasn't what I had in mind at all.' Tony cleared his throat. 'It's too early to propose to you, although I can't get you out of my head, but I thought we could try moving in together; a sort of trial to see if it works, and then who knows.'

Cathy was stunned. She opened her mouth but no words came out. Tony, ignoring the amused looks from the other customers, leaned over the table and kissed her full on the mouth.

'Shall we skip dessert,' she replied huskily.

'Good idea!' he replied a smile creeping into the corners of his mouth.

Here is a review from the Historical Novel Society for *Riduna,* the first in Diana Jackson's *Riduna Series:*

RIDUNA

Life was picturesque growing up on Riduna on the Channel island of Alderney, before the second World War. It was a place where the old ways remained steadfast even though "outsiders" were slowly creeping in. Lifelong friendships develop and, in the case of Harriet and Edward, these friendships blossom into love. As the two grow into adulthood, they find that their love will be tested, when each desires a different path for their futures. Edward's dream of becoming a sailor finally pays off, and he finds that life onboard a ship is very different from the strict morals of Riduna. Harriet has decided to wait on the island for her sailor boy to return, and during his Christmas visit, their actions lead to a possible pregnancy. After discovering that it's a false alarm, both are relieved. After an unfortunate accident that shakes Harriet's world, Edward becomes more distant as his taste for the sea takes over his life. Throughout their journeys, both Harriet and Edward must make sacrifices and decisions that will forever change their lives.

Riduna speaks volumes about the power of love and loss and is beautifully written with a fluidity that speaks to your soul. Author Diana Jackson's ability to portray the everyday ordinary yet life-changing events of those in a community is amazing; you get a true feel of what it must have been like living in Riduna during that era. Fans of *The Guernsey Literary and Potato Peel Pie Society* will fall in love with *Riduna*. -- Angela Simmons

Ancasta ~ Guide me Swifty Home is the sequel to *Riduna*. This review was posted on 'Readers' Favorite':

ANCASTA ~ GUIDE ME SWIFTLY HOME

Ancasta is the continuation of the family saga that began in Riduna. Harriet is now a widow with four grown children. Edward is still traveling the seas, enjoying his freedom. As the world starts to change and a war looms, we follow the former childhood friends and sweethearts as they deal with the ravages and realities of war in England. No one is untouched by the war, as Harriet will watch her twin sons both volunteer for service along with her daughter's husband. It will also be a time to reunite with old friends; Jane, with whom she had lost touch will become the steady rock of a friend that Harriet leaned on before she had Joe. Now with Joe gone, Jane will again become that rock. Diana Jackson doesn't pull any punches with the tragedies and realities of war and what it was like. Still, that does not diminish the glow of the story of a family once again facing the idea that dreams change and life goes on.

In first Riduna and then Ancasta, we follow Harriet and Edward, who always thought their path in life would be together, but the reality of life was that it was not meant to be. Finally, in their retirement years, are they able to realize that it wasn't them who changed but the world around them and that things happened to them to make the dreams change. Diana Jackson weaves a story that is real and true and makes you feel that you are right there living it. It is a wonderful mix of the romance and realities of life with some of the technological advances of the historical time period of the novel. It is definitely a novel of moving on and never giving up, one any reader will enjoy.

Reviewed by Michelle Randall for Readers' Favorite

Diana Jackson writes:

If you enjoyed '*MURDER, now and then*,' and would like to hear about my writing projects I would love to hear from you. My email address is

diana@dianamaryjackson.co.uk

It would also mean a great deal to me if you would spend a few minutes writing a review on Amazon, Goodreads, Shelfari or on any other book site.

Heartfelt thanks
Diana

To find out more about Diana Jackson's writing check out her website:

www.dianamaryjackson.co.uk

Her two blogs:

www.dianamj.wordpress.com

http://selectionsofreflections.wordpress.com/

Riduna on Twitter

https://www.facebook.com/DianaJacksonauthor   on Facebook

Made in the USA
Charleston, SC
07 January 2015